BEN LIEBERMAN

- NOVEL -

Odd Jobs

SterlingHouse
Publisher, Inc.

Pittsburgh, PA

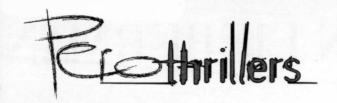

ISBN-10: 1-56315-472-2
ISBN-13: 978-1-56-315472-0
Trade Paperback
© Copyright 2011 Ben Lieberman
All Rights Reserved
Library of Congress # 2010927992

Requests for information should be addressed to:
SterlingHouse Publisher, Inc.
3468 Babcock Boulevard
Pittsburgh, PA 15237
info@sterlinghousepublisher.com
www.sterlinghousepublisher.com

Pero Thrillers is an
Imprint of SterlingHouse Publisher, Inc.

Cover Design: Nicole Tibbitt
Interior Design: Jessica A. Hilderbrand

Printed in Canada

CHAPTER 1

Just when I thought I could pull it off, I let out a double tequila burp. I can't stop tasting the shit. I'm in the ultimate purgatory; that place simultaneously blending being hung-over and being drunk. What seemed pretty manageable last night has a whole different view from this bus. Man, I just went out to meet Ray and Cindy for a few Margaritas at Rio Bravo and just like that, it's two in the morning and I'm doing shots of Wild Turkey in the Blarney Stone, arguing politics with some toothless 80-year-old guy.

The sun is coming up, and somewhere someone is thinking how beautiful this is and what a great day it's going to be. That's not me. The bus turns left onto Industrial Road and passes a huge cemetery that is jam-packed with acres and acres of tombstones all on top of each other. It's fuckin' packed tighter than the six-train. Some low budget tombstones are actually outside the metal fence. I guess they got a discount. A guy is walking his dog and the dog is taking a leak on one of the exterior tombstones. This gives me a degree of satisfaction, as someone is having a worse day than me.

These buses are a piece of work. They all smell like piss. The guy next to me weighs at least 300 pounds, and he doesn't smell too good either.

When I graduate from State and get a real job, I'm buying a Maserati GranCabrio. That's what I tell my friend Cliff Tsan sometimes. He keeps me down to earth and tells me to start liking buses, because I'll never have any job but odd jobs, like the one I have now, carrying beef carcasses. "You know why they're called odd jobs?" he says.

"Because they're really strange?" I answer.

"No, asswipe," Cliff says solemnly. "Odd comes from an Old Norse word meaning the tip of a spear. Therefore, an odd job is a job that makes you feel like you're being stabbed with a spear." Cliff is an English major whose father is a famous novelist, so maybe he's right; then again, maybe he's just busting my balls.

The bus hits a pothole, and my neck goes right through my brain. That's what it feels like, anyway. I don't know why I go out drinking with my friends on a work night, but sometimes I do. Like last night. It's not like I can even afford it; I'm supposed to be saving money for school. But I don't want the guys to think I'm an asshole.

Through a red haze of pain I see the dairy factory on the left, pink and gold in the light of the rising sun. I wish had a job there. I could run the machine that separates the milk from the cream, or drive a tanker truck. Nice clean jobs. But no, the part of Maspeth, Queens, that I claim as my little piece of heaven is staring right at me. In front is a honkin' big sign in hemoglobin red and raw bone white reading Kosher World Meat Factory: The highest standards in this world and beyond.

I don't belong on this bus, and I don't belong at Kosher World. But I don't belong with the hard-drinking, money-hemorrhaging crowd either, like Cliff and his friends. So where do I belong? That is the million-dollar question, Regis. But first I've got to try to do something about my current situation.

My watch reads 6:15 a.m. as I enter the building and get struck in the face with the stench of blood, tripe and oozing intestines. Miraculously, my stomach stays where it's supposed to be. Better yet, I'm on time. It's June 23rd and I'm bundled in long underwear, flannels and a thick orange jumpsuit, the uniform of the serious meat handler. I'm sweating like a racehorse. Christ, this is so unnatural. But the money's good, real good. There's no one back at college making this kind of money, at least not legally. Cliff and Mike Katz have internships at a swanky law firm, but you can't eat prestige. I'm pulling down $18 an hour, plus time and a half for each hour of overtime and double time for Saturday nights and holidays. I know if I bust my ass and stay focused this summer, I can cover a decent nut on my school expenses for a semester or so. Finish my last year of school and start making some real money. Hell, I've handled this crap for a whole month so far. Now, if I just get through the day without getting fired, and hopefully without puking, I'll be golden.

A couple of guys pass by and mutter 'hi' under their breath. I say 'hi' back, still trying to hold down the contents of my gut. There's a lot of noise – men yelling, trucks roaring into the yard, the thumping of the packing machines. My head feels like a boiler under way too much pressure. I shuffle off in the direction of my work station, but I'm taking my time, trying to ignore the damn smells and noises.

The essence of my job is twofold. I am a grunt. I unload sides of beef off trucks in the mornings and in the afternoons take huge racks of hotdogs off a washing apparatus and load them onto a conveyer belt for wrapping.

I got this job through a connection and basically get paid as a union guy but don't belong to the union. The union, by the way, is poetry. They have negotiated time off, vacations, breaks and benefits out the wazoo. You don't want to work too hard or you can hear it, "Hey fuckin' college boy, are you getting paid by the box or the hour?" You see, all the nice gentlemen here would like to work at least one hour of overtime a day. At time and a half, working one hour extra a day means getting paid six days for five days of work. Seems pretty slimy to me, but I don't have a wife and kids to support. Plus, management ain't exactly angels either.

My stomach gurgles menacingly. I know for a fact that I am so sick that I'm not going to make it today unless I get away from the stench that's weaving its way into my nostrils and into my digestive tract. Maybe I should have called in and taken my chances, but they just don't take that weak stuff from grunts. I'd be gone and I need this job. But if I get sick on the meat, I won't have much of a future either.

I decide to face up to my problem. I see Severan Reynard giving directions to two guys carrying a crate of ribs. Sev calls the shots on the floor. Sev doesn't say much and he really doesn't have to. He's 5'11" but seems bigger. He's got a body as wide as a truck with a decent size gut and skin so dark it actually looks black. His goatee is black and so are his eyes. His eyes are what do the commanding. When he wants something done, he opens those black eyes wide and points. The whites of his eyes are such a contrast to his other features that it shakes people. It's fuckin' freaky.

The funny thing is, Sev runs the place but he's not the real boss. Supposedly, there's a foreman. I haven't seen him yet but I heard he's some lazy sack of shit that got "put" in the job. Sev doesn't have the title, but I guess running the place beats taking orders from someone else. Everyone, including the foreman, knows Sev's the best guy, so it just works. Word is he did some wild stuff in the Marines like 15 or 20 years ago. Obviously the guy has been around. Supposedly he's a pretty straight shooter; I figure that if I go and talk to him and let him know how sick I am, maybe I can pull some other duty today.

Sev is talking to Sal and Frank in the doorway of the employee lounge. The lounge is a large room with 20 foldout cafeteria tables. In the corner there is a soda machine, a candy machine and a table with a microwave. It doesn't look like the guys are saying anything monumental, so I figure this is as good a time as any to talk to Sev.

"Sev, can I grab you for a minute?" I ask.

Sev shoots me a glance and then quickly turns back to Sal and Frank. Frank is telling Sev that we are behind in

June production. But this is good news for Sev because being behind schedule means overtime and some double time. The boys in the trenches are going to be happy.

A minute or two later, Sev looks over and says, "What's up?"

"Sorry to hassle you," I answer. "Uh, look, I'm having a little trouble today. I'm uh, kinda sick. Is there any other area I can work today?"

Sev is staring straight at me and his mustang eyes are getting pretty wide. He's not saying anything, but something is going on. Frank looks surprised and Sal grins. Immediately I know that I'm making a mistake.

"Motha-fucka!" Sev says in the loudest voice I have ever heard him use. "What the fuck do you think you're pullin' here?"

"Really Sev, I'm not trying to pull anything," I answer, trying to avoid those eyes.

"You think I'm a moron? You think I don't smell the liquor on you? You think I'm blind and I don't see you stumbling like a fool?"

I don't answer him. Even if I were on my game, he is pretty much right.

Sev is really going now. "What? You think this is a damn joke?"

I try to recover. "I'm really sorry, I made a mistake. I'm not looking for any…."

Sev interrupts. "Look, you want to go out late, fine. But don't go out at night barkin' like a dog if you're gonna be pissin' like a puppy in the morning. It don't happen like that in my house. Now get the fuck outta here, you're done."

I look around. It's pretty quiet now. I seem to be the center of attention, and everyone seems to know what just went down.

"Get the fuck outta here," Sev barks.

Sal steps up and says, "Sev, maybe we should wait a minute." Sev's eyes close just a little. "The kid got the job through Jimmy Balducci," Sal reminds him. "Why piss him off if we don't have to?"

"I got a floor to run and this little snot deserves to be canned."

"No doubt," Sal agrees. "But the kid's actually been doing all right. He's a hard worker."

"So I'm suppose' to put him on line where he can kill himself or, more importantly, one of my guys?" Sev growls, "Look at `im! He can barely stand up!"

"Why don't we give the kid a break from the hard labor and give him a nice, easy job today?" Sal says. "I got a great place to nurse a hangover that always needs a few more workers."

Sal pulls Sev to the side and mutters something. I can't hear what they say, but whatever Sal says causes Sev to do something I haven't seen since I began working here. Sev smiles.

Sal and Sev talk for a few more minutes while I just stand there like an asshole. Eventually Sal walks past me and says, "C'mon kid."

He's walking pretty fast—at least it feels like he's walking fast—but eventually I catch up to him. "Thanks a lot for saving my job back there," I say.

Sal laughs. "You are so fucked up, you have no idea what you're in for. Don't be thankin' me, kid. I'd ask your name but it doesn't matter. It's just a matter of time before you quit."

"I'm not going to quit, and you know my name is Kevin."

"Whatever."

"Why do you think I'll quit?"

"You, young stallion, are on Sev's shit list. You are

past the point of no return. You can't possibly imagine the shit detail you are going to be pulling. I've been working here 12 years, I know exactly what's going on, and all you are right now is sport."

"What do you mean?"

Sal tells me that the guys are making book on my estimated time of departure; lots of money changing hands as we speak. In here, he says, they bet on anything they can think of; it helps the day pass quicker. "And today we got you."

"Just great," I mumble to myself. A small man in a black outfit and a long dark beard bumps into me. Or maybe I bump into him. "Sorry," I say. He just mutters something to himself and walks on. I can see he's wearing a skullcap.

"What's up with him?" I ask Sal.

"Rabbi," he tells me. "You've never seen him before, wandering around? I wonder if he has any action on you yet."

We continue to walk past different huge refrigeration and freezer rooms. They all have names, like pickle box and curing room. We are walking in areas I've never been before.

"Why is there a rabbi here?" I ask.

"It's his job. This is what he does." Sal pauses. "He blesses the meat."

"Really?"

I'm not sure if Sal is starting to like me or, he just likes the sound of his voice, but for whatever reason, he explains the situation to me. "Kid, it's Kosher World, right? Someone has to make the meat kosher. Now, you have your all-star rabbis that lead congregations and save souls. Your B-team rabbis do other stuff like performing a bris on baby boys. I think they're called moguls. Then you have guys like our Rabbi Silver. He spends his day blessing meat. He has a congregation of dead carcasses."

Sal and I pass the smokehouse and finally get to the last room on the floor. Sal opens the door and immediately I'm engulfed by a strange smell. It's a cooked smell, almost like sanitary cleanser, but definitely cooked. It actually seems a lot tamer in here than the loading dock and the sides of beef I usually haul. I can pull this off.

Sal and I are the only ones in the room. He looks at his watch and informs me the gang will be here in less than two minutes. They start at 7 a.m. today. I ask what they'll be coming in to do, exactly.

"Kid, you are going to help in bringing a popular and special Jewish delicacy to your local restaurant and delicatessen. You should feel very honored."

"What delicacy?"

Three people walk into the room, all wearing big white smocks over their orange jumpsuits. "Heya Sal, what brings you to our corner of the world?" one of them asks.

"Morning, George; wanted to bring you a little help today. You're always looking for a little help, aren't you?"

George starts looking me over. George is maybe 5'5" tall and could possibly be 5'5" wide as well, but his most noticeable characteristic has to be his ears. They are the hairiest ears I have ever seen; there's a forest coming out the sides of his face. I stare at him dully.

"What's the matter with him?" George asks.

Sal tells him I am a college intern who just wasn't up to the heavy labor today, so he thought George's line of work might be a better match for me. Then Sal excuses himself, leaving me in the capable hands of George Skolinsky, who introduces me to Felipe Cortez, Ramon Pizzaro and Lily. They are talking and getting ready for what must be the task at hand, but the whole thing has a weird feel to it. After all, Sal did say something about a shit detail. I look around and notice that everyone is a little…odd. There's George with his hairy ears, and Felipe, who walks with a bad limp, as if one leg was 12 inches shorter than the other. Ramon isn't talking at all and I'm not sure if he doesn't want to be part of this group or just can't follow the chatter. And then there is Lily, who is extremely heavy and has the most god-awful dyed red hair ever. It's more orange than red. She has on orange lipstick that perfectly matches her hair, but there's more lipstick on her teeth than on her mouth. What is this, the detail of the damned?

George barks, "Let's get started."

Ramon wheels in a huge, tall vat while the others circle around a stainless steel table. There is steam coming from the vat and something is obviously boiling. Between the boiling vat and the cold of the refrigerated room it looks as though the vat is on fire and smoking up a storm. Felipe has a ponytail, and it looks pretty funny when he puts on the plastic sanitary hat that they all begin pulling on. Everyone looks pretty silly; it's like an operating room.

"Here you go, sweetie," Lily says as she gives me a hat.

"Don't try too hard, Lily. I don't think he's ready to marry you yet," George says with a yellow-toothed grin.

I put on my hat and watch as Ramon wheels the vat next to the table. He gets on a step-stool and, wielding a huge spoon the size of a shovel, begins scooping something from the vat. The water strains from the holes in the gigantic spoon and he dumps these slimy things on the table. They just slide toward the middle. Within about three minutes there are dozens of huge pink blobs on the table, roughly the size of an NBA basketball player's foot. Then I recognize them. They are rock-solid huge tongues. I might still be a bit buzzed, but it looks like these tongues are aimed at me, taunting me.

George sees my amazement. "Tongue," he says.

"I can see that, but from what?"

"Cows, moron."

I'm watching as the group begins working with surgical

precision. Hands move fast and each huge tongue is processed in about three minutes.

Lily is complaining about how the government is too soft on crime and how she can't even walk two blocks in her own neighborhood. She keeps at it for a few minutes. Man, she can go.

Finally, Felipe interrupts her. "The men in your neighborhood must be all over you. They can't get enough of you."

George and the others start laughing. It's a bit sad that they are having such a good time at Lily's expense, but I have to admit, I'm grateful that Felipe got Lily under control. Just listening for a few minutes, I could tell she is a runaway train.

Georgie notices me and says, "Someone get the kid involved."

"C'mon over here, hon, I'll help you," Lily offers.

"Quiet down, Lily, I got it. Stand over here, kid," Felipe says.

That's a relief; the last thing I need is to be cornered by Lily. Felipe begins to show me the ropes. He lifts one of the gigantic tongues, tosses it up a few inches and catches it again with the back facing him. Now the tongue is sticking out straight at me. I'm doing everything I can to keep down a pint of tequila and Wild Turkey.

"Okay," Felipe begins. "Three steps, simple as that. First, you take the bone that attaches this lovely tongue to the rest of the beautiful bovine." Felipe digs his thumb and middle finger into the back of the tongue and pulls on a four-inch bone. It gives him a bit of resistance but he finally yanks it out. "Next, you turn it over and scrape off the USDA grade that was stamped on the bottom part." Felipe takes a short, sharp knife and begins to whittle at the stamp. Small pieces of flesh begin to drop onto the stainless steel table until the bottom of the tongue no longer has a mark. Watching him is mesmerizing.

I'm staring and getting a fuzzy head.

"Here's the fun part. This thing has a tough cover of skin that needs to be removed before it can be eaten." I stare at him and the tongue, wondering who was the fuckin' Einstein that came up with the concept to eat cow tongue in the first place? And who was his friend that said, "Yeah, great idea."

Felipe continues. "Some amateurs will try to get the skin cover off by using their knife, but that's too slow. The tongues get these blisters from boiling for hours. You have to find a blister on the tongue, pop it and work your thumb underneath. Zip up, and the skin peels right off. Just like this." He demonstrates as I try to watch. I'm getting a bit dizzy and definitely queasy. Felipe slides a tongue at me and says, "Time to peel some tongue, kid."

I go to pick up the repulsive thing, but nature is taking over. My stomach is heading for my throat and I have to get out. I drop the tongue and race toward the door. I have to find a bathroom. Fast. I don't remember if it's to the left or the right, but before I can make my decision, bam! I collide with Rabbi Silver, who is walking in. We're both sprawled out on the floor. Now I have no shot of making it to the bathroom.

Jumping up, I quickly glance at Rabbi Silver, who is sitting up and muttering something. I don't have time to apologize. Where can I go? I look around and spot a vat in the smokehouse room; it'll have to do. I scramble over to the vat. I have no idea what is in there but it's out of my hands. Then it's out of my stomach. Violently, a yellow liquid filled with unrecognizable lumps cascades out of me. When I start getting control I realize I have heaved into a vat of cow by-products – eyeballs, spleens, bladders and some pink things that could be reproductive organs. The smell reminds me of the men's bathroom at the bus depot, now combined with the stench of half-digested food. I'm hoping that the lunatics who eat tongues aren't eating this stuff, too. I figure if it's garbage I can keep my job. If it's another ingenious delicacy, I'm toast.

My clothes are wet with perspiration; it's like 20 below, but I'm drenched. Wow, I feel good, almost like a human being again. There are about 15 guys around me and they're all cracking up. They got some show from me this morning, and it's not even close to 9 a.m. yet.

It's hard to imagine I still have a job, but until they tell me otherwise, I'm working. I pick myself up and head toward the bathroom to clean up. The guys are still laughing. Some are patting me on the back and others are making comments like, "What a loser."

If they're going to can me, I hope it's sooner rather than later. I wash up and look in the mirror and say, "Let's peel some tongue."

Walking back to the Tongue Room I notice Bino walking toward me. His real name is Russell Binoheitzer and since there's no time for all that, everyone calls him Bino. He's an ornery red-haired guy with real fair skin. After working in the freezer for a few hours, he looks like he's been dead for a week. All us grunts were given fair warning to avoid this guy and stay off his radar. As Bino passes, he nails me with his shoulder and nearly knocks me over. He says, "What a pussy. I lost 350 bucks because you couldn't make it 'til lunch time."

Yup, I'm pretty stealth flying under the radar, I say to myself.

Inside the Tongue Room, life isn't much better. I'm ripping bones and peeling off skin like a pro, but the comments keep flying at me. They're examining my every move, and Old Ear-hair is really starting to ride me. "Let's go, college-boy. I never finished high school, but I calculate that you're about five tongues behind the rest of us."

Felipe says, "You think you're too good for this, don't

ya?"

Why did he say that? This guy was helping me before; how did I lose him? I don't have any problems with these guys. Christ, they're all making an honest living and trying to get by. I appreciate that. All us college interns start with two strikes because we're getting money without paying union dues, but I always show respect to the guys. I thought I was okay with them. It's amazing how many places I can't fit in.

I'm trying to stay low and not get into it with anyone, but the shit just keeps coming. Felipe thinks it's funny to call me princess and he won't stop. "Here's another tongue for you, princess. You missed a spot on this one, princess. Your highness, are you ready for another tongue?" I have to start defending myself.

"Shut the fuck up, Felipe." I can see this outburst catches George by surprise. "I'm working like everyone else. I've always done my job and never gave anyone a hard time. I got banged up last night and I fucked up. It's not your business and it doesn't affect you, so stay the fuck out of my face."

"You put that face knee-deep in animal parts and you're worried about me being in your face?"

The others start laughing, Lily the loudest. So much for trying to defend myself.

Even the tongues are copping an attitude with me. Look at that one, just dying to chime in. That's what I need, talking cow tongues. I can see what this fat bitch is thinking. *Why does every situation turn out like this? Can't you deal?* I hear it saying.

I'm thinking, *Like you're one to talk. You're about to land on some shriveled old man's rye bread and you're giving me advice?*

Don't take it out on me. Live your life, don't live someone else's, the tongue replies. Look, you hold down like 80 jobs to get through college, but you don't give a shit about college or your classes. You just want a piece of paper so you can make big bucks, like your friends.

    And the problem is…?

    I can see its smug expression. *You're too impressed with money. It's all you think is important, and you keep chasing it, like a stupid hamster running on a wheel. Not only are you missing out on what's important, but you keep winding up in the Tongue Room. You always end up in the Tongue Room, one way or another.*

    I can't let a fucking tongue talk back to me like that. *Listen up, Tongue. I'm not asking anyone to give me anything. I'm willing to do what it takes. I'm doing the work. I don't have to just fall in line with everyone else. It's not a sin to want more, to make a situation better.*

    Dude, when have you ever made the situation better?

    I get things going. I've done stuff, I answer, feeling a little defensive now.

    Yeah, you get things started, but that's it. You get used or you blow a good thing and, of course, you wind up in the Tongue Room.

    Maybe this time I learned, I think. *It can't get lower than the Tongue Room. Things can't get worse. They gotta get better. This, you fat, slimy, ugly tongue, is the low point; it's all up from here.*

    Bullshit! counters the tongue. It's sneering at me; at least I think it is. *All you had to do here was some simple manual labor. Just bite your tongue, pardon the expression, and do your fuckin' job. But you want to go out with your fancy friends and whoop it up. Problem is, they have bucks a-go-go and you have squat. While you're here peeling tongue, they're drinking Mimosas. Was it worth it?*

    Hell no, but I didn't think everything would come down like it did.

    The tongue is laughing now, and it's not a very pretty

sound. Think? Kid, that's the trouble: You don't think. You made an asshole out of yourself in front of the whole place. There isn't a worker in Kosher World who doesn't know who you are – Puke-Man, Rabbi-Crusher. Can't you be anonymous anywhere?

I don't know, I tell myself. Being anonymous is kind of over-rated.

You should try it sometime. It might fit you better.

It's depressing to think that the tongue gets the last word.

CHAPTER 2

After the Tongue Room debacle, I hear a ton of comments all the time at work, but at least no one taps me with a pink slip. I know that's because Jimmy Balducci brought me on.

I keep remembering something Jimmy Balducci told me once, and it makes me feel better. He said that these jobs are more about building character than about the money. Sure, some people go to Exeter, Harvard and then Goldman Sachs, but those are the dorks who got their books knocked out of their hands every day. The real successes come from the people who claw their way up, people like Jimmy. "Trust me," he said. "Guys who are big shots today jack off to the good ol' days when they were digging graves or selling ball bearings. You look back at the shit-work you had to do and it gives you satisfaction. Real satisfaction; it's something you can't get from any drug or any broad."

Around 7 p.m. I manage to get to my mom's house in Hempstead. Hempstead is a less-than-affluent town on Long Island. Long Island is kinda funny that way. There are some real nice areas, but I guess the people who work in the nice areas need a place to live, and Hempstead serves that purpose. Which is fine. I used to not have a problem with the thought of being a cab driver, working construction, or peeling tongues at Kosher World. It seems to be what people do, and they deal with it.

Then along came Harris North IV of the Remington Academy. What a piece of work. He brought me into a different world, and I had already done a few 180s with my other worlds, so I guess it shouldn't have mattered. To be clearer, when I was 10 years old, my father was an up-and-coming prosecutor in the DA's office. We didn't have a ton of money. We had a small home in Manhasset, but we were heading places.

I'm not going to try to say life was like the Brady Bunch but fuck, it wasn't that far off, either. My dad put in a lot of hours, as upstarts in the DA's office tended to do. On the weekends, though, my mother wouldn't let him get away with any of that too-busy crap. She was always booking day trips or weekend trips. Our family was always exploring some Renaissance festival or museum or paddling rafts down some white-water rapids. She kept us busy. Dad would roll his eyes when he heard her plans, but at the end of the day, he probably had a better time than anyone.

The time we spent together wasn't enough for me. I couldn't get enough of my father, so I badgered him to coach me before work on the weekdays. If I wanted to spend more time with him, basketball was the perfect excuse. He was a huge hoops fan and a pretty decent player himself.

"Okay, okay," he said, finally giving in. "If you're willing to set your alarm clock, I'll work with you from 6:30 till 7:30, but then I've got to leave for work. Is that fair?"

"Yeah," I said.

"I'm not going to wake you up and start haggling to get you out of bed. If you're willing to meet me at 6:30, I'll be waiting for you. Deal?"

"That's a deal, Dad," I enthusiastically shot back.

The waking up early thing was harder than I thought. The first morning I rolled over and shut the alarm clock off, only to snap up at 7:20. I scrambled in a panic and shot down the stairs, trying to put my sneakers on as I was stepping on the stairs. That moronic combination caused me to skip the bottom four steps. I splashed down in Superman flying style, landing spread-eagled on the floor. Still determined, I rolled onto my

feet and in the same motion sprinted toward the front door. My
father had just pulled his car out the driveway when I startled
him with my scream, "Wait, waaaaaaait!"

He stopped the car, rolled down the window and gave a
half smile. "I know, it's tough waking up earlier in the morning."

"But…but I'm here now," I said in near panic. "Let's
play now!"

"Sorry pal," he explained. "I have to get to work.
We'll give this another try tomorrow."

Tomorrow? Tomorrow? You can't tell a kid tomorrow.
You might as well say in 15 years. "Nooooooo. Let's play
today! I'm here!" I wailed in desperation.

"Pal, I have to get to work," he said calmly.

"Why, why now?" I demanded.

My father smiled and said, "Because I have to work on
putting the bad guys away." He was so proud to talk about that
end of the job, that he was a lawyer who helped put the bad
guys away.

"But you need to help me today. Won't you play?" I
pleaded.

He saw my heart was going to explode so he said,
"Okay, this is what we'll do. Fifteen minutes today—we'll call
it a warm-up. Heavy training starts tomorrow. You meet me at
6:30 a.m. sharp. Got it?"

"Really, we can play today?" I asked.

"Yeah, we can play for 15 minutes. Only if you agree
there's not a minute more than that today. The bad guys won't
mind waiting a few minutes I'm sure."

Almost missing that opportunity to play with him put
the scare in me. We did our "warm-up" that morning and I
never overslept again. I was there at 6:30 sharp the next day,
and my father was out in the driveway, waiting for me.

I learned that you have to be careful what you wish for.

I thought I was going to be playing basketball with my dad, and my father thought this was the beginning of my NBA career. I thought I would be shooting around and maybe playing some one-on-one with him, and he had all these drills planned. I didn't dare complain because I was just happy to be with him.

"How about we work on shooting today, Dad?" I asked.

"That will come in time, but first you need to work on your vision," he stated.

"Vision? I can see fine. What's up with that?"

"Kevin, I'm not talking about needing glasses. You need court vision to play this game. You need to see things other guys don't. That's what makes some players great. Now, you want to learn about vision?"

"I guess."

"Well, first of all, right now, you and a lot of the guys your age dribble with the palm of your hand and your head down. But if you do that, how are you going to see the open guys?" my father asked. "How are you going to make those miracle passes?"

"I dunno." At that point in my life, who thought about passing the ball? We all just wanted to score. Actually playing the game was a whole different level.

"Okay," he said patiently. "You need to dribble the ball with your fingertips instead of the palm. If you use your fingertips you get much more control. And keep your head up. Wouldn't you rather watch the game instead of your hand?"

I shrugged. "Sure, I guess."

"Son," he said earnestly, "there is a whole world beyond your hand. There is a whole story developing, and things aren't always as they appear. Always learn to see beyond your hand. When you're confident the ball is under control with your fingertips, then you can see who is open and, equally important, who is going to be open. In this world you can't just look at yesterday and today; you need to see tomorrow. Keep your head up and soak in the whole picture."

I didn't quite understand his point then, but I'm glad I always remembered it. That week we did a bunch of drills and I learned how to keep my head up and dribble with my fingertips. I got the hang of it and felt pretty good, so one day I had the balls to ask if we could do some shooting. I mean, after all, wasn't that basketball?

"Oh, you think you have this mastered?" my father asked.

"Yeah, I'm good at dribbling and keeping my head up. C'mon, Dad, let's do some shooting."

"Okay, here's what we'll do. As soon as you master the steps, we'll move over to shooting." My father grabbed the ball and walked us over to the side of the house where 11 cement steps separated the front yard from the backyard. My father then instructed me to dribble down those steps with my head up, using only my fingertips. It didn't work out too well. Anytime I bounced the ball on the corner of a step, the ball shot free like a champagne cork. My father said that when I could get up and down the steps 10 times without losing the ball, we could move on to shooting. It turned out to be no small feat, but during that long and difficult process, my dad and I had some of our best conversations.

"Dad?" I asked.

"Yeah, pal."

"You said the great players have vision, right?" I asked as I dribbled up the steps for my third lap in my attempt to get to 10.

"Yup."

"Well, who was the best? Who had the most vision?"

"Oscar Robertson, maybe Jerry West," he said.

"I never heard of them. Were they the best ever?" I asked.

"Maybe; they sure had the vision, and it made them great."

I bounced the ball carefully and felt like this would be the winning lap. Still, I wanted to keep the conversation going, so I asked, "Does that mean they were the best basketball players of all time?"

My father thought for a moment. "Michael Jordan had the vision and everything else you can imagine."

I finished the fourth and fifth laps and my rhythm was great; I knew I was going to do the 10 laps. "Michael Jordan?" I challenged. "He's not better than T-Mac."

"Better," my father answered.

"Not better than Dirk Nowitzki?" I shot back.

"Much better," my father said, smiling.

"Okay, okay not better than Shaq!" Because that I wouldn't hear of. Shaquille O'Neal has always been my idol.

Now, my father knew he was sharing idol status with Shaq, so maybe this was his opportunity to get an edge. "Please, not even close."

"Not even close? How could that be?"

"Shaq might be twice the size of Michael Jordan, but he's half the player."

"C'mon," I whined. "Half the player?"

"Keep dribbling," my father encouraged me. "I'm telling you, Shaq is half of Michael Jordan in his prime."

I couldn't help but imagine what half a player actually looked like. I started my seventh lap dribbling up the steps. "So if Michael Jordan in his prime is missing his arms, who wins? Michael Jordan or Shaq?"

My father laughs at this imagery. "Lessee...Michael Jordan with no arms versus Shaq. Michael Jordan wins."

"Dad!"

"Kid, you're talking about Michael Jordan."

"How about if Michael Jordan didn't have his arms or

his legs?"

"He'd still win," my father said quietly.

"Get out of here, you're crazy!" I said.

"Son, I know it's hard to believe because you've never seen him play, but if Michael Jordan played against Jerry West, Oscar Robertson, Dirk Nowitzki and your beloved Shaq, all would lose to Michael Jordan, even if Michael Jordon was just a nose on a table. That's how great he was."

The sight of a nose on a table beating all those basketball greats was too much for my 10-year-old brain to take. I laughed so hard that the ball I was dribbling hit the corner of the step and shot away. I only made it to my ninth lap and the stair torture test had to continue.

"Ha!" my father said with a snort. "That's why you need the vision. There are always distractions that can stop you. You've got to fight through and keep your eye on the ball. Keep your eye on the ball in your mind and watch the court. See it develop. I'm going to work now. Keep working on the stairs, and maybe tomorrow will be your day."

It wasn't the next day that I won the stair challenge, nor was it the day after that. Looking back now I can't remember how long after the Michael Jordan's nose debacle that my accomplishment came, but I do remember when it happened I kept my mouth shut and took care of business.

There was that time in life when things fell into place. When if you worked hard you beat the stairs. It was a great theory, that is, if you worked hard you got what you needed. Then there came the time that no matter what happened and how hard you tried, the stairs beat you. Looking back, I can't remember the day I beat the stairs, but I can point to the minute in time when all the stairs of the world started beating me, when everything changed and never went back, no matter how hard I tried.

My mother was running some errands and my father took me and my little sister Katie into town to get a few things to start the new school year. I needed a haircut and Katie needed shin guards for her first season playing soccer. While I was getting a haircut, my sister was combing her doll's hair. The doll, Karen, was wearing the same pink skirt and white shirt as my sister. The doll also had the same blonde curly hair that Katie and my mother shared.

As I sat in that chair getting my haircut, in the mirror I could see Katie grooming her doll and I saw my father staring at the newspaper in his lap. I don't think he turned one page. His eyes were on the New York Times but his mind was back in his office, working. We caught his mind there all the time.

After my haircut, Dad bought Katie's shin guards and she and I conned him into getting us some big sloppy ice cream cones. Then we were ready to go home. We went back across the plaza, and when we were about to cross the street to our car, my father warned Katie to be careful not to get any ice cream on her doll. But Katie had left Karen in the ice cream shop. When she realized her loss, Katie let loose a shriek that I swear could have melted our ice cream faster than this unusually hot late August day.

I told them both, "It's no problem. I'll get Karen and meet you back at the car."

"Thanks, Kevin," Dad said. "We'll wait for you right here."

"Naw, you don't have to do that," I insisted. "You guys wait in the car and get the air conditioner cranking," I suggested.

Katie screamed. "No, I want to see Karen." Her face was red and her eyes glistened with tears. She was past the point of no return, so there wouldn't be any reasoning with her.

"Okay," I said to them both. "I'll get the doll and wave to you from the ice cream store and then you guys get the AC going."

"That sounds like a plan," my father agreed. "Hey," he added, "make sure you're careful crossing the street."

"C'mon, Dad, I'm almost 11. I know how to cross a street."

"Of course you do," he said and smiled. "I'm just saying it because I care about you."

I sprinted over to Chico's Ice Cream and saw Karen perched on the counter. I grabbed the doll and stepped outside. I waved it in the air back and forth and my father and Katie waved back. I couldn't see Katie's face but I try to remember how relieved she must have felt. She knew Karen was safe and she could enjoy her sloppy ice cream cone. I also always remember what my father said about caring about me.

A black car zoomed around the corner faster than any I had ever seen. Oddly enough, everything happened in slow motion. The windows on the car were smoked dark, but one window wasn't completely closed and you could see long red brittle hair in contrast to the dark car. There was screaming and hollering coming from that open window. The car swerved in all directions, then it veered right toward my father and sister. It lifted my father clear in the air and rolled over Katie. The car never slowed down and careened out of sight. Katie's cone was still intact on the pavement but the ice cream had been separated and was unrecognizable amid the crimson mess. How could it be? I thought, unable to process what I had just seen. Dad and Katie lay on the sidewalk like broken mannequins, but the ice cream cone was still intact.

A hit-and-run accident. They never found the guy. Drunk driver, they hypothesized. Broad daylight and everyone could see it but no one saw it but me. The whole process was only a few freak seconds. Did the delay waiting for the doll cause a bizarre juxtaposition that couldn't be reversed? It was just a few seconds. Yet those few seconds caused a disruption that ended two lives and sent two others spiraling in a completely different direction than they were headed before.

I guess every minute is a defining moment somewhere in the world. Ten minutes ago, Billy Bob Buttfuck in Ohio just bought a winning lottery ticket and the next minute Igor Roganovich got hit by lightning in Croatia. Good or bad, is the new direction permanent? For me, every day since those brutal moments has been a fight to get back to where I was. Where I want to be.

For the next few years, my mother was a virtual zombie. She barely had the desire to get out of bed to go to her bookkeeping job. Mom was there and I was grateful, but damn, I missed her. If I weren't around, my mother would have offed herself long ago, I'm sure.

Any extra money I made after the accident went to maintaining our shoebox of a house in Hempstead and buying her medication, but there was rarely enough money for both. Then, when there was some extra cash, instead of putting it away for a rainy day like I should have, I'd be too tempted to go out with my friends and see a movie or grab a burger, anything to squeeze in some "normal." And those little things add up. The extra pressure of a stupid thing like money was killing us.

Harris North IV changed all that, though.

I remember the first day I saw him. I was in my last year of middle school and Harris North IV was watching me play basketball at Hempstead Park, a hotbed for street basketball. There were 30 or so shirtless basketball players wearing long shorts and high-top sneakers. Along the tall brick wall were another 20 hand-ballers wearing long pants and wife-beaters. Also lounging around in the vicinity was an assortment of old-timers with scraggly beards and dental issues. Then there was this one guy sporting khaki slacks, a pink golf

shirt and Gucci loafers sans socks. Yeah, he was some chame-
leon. Fit right in.

His Gucci ass showed up at my house and he started
talking to my mother about giving me a great education. This
guy was actually scouting parks looking for people to put his
school on the map. I wasn't any better than my buddies Loot
or Carey, but Harris wanted me because I played b-ball pretty
good and I was white. I found out later that the school had
this whole strategy worked out. A football team had too many
players and too much equipment, so a major football program
wasn't worth the trouble. With no expensive equipment and
only 12 players to award scholarships, hoops was just what
they needed. And what they really wanted was lily-white players.

This guy really laid it on thick for my mother. Hempstead schools couldn't compare with a private school like Remington. I would be a target for drugs and in a bad element if I
stayed where I was. He could open up important doors for me.
This grown man with a pink shirt, hanging out in shitty parks,
was gonna open doors for me?

It wasn't like I bought into North's visions; I had no
choice. The guy had no idea what buttons he was pushing.
After all, my mom had just lost two of the three people dearest
to her in the whole world. She sure as hell wasn't about to lose
the third – me. And if Harris North IV had the solution, she
was going to take it. While speaking with him, Mom came out
of her trance and flat-out demanded that I go to the academy.
If something like sending me to a private school moved her, I
wasn't going to argue. I just wanted her to be happy, not that
she ever could be. Not like she was.

Looking back, though, Remington Academy was fine.
It showed me some stuff I never would have seen. On the
other hand, it made me want stuff I didn't know I wanted. Bottom line was that I was in a packed 10-cent candy store with

only nine cents to spend.

The funny thing was that this bozo Harris North IV sold Mom on getting me away from all the drugs in Hempstead. Meanwhile, you can't believe the drugs rich kids get their hands on. While we were scoring dime bags in Hempstead Park, the guys at Remington were getting blow, X and 'shrooms like they were renting movies from Blockbuster. Their money made all the difference.

These guys lived in a different world, and for a while I got to live in it. I liked living in it. They showed me there was another world outside Hempstead, and I couldn't help it, I wanted in. I got a front row seat courtesy of Constance Wendy Wellington. Everyone called her C.W. You're not really allowed in this world without a weird name. It's like a password at the door. No lie. We had a Bunny, Potter, Bucky, Rip, Chip, A.J. and every combination of initials possible in the alphabet, landing me right with C.W.

I remember always trying to have an excuse to talk to her, to find any reason to see her. I can practically still feel her straight brown hair that was so silky and shiny that it drew in the light and sent it back out with a subtle glow. While the rest of us were fighting the good fight versus a tsunami of zits, C.W.'s skin was flawless. Her dark complexion managed to look tan in the winter. Beautiful green eyes and a mouth that was inviting in a plump and seductive way accented it all.

It was hard not to be drawn into C.W.'s world. She would talk to me about basketball and the games we had coming up. When she talked to me about hoops, I was pumped. I tried to fit in. In my second year at Remington, I actually busted my ass to nail down literature class. To make things even tougher, her favorite author was Charles Dickens, so besides the regular reading, I tried to tackle Dickens. I didn't give a flying fuck about literature, but it was C.W.'s favorite subject. Girls make you do some weird things. English Lit was hard

enough to grasp, and they didn't make it easy for a guy like me.
We were reading books in class like *The Catcher In the Rye,*
A Separate Peace and The Great Gatsby—stories about these
characters with tons of money and fancy lifestyles, perfect for
the Remington crowd. For them, it was like reading about their
next-door neighbors. For me, it was like reading a story about
aliens from the Planet Zeron.

Later on, C.W. admitted that's what got her really liking
me. I'd like to think I charmed the fuck out of her, but that's a
reach. She knew I couldn't care less about this stuff but I was
doing it for her. I never minded doing the work to get what I
want but when I looked around, everyone else was either getting things handed to them or expecting to get things handed to
them.

I spent a lot of time at C.W.'s house…if you want to
call it a house. The damn place could have had its own ZIP
code. I always knew people had swimming pools and tennis
courts, but the Wellingtons even had a stable and horses. It was
her mom's "hobby." This hobby could drain the economy of
some small countries.

C.W. had a great relationship with her mother. I would
meet them at the Piping Rock Country Club and they would
be there downing Southside cocktails, watching the tide roll
in. They would spend hours together before I got there. It
wasn't that I thought it was so hip that C.W. was having drinks
with her mother. It was that she was having anything with her
mother. My own mother was so out of reach. Her hobby was
jumping from one antidepressant to another. If that hit-and-run
didn't happen, maybe my life wouldn't have been horses and
cocktails, but it wouldn't have been Hempstead either. I appreciated what I had and I tried not to be jealous of the Remington crowd, but it was hard to fight what I really felt. It's not
like I needed to drink Mimosas with my mother, but I didn't
need to be feeding her tranquilizers either. Shit didn't have to

turn as far left as it did.   It didn't always have to be that way, I
thought. I could learn to win. Like I said, I was willing to do
the work.

Buster Wellington, C.W.'s father, was a tough read for
me. As the president of the board of trustees at Remington,
he was so active with the school that you could almost imagine him taking calculus with us. When he saw me around the
school, he barely gave me a look, let alone have any conversations with me.

Buster liked the basketball games, though. He was a
real sports fan who had four daughters, C.W. being the oldest.
While their girls were all good equestrians and field hockey
players, old Buster was pretty bummed he never had a super-
star lacrosse player. On that point, he treated me pretty well.
He was at all the Remington hoop games and would spend
some time talking basketball.   I don't have a ton of experience
with fathers. Maybe I thought he could bring me into the fold
a little more, but that was probably my own frustrated desire to
have a father. Plus he had a natural desire to keep me out of his
daughter's pants.

C.W. must have done a great selling job on him though,
because one time he took me with them on a family vacation.
We went to Nevis, an unbelievable island in the West Indies.
Just to get there, we flew to Puerto Rico, then took a tiny plane
to St. Kitts and then a 45-minute ferry boat ride to the resort.
C.W. and her 15-year-old sister Missy had one room, while her
younger twin sisters shared another. I, the king, had my very
own room. It was nice stylin'.

However, the separate rooms thing didn't really work
out the way Mom and Pop Wellington had planned. The vacation at Nevis turned out to be where C.W. and I did it for the
first time. After scouting out several romantic moonlit locales,
we decided on the big laundry room where all the beach towels
were washed. We broke in and turned on the dryers and lay

on top of them. It was like having a vibrating bed in a seedy downtown motel but we didn't have to pay any quarters. Pretty ingenious, I thought.

The laundry room was C.W.'s idea; you never knew with her. She had an unbelievable appetite for fun. There were a lot of laughs and some great sex in the laundry room that night. We did pretty well a bunch of nights after that. We even managed to find a bed sometimes.

So there I was, living large with all the beautiful people, having the hottest girlfriend in history, enjoying great sex, playing basketball and even making some connections. Obviously, you should never get comfortable on the top of the world. The landing can be a real bitch.

After that vacation, I got a part-time job in a sandwich shop. One day my boss let me out two hours early, so I went to surprise C.W. When I got to her house, she and her father were heading toward their stable. They were pretty bundled up, but I was sure it was them. They didn't see me come into the stable, and I didn't mean to eavesdrop, but I heard my name. I stood still where I couldn't be seen and just listened.

"I know where it's going and not going," I heard C.W. say. "I know what your expectations are of me, and I know what they are of myself. There's a certain life I want to lead and a type of person I want to share it with. There's a place for Kevin, but it's not long term. I'm not going to have baggage in college next year."

Holy shit, I thought. *I'm a fuckin' boy-toy.* I thought maybe she was just telling her father a story, you know, to get him off her back. But that wasn't the case.

I left the stable so quietly they never even noticed me.

Right around the end of basketball season was when it happened. Oh, she was nice as could be, this culture has a way of having the brightest smiles when they drop the biggest bombs. She said she wanted to break up and stay friends.

Man, it hurt so much. Worse yet, I soon realized it was pretty much over for me with everyone at Remington Academy. It was like I used up my value when basketball season was over. At the end of the day, I was just the hired help. Just a fucking birthday party clown.

So C.W. went off to her liberal arts white-bread college. Maybe she thought of me when she saw a basketball game or a clothes dryer but probably not much more often than that. For me, it was different. Not a day passed when I didn't think of her at least once. When I went off to New York State in Albany, I still tried to hang with that money crowd. Once you get a taste of that life, it's hard to settle back in.

I took on odd jobs to get enough money for drinks and even some clothes to go clubbing. I had a dozen different jobs, anything that paid. Sometimes I would caddie at the country club. I'd hump golf bags and listen. One day I would hear political power brokers lobbying prominent state politicians. The next day it could be a hedge fund manager with his airtight arbitrage siphoning off affluent investors. They all pumped each other for resources and lied about their golf scores. There was a kingdom out there, and everyone was fighting for their share. Why shouldn't I?

I worked my ass off during the day so I could get to the clubs and fake being cool at night. I didn't have the Porsches and BMWs the others were getting from their folks to take me to the clubs, but I managed to go there sometimes. Mostly I was trying to find another C.W., but no luck. As soon as I discovered any quality in these girls that was different from C.W., I ended it. I had some short relationships but nothing satisfying. Sometimes, when I stopped and thought about it, I wondered what I was doing. Why was I searching for another girl to say "fuck you" with a gentle smile and a kind word, the way the rich do it? But even that realization wasn't enough to make me stop longing for the good life.

CHAPTER 3

I sleep like I am in a coma on the bus ride home. Walking into our house, I notice two voicemails on my cell phone.

"First message." Beeeep. "Kevin, it's Loot. Great action tonight at the park, bring your jump shot, we needs you, lots of dough-ray-me for the takin'."

"Second message." Beeeeep.

"What up, Kevin? It's Ray. Man, were you wasted last night. What a pissa! Cameron has an 'in' at a serious after-hours club in the village, lots of ladies. Gimme a call. It's gonna be awessssomme!"

I stare at the cell phone for a few seconds and say, "Fuck you." I grab some food and fall sound asleep by 8:30 p.m.

I make it through the next day at Kosher World and the next week. I guess they're still betting on when I quit. The work and the abuse pile on. Every shit job that has to be done and any miserable mess that needs to be cleaned up, I'm the man.

Sev has me clean the bathrooms one day, all of them. He thinks it will help me learn their locations so when I have my "stomach problems" I won't be such a disturbance.

Yesterday, Bino corners me in one of the factory corridors. He's got this smirk that's so freakin' weird. The pale fuck is wearing a white butcher's apron over his jumpsuit and he seems to melt into the sanitary white walls of the corridor. All you can see are some dark red lips that have been freezer burned and orange hair effortlessly floating above. But that's all you can see, lips and orange hair. The rest is there, but you hardly notice any other feature. I feel like laughing, but I know that every time I see this guy, it means trouble.

Bino says they have a job for me. He should have said he has a job for me but he chooses to say "they." Bino brings me to the lounge area; coincidentally, it happens to be when the place is on break, so it's crowded in there.

Bino pulls out a toothbrush and says, "Hey, dipshit! I doubt you ever seen one of these. It's a toothbrush."

I'm thinking, *Thanks, Mr. Rogers, can you show me what a comb looks like?*

"The room needs a good cleaning in those hard-to-reach corners, so get going," Bino says.

So instead of having a break, I'm cleaning corners with a toothbrush and steaming under my breath. Bino sits down with his friends and occasionally barks at me to hurry up because there are plenty of corners in Kosher World. Who gave him the authority? Man, I hate that pale fuck.

The other two grunts are loving life. I make their job so much easier. All the crap used to be divided among the three of us, but not anymore. I managed to invent a new job. I've become a grunt's grunt. I keep telling myself it's just a few months, but I'm kidding myself. I have to figure out a way to make it stop.

At lunch, Bruce Nissen, a college grunt from Hofstra, tells me to watch out because Sev is really on the warpath.

"Why is today different?" I ask.

"They have these matches set up once a month against some of the factories on Industrial Road and even from outside the area. It's a real big deal, lots of gambling. Everyone takes a lot of pride in it."

I guess I should have known about it, but no one talks to me. "What kind of matches?"

"Boxing matches, except without any gloves. Sev's man Hector had to bail today, and Sev has egg on his face.

There's no one he can get on short notice. Man, is he pissed."

"I know Hector Pinto. He works in the butcher block. What happened to him?"

Bruce tells me that Hector practically cut off his entire index finger. "The butcher block is brutal," he says. "Those guys are cutting up the same exact piece of meat day in and day out, 12 hours a day. It's hard to concentrate. You know, one minute you're thinking about some hot girl on a beach and the next thing you know, wham. You're missing a digit."

"The fact that he was going to get the crap beat out of him today probably had a lot to do with it," I say. Hector's a nice guy, but he doesn't look like much of a fighter.

"Supposedly, he needed the money."

"What kind of money?" I ask.

"Depends on what's bet. Guys who lose a bet have to kick in an extra percent, you know, a vig. The vig gets split between the winning fighter and guys who are set up as book-makers. I hear the winning fighter usually gets around two to three grand."

"No kidding. What's the loser get?"

"Usually stitches."

We were both quiet for a minute or two and then Bruce says, "Sev is really bummed because he hasn't been winning lately. Now he's gonna be a no-show."

I say good-bye to Bruce and go looking for Sev. Already I'm making plans.

There are only 10 minutes left before lunch is over, and I'm due at the Smokehouse to clean the scraps. I poke my head into all the different rooms as I search for Sev, but he's not in any of them. I head to the lounge.

The lounge is still pretty packed considering there are only five minutes left in the lunch hour. George is standing and talking to a seated Sev, who is flanked by Frank and Sal. I have less than five minutes; George will have to be interrupted.

"Hey Sev, put me in for Hector Pinto tonight." I say it loud enough so Sev, Frank, Georgie and the masses can hear me.

Sev looks at me, irritated, and says, "Go away. There's no throw-up events that I know about." Sev gets some laughs from all the ass-kissers there, but this chance is too good to be true. All the laughter is going to stop now.

"Hey, right now you have nothing tonight," I insist. "You want to save face, get me in. And if you had any real balls, you would put a ton of wood on me."

There are a couple of blank stares from the guys in the room, then a couple of "holy shits," then just outright howling and whistling. I love it. The place is going berserk; no one talks to Sev that way. It's not like I have a particular desire to show him up; it's just that I need some results here.

Sev has no choice. "I don't give a shit whose bitch from management you are," he says. "You want in, fine. I hope he kicks your teeth in."

When word gets out a few hours later that I'm representing Kosher World, I don't amass much confidence. Hector was a three-to-one underdog; now I'm going off at five to one. At least I'm not ten to one.

The bout is at our courtyard and my opponent is from the Dairy King Milk Factory. But there are plenty of people here from all the factories, like Moonbeam Cheese, Country Boots and Foliage Coffee. It's probably one of the biggest crowds I ever fought in front of. Pretty cool considering a few hours ago I had no idea I was even doing this.

Being how it is our "home game," practically our whole factory is here. The Hot Dog Room is the only area that can't come. They have to work through the night as we are approaching the July 4 weekend, the go-go time for hotdogs.

It's amazing watching the courtyard fill up. The fences around the perimeter bend as the group continues to expand.

The activity at the bookmakers looks like a combination of circus ringmaster and the New York Stock Exchange. It's serious stuff.

I hear the other fighter's name is Butch Bombart, but I can't be sure. I'm waiting for a ring announcer but there isn't going to be one. Hell, it would be nice to have a guy in the corner with me, but I guess I'm such a joke that no one wants to associate with me. Butch steps out in the middle of the ring and takes off his shirt. He is a stocky black man about 5'9" and maybe 195 pounds. He must be in his early 40s. He looks strong, but at least I have the reach on him.

Someone taps me forcefully on the shoulder and I turn around. It's Sev.

"Let's go, Peter Pan. They're waiting for you at Never-Never Land." He doesn't smirk, wish me luck or check my medical insurance options; he just points to the circle created by the crowd.

"Hey, Sev, any rules I should know about?"

"Hands and feet. I don't think you can bite or use any foreign object."

I get to the ring and unzip my orange jumpsuit. I take off my flannel shirt and my thermal undershirt. As I take off my shirt, I hear Felipe say to George, "Holy shit, the kid is ripped." I'm standing bare-chested in my jeans. I guess this is the first time anyone really sees what I look like. They should see me when I'm really in shape. But I should be okay for this guy. I probably weigh the same but I have a good 4 inches on him. I love having a reach advantage.

My heart is hammering now, as it always does when I fight. Is it the raw thrill or the fear of getting your head kicked in? Whatever causes the rush, it's exciting, real exciting.

Butch and I circle around each other a few times. I wish I had seen one of these street fights before; I am definitely at a disadvantage here. I keep him at bay. Then jab, jab, I get him twice on his forehead. I open up a quick cut on his head, but I think I hurt my hand more. This is different than with boxing gloves. I need to adapt. I jab again and get him in the face again. This guy is so dumb and slow I should be fine.

Butch lets out a huge growl, charges me like a bull and tackles me to the ground. The crowd is going wild, as I am clearly not the fan favorite. He drives me so hard and far that the crowd has to shift to accommodate our new position. This guy is strong; he's got me on the ground. He gets me in some kind of wrestling hold. My face is smashed against the ground and he's trying to twist my arm behind my back. I feel my face scraped raw along the blacktop. I have to get up; I'm in trouble on the ground. Butch punches me in the back of the head. Damn, this hurts! I can't let him do this anymore. I'm getting scared now; this is no joke.

Butch is on top of me, trying to get me on my back; I'll be more vulnerable face up. He pushes me to the right and I resist. I push left with everything I have, and he continues to push hard right. I keep pushing real hard to the left, and then suddenly, on purpose, go limp. His ferocious pushing and all the momentum turn me over much quicker than he expected. We both roll over completely and I am able to pop up free. I am not going to make that mistake again. This guy will never get close to me.

Butch slowly gets to his feet and the crowd jeers at him. He had me in his crosshairs and he couldn't finish me. I'm getting tired. Wrestling is tough and I don't have the stamina that I used to. It's not like I've been in any kind of training lately.

We circle each other. I keep him away. Then I jab. *Got him*. His face pops back and he keeps coming. Jab, jab, fake, jab jab. I'm connecting. He throws a wild left hook but I duck down easily and then jump up. Jab, jab. He can take that with him, give him something to remember. Keep working. Jab, right, jab, hook. I connect on two of them. He's bleeding from his left eye, so I keep working his left eye. He throws another wild left and I duck.

Jab, jab. It looks like another left. No, it's a right! Damn!

My face is in the pavement again. I can't believe I let that asshole connect on a haymaker overhand right like that. He's about to pound on me.

I tuck and roll away as fast as I can. He's catching his breath, he's winded. I pop up fast and I know there's no more fucking around. I'm winded too, much more than usual. But I can't let him catch his breath; it's go time. I pop two more jabs and get him to throw another haymaker. I duck underneath and come up with everything I've got. I throw lefts and rights, fast and hard in constant combination. I guarantee it's faster than anything these guys have ever seen in person.

Butch is taking them but the stubborn son of a bitch won't go down. Still, he's dazed and harmless. I duck down and snap my whole body into a left hook that lands square on the right side of his face. Two teeth fly out and blood splatters. That's enough. Butch goes down hard and I raise both fists in the air.

I'm exhausted. The guys at Kosher World are cheering and patting me on my back. A couple of guys are helping Butch out, and I can't help but wonder how they would have treated me if I were knocked out. Tommie Doyle, the bookmaker, catches up to me and hands me a wad of money.

"Hey, kid, $4,200, awesome take. You were such an underdog, the losing bets had to really shell it out. Really nice numbers."

"I get this four grand?"

"Yep, I already took my cut for making book."

The crowd is still hovering around the ring, giving me the impression there is at least one more fight. I guess I wasn't the main attraction. I have to clean up and get my shit together.

I glance around and see Sev looking at me. He's actually smiling. I feel like Santa Claus; I'm the only fuckin' guy that can make Sev smile.

I walk through the courtyard and into the factory. The Hotdog Room is cranking and full of people. I head to the bathroom and wash my face. I'm pretty bloody from getting scraped against the pavement, but nothing major. And that four grand goes a long way to making me feel better.

I clean my bleeding face with water and it really stings. I am so tired right now; I need a minute alone. I slump down on the tile floor next to the last of eight sinks and lean my back against the wall. There are some loud grunts coming from one of the bathroom stalls. I guess I'm not alone in here. The guy sounds like a giant animal stuck in a trap. He's apparently in a bigger battle than I just fought against Butch Bombart. A pungent aroma fills the large room. I can't imagine who could be making these sounds. Maybe someone seven feet tall. I'm too tired to get up and leave, though. After a few more minutes of bestial noises, the toilet flushes.

The door of the stall opens and out walks Rabbi Silver; he gives me a confused glance, zips his baggy black pants and shuffles out the door. You would think he might consider washing his hands before blessing the meat.

CHAPTER 4

On Monday the workers are treating me differently.
Not only do I exist but I'm also back to my old routine, the one
I had when I started. I spend the morning unloading sides of
beef for transport to the butcher block. I now have breaks like
everyone else and am even offered some coffee. How 'bout
that? Someone offered me coffee. I feel like I'm fuckin' roy-
alty.

Throughout the morning, guys are telling me what a
good fight I had. I'm having the best morning since I began
working here. I would be happy to be left alone, but I can dig
the celebrity treatment.

At lunch I go to the sandwich truck that is parked outside the Kosher World courtyard. The old guy inside the truck
is drenched. While we work in the freezers all day, this poor
slob has the opposite problem. He's stuck in a silver metal
truck in the mid-day sun. I order a ham and cheese on a roll
with a soda. It's hard to imagine what's sweating more: this
old guy or the ham I'm about to eat. I put down $10 but the
old guy in the truck pushes it back. He puts my sandwich and
soda in a bag, but before he hands it to me, he drops in a packet
of cookies and gives me a nod. I am the man!

As I head to the lounge to eat my free meal, I'm thinking about one issue that needs to be addressed. Just then Felipe
catches up to me. "Yo, nice fight. You really surprised everyone."

"Thanks. Thanks a lot."

There is a shortage of real estate at the long cafeteria
tables in the lounge, just a few scattered seats here and there.
Sev is seated in his usual spot toward the corner with his cap-

tains Sal and Frank. I spot Bino the ball-buster sitting dead center.

"Are you going to fight again?" Felipe asks. He asks loud enough so the others in the lounge can hear. A few of the guys turn to hear my answer

"I dunno, I haven't been thinking about it. Maybe. You gonna spar with me, help me train?"

Felipe laughs. "Not me, man. I'm a lover, not a fighter."

"Okay, Romeo, check this out. I got to take care of something and at the same time, maybe I can scare up a sparring partner."

I walk toward the center and, interestingly enough, Felipe follows. I weave my way around the large cafeteria tables that occupy the room until we are standing directly in front of Bino. The jerk looks up and sees me standing there; he gives me a quizzical look and then goes back to his bright orange macaroni and cheese. It's time to really start leveraging off all my recent good fortune.

"Hey asshole, you're in my seat," I say loudly and firmly.

Bino and some of the others look up, surprised by this unprovoked comment. The room is starting to quiet down a bit; I figure maybe half the guys know what's going on. But for some reason, Bino looks perplexed.

"You ugly pale fuck, get out of my seat." I stare at him intently, refusing to let myself blink. I just keep thinking about how that cocksucker has been giving me such a hard time, just for laughs.

Bino gives me a blank look. He has no idea what to do. The lounge is even quieter, and in his confusion Bino turns and looks at Sev. Sev is staring straight forward, trying to chew on his sandwich, obviously doing everything he can to hold back a smile at the same time. It's not working, and Sev's smile grows wider and wider. It's getting pretty easy to get him to smile. Clearly, Bino ain't getting any help from Sev.

With an open hand, I slap down hard into Bino's plate of macaroni and cheese, sending the crap all over the guy. I know it's more third grade than it is OK Corral, but fuck it. I'm gonna send a message that I can push back. Bino's in a pretty bad spot. He should do something, but if he goes after me, he knows now that I'll put the hurt on him.

Bino looks at himself wearing his lunch. He stands up and is trying to say something. The fucking guy is so embarrassed that his pale skin is turning red. Maybe I did him a favor here. Someone should screw around with him 24 hours a day; with the surge in blood flow to his face, he almost looks human. He finally blurts out, "Fuck you, man! Don't think I can't get you back."

With that comment he storms out. The guys in the lounge egg him on, saying "Oooooooo" in unison.

When Bino is gone, practically the whole lounge is laughing. The guys who were sitting next to Bino scoot over a bit to make room for Felipe and me. I brush off some of the macaroni and cheese that landed on the long bench. I know the guys bitch about what an asshole Bino is. I have a hunch taking care of this will go a long way. Maybe it's a stupid risk, but I think I just made life better. In any case, it feels real good.

I've just swallowed the first bite of my sandwich when Lily comes screaming into the lounge. She's in a panic and wailing uncontrollably. Felipe turns to me and says, "Man, can she be dramatic."

I can't make out what she is trying to say but I'm sure it's nothing good. Everyone is trying to go about their business rather than get involved with Lily. Finally Amy Horwitz from packaging tries to get her under control. Lily's face is bright red and she's breathing like a cow giving birth. I've never seen hysteria like this.

Finally Lily calms down enough to tell us what happened. She says she went to the women's locker room to start her shift and opened up her locker. What she found was her boss George and his hairy ears staring at her. The problem was, George wasn't all in one piece. His severed head was gazing at her from the top shelf. The rest of him was in her locker too. Apparently someone shot George, hacked up his body, put him in garbage bags and stuffed him into Lily's locker. They put his head in a clear plastic bag and left it on the top shelf of her locker for maximum effect.

It takes the police about 20 minutes to get here. They are taping off areas and questioning everyone. The police are amazed it took till noon to discover George, as he'd been there overnight at least. The other women apparently smelled something rank in the locker room but just figured it was Lily being hygienically challenged. Kosher World is shut down for the day, but we all have to hang around in case the cops want to ask any questions.

The next day they get us working as soon as possible. Sev tells us, "Let the police do their job and you do yours." It's a surreal atmosphere. People are milling about like little kids at a party for adults. I stumble like a zombie to my spot in the Hotdog Room.

No one wants to talk about the murder. I'm getting the impression this didn't come out of the blue. People are upset, but nobody's shocked. No one will tell me anything, either. Just when I think Kosher World can't get any weirder, it moves up a rung on the weird ladder. And while it was never really safe, it feels downright dangerous now.

So I just keep to myself and do my job, trying to pretend nothing awful has happened. People are doing their jobs and leaving me alone, so I can't complain too much. Throughout the week some of the shifts are pretty thin as people go to George's funeral and pay their respects to his wife and two

daughters. I am more relieved than ever as this week con-
cludes.

CHAPTER 5

It's only been a week since George was killed and it's
already business as usual. Sort of. No one is talking about
the murder, as if it didn't happen. I don't get it; not only was
George a co-worker, but he was also one of the guys in charge.
I know less than everyone else, but one thing is clear to me:
It's not smart to talk about George now.

It's time for me to leave, and I can't wait to bounce. By
the end of a day here, I need a nice hot tub and massage. But
I'll settle for pizza in Hempstead and watching my mother
stare at the stupid shows on the Game Show Network. Then I'll
crash for the night and do it all over again.

I leave the courtyard and lock eyes with a man in a light
blue warm-up suit. He's a strange-looking guy, sunburned with
a bushy, bright-blond beard, big gold chains and a huge gut.
No doubt he is looking at me. I walk past him, but even with
my back toward him I can feel him looking at me. What the
hell is he doing?

As I turn the corner on Chet Boulevard, I forget about
the guy. I must have just missed the bus. There's only one
person at this usually crowded bus stop. Standing there by his
lonesome is one of my all-time favorite people, Sev Reynard.
I know Sev doesn't live in Long Island, so there's no reason
for him to be waiting for the Grand Central Express. Maybe
I missed some corned beef scraps when I was cleaning up a
room.

I walk up to the bus stop and without saying a word I
stand behind Sev. We both stand there, weighed down by that
awkward silence that is always found in elevators, at chance
meetings with old girlfriends and in the company of factory

bosses who torture grunts. We just stand there. The first person who talks loses.

"Hey, Kevin. You in a hurry or you got a few minutes to talk?"

I look at Sev for a moment and say, "I'm not in any hurry. What's up?"

"There's a bar two blocks away. You up for a drink?"

"Sure, but I never saw a bar out here."

Sev motions with his eyes to the left. The outdoor light drains some of the contrast from his white eyes and dark black skin but he's still got a commanding look. Sev starts walking past Chet Blvd. and I follow without talking. We go south on Roogie Avenue. Sev says, "It's in an alley next to Moonbeam Cheese. You won't see it unless you know about it."

But there it is, a simple red brick building with a neon Budweiser sign and, I have to admit, a pretty good logo painted on the glass. The logo is a huge blue train, but the front of the train has an angry human face. A cloud of green smoke billows from the irate mouth and in the smoke are the words "LOCO-MOTIVE BREATH."

From the inside, it looks just like the Blarney Stone I was at a couple of weeks ago. The only difference here is the rock star posters covering the walls. There's Led Zeppelin, Grateful Dead, Eric Clapton and a bunch of others I can't make out.

"There's the guy that owns the place, Harv Hatch. We call him 'H'."

I turn around and see H standing behind the bar and pouring some pretzels into a bowl. He's wearing a shirt with a Confederate flag and the name Lynrd Skynrd. H stands about six feet tall with a scrawny frame and concave chest that looks way out of proportion because of his bowling ball gut that protrudes above a large metal belt buckle. He has a scraggly beard that can't cover all the places it's supposed to on his face.

His long, dirty-blond hair actually is dirty and doesn't cover his head much anymore, either.

"H is a big rock fan," Sev offers. "He mostly likes the classic rock crap, you know, like the Stones and the Doors."

A waitress walks to our table and looks at Sev. "What can I get you, Sev?"

"Tina, I won $2,000 on my boy over here and it's burning through my pocket. How 'bout two beers and two shots of 151?"

"You actually bet on me?" I ask as Tina saunters away with Sev's order.

"I didn't have a choice. You were my guy; you know, from my place. I had to do it even though I thought I was donating it."

It's hard to imagine anyone making this guy do anything, but at five-to-one odds, Sev must have bet $400 on me.

Sev looks at me and asks, "Where did you learn to fight? You knew what you were doing with Butch."

Tina shows up with her bar tray filled with goodies. There's an entire bottle of rum, the 151 version—it's as close to pure grain alcohol as you can get. She places two long beer glasses filled from the tap onto the table along with two shot glasses. She pours two shots of 151 and then clicks her cigarette lighter and touches the flame to the top of the shot glass. The rum catches fire and Tina says, "Enjoy," and walks away.

"What's with the fire?" I ask.

"It's kinda gotten to be a tradition you know, working in the Kosher World freezers all day, the guys found this helps warm the bones."

"Wait, you mean you guys think this warms your bones?"

"What are you a fuckin' doctor now?" Sev snaps.

"I'm not saying anything Sev, it makes sense, I just never thought of it before." Holy shit, just when I think I'm getting along with the guy.

Sev takes a sip from his cold beer, puts the beer glass down, picks up his flaming 151 shot and throws it down his throat. So I pick up my shot glass and I'm telling myself, no matter what, don't cough or act like a pussy.

I swallow and real quickly chase it with my beer. It's as rough as I expect but I maintain some degree of dignity.

"We got two more fights over the summer. You got any more in you?"

"I don't know, Sev. I kind of did this one spur of the moment. I'm not sure how a planned one would work out. Me fighting…is that the only way the shit treatment is gonna stop?"

"No, that's done whether you fight again or not." Sev motions to Tina for more drinks. "You're all right. The job's tough enough and I piled a load of shit on you. You handled it, plus some. We couldn't believe you didn't bail. You do your job now and things are gonna be fine. If you want to fight, it helps us. If you don't, we'll just sew Hector Pinto's finger back on and get good odds."

Look at my boy Sev trying to tell a joke.

Tina walks over to the table and pours two more shots. Tina has a look like she's seen everything ten thousand times. She doesn't seem to have an attitude but she's not too sweet either. Her face is hardened from too many asshole drunks, but you can see that once upon a time she was a looker. Yeah, I'm pretty sure Tina is attractive; I haven't had enough of the 151 to distort her favorably.

Sev picks up his shot glass and I do the same. He says, "Nice win." We just tip the shot glasses in each other's direction because you definitely don't clink glasses here. We simultaneously down our drinks.

"So where did you learn to fight?" Sev asks as he motions to Tina for some more rounds.

"It's kinda weird. I blew my knee out during a game and couldn't play hoops anymore. I used to play a lot of basketball. I even got a scholarship to play at high school."

"Bullshit, they don't give high school scholarships."

"Yeah, they do and I got one. I got one to play at a real ritzy school in Locust Valley, Long Island. Before that I almost spent my whole life playing hoops in Hempstead Park."

"I know Hempstead Park. It's not Rucker Park or West 4th Street but it's on the map."

"Yeah, that's it. Me and my boys were always there."

"So how was the school?" Sev asks as we throw back two more shots.

"School was okay." I hold back a 151 cough and say, "I got through it. I learned what I needed in class and saw a different way to live. We got a decent hoop team out of it and I had some colleges looking at me. But my timing sucked. I tore my knee up in the playoffs of my senior year. No time to show I could heal up and it killed the college interest I was getting."

"Tough story about your knee. But Homer, didn't I ask you how you picked up fighting?"

Wow, I'm rambling. I know what he asked me, but it's the first time I ever really spoke to Sev. He's the boss; why does he give a shit about me? Man, I'm getting buzzed. Tina walks over with two more shots. At this point I welcome the shots and damn, Tina looks good.

"Sorry," I say. "They're kind of related. Despite my knee injury, my high school coach put in a word for me at New York State University where he had some connections. They offered some financial aid and some bullshit job that I didn't even have to show up for. It was enough to get me by. They called it a 'soft scholarship.' I was going to be a walk-on player. It was the best I could do with a bad knee.

"When I got to school, way the fuck up in Albany, the

'soft scholarship' got pulled from me and six other prospective players. Only one guy really had a shot for the team and the rest of us were like insurance. It's the same as an airline over-booking a flight. So here I am; if I want college, I got to pay for it. If it's not college, it's back to Hempstead. So I started working a bunch of shit jobs to make tuition and pay bills. Then I lucked out. They had this crazy old coach who took guys like me and trained us for club fights. When we won, he got a third of our prize. I got to learn how to box and make some decent bucks. But to tell you the truth, I dug getting the attention again."

I'm surprised Sev's asking but more surprised he's listening. I'm feeling weird telling Sev about this shit. I wouldn't mind not talking anymore. As a matter of fact, I can use some answers myself. *Fuck it,* I tell myself. *Let's see if I can get some info; worst case, if he gets heated up, I blame the 151.*

More of the liquor magically appears at our table. Tina lights them up. It dawns on me that she's probably lighting them right at the table as opposed to the bar so that the blue flames won't lap up the booze before we get our chance. It's a pretty good observation. I'm thinking that this stuff might actually be making me smarter. "Sev, can I ask you something?"

"Yeah, what's up?" Sev seems to be more relaxed than I've ever seen him. His head is bopping slightly to the Allman Brothers song, "Sweet Melissa."

"Who whacked George Skolinsky?" I ask.

"Good question, but it's not one I'm gonna answer. You got any other questions, wiseass?" Before I could ask anything Sev blurts out, "Say, how did you get into Kosher World anyway?"

"I got friendly with Rich Balducci, Jimmy Balducci's son." I told him how we started at the Remington Academy together. We both really stood out, I said, since everyone else there practically came off the Mayflower except for the two of us. "I got in for hoops and Balducci's old man donated a building or something. The kids let me alone but they really hassled Richie. I kinda looked out for him and even got him on the basketball team. His father always appreciated that, and every now and then he did some nice things for me. I still stay in touch with Richie, and when his dad knew I needed some money over the summer, he did me this favor."

"He gets you in Kosher World and considers that a favor?" Sev chuckles quietly.

"You laugh, but I'm always looking for money," I say. "This is as good as it can get for me as far as the dough." We both fall silent for a minute, and I figure I can try again. "How come nobody can give me a straight answer about where you were before Kosher World? Did you do any fighting?"

This question seems to intrigue Sev and I can see his normally powerful eyes are starting to get glassy. "I don't know…. Is it just you asking?"

"Yeah, just me. Who's gonna listen to me anyway?" I say.

"It's funny, but no one's really had the balls to ask me to my face for years," Sev says. "I never told anyone before either. I just preferred it that way. Truth is, though, I can help you, and so I'll tell you something. I was star linebacker at a high school in Detroit. I went to the Marines after high school, and if you think you got involved in a whole different world, it was nothing like I saw."

"Vietnam?" I asked.

"Just after. As far as the world knew we weren't fighting wars anymore. The problem was, we were fighting in wars and I was fighting in them. You probably don't even know about Biafra, Congo or El Salvador, but I fought in places like that. We were trying to take out governments, and the shit I saw and did make what happened to George a walk in the park.

The fucked-up thing is when we were finished we became a problem. The CIA didn't want us around anymore. They couldn't use us and they didn't want anyone to know about us. So they started taking us out."

"When you say out, you mean…."

"Out is out. It was sick shit. Luckily, I did a few really big guys some huge 'solids' in my day and they ended up doing the right thing by me. They got me to disappear. You know, become invisible."

"Invisible, like Kosher World invisible?"

"Exactly. Nobody here knows my past, so if somehow, someone has a great discovery, you and I are gonna do some discussin' and I ain't as easy as Bino."

"Sev, I'm not gonna say anything, for real. Why do you think this can help me?"

"You remind me a lot of me. Different worlds but, at the core, more or less the same. You're gonna have some choices, some roads are gonna fork. I thought I was a bad-ass, and I ended up killing guys that I didn't even know. Why? Because some colonel told me to. Then they turn around and try to waste me and my buddies. You can do better. Look at me. Do I look like I'm fulfilling my potential?" I have nothing to say to that, so Sev continues. "That shit with Bino in the lounge, it's a waste."

"C'mon, Sev, that guy…."

Sev interrupts me. "That guy is a fuckin' pimple on your ass. He probably was done bustin' your balls like the rest of us. You just had a hornet up your ass and you weren't smart enough to let it go. I'm sure it felt real good to grind him down in front of everyone. But now, you know he's gonna try to do something back at you. The thing is that if you keep doing that kinda crap, then you become Bino. How do you think Bino got like he is? The point is, don't make enemies you don't have to. Keep piling up worthless enemies and you'll never know who puts a cap in your head when you're not looking."

Sev pauses and looks over at Tina. There are three workers from another factory, and one of them keeps trying to pat Tina on the ass. Sev kinda half stands up, leans over the table and barks out, "Yo." He glares at the three guys. "Everything okay, Tina?"

"Seems to be fine," Tina says. "I got yours here, too. I'll be right over."

Sev turns back to me and picks up where we left off. "You and me, we have some inner demons. If you're gonna be better than me, then control those demons. Do you want to fulfill your potential? Listen up. You are gonna kill someone sometime. Maybe you think I'm on crack. How can I know something like that? Because I've been around, that's how. I was the same lost hotshit with a big set of balls and some ambition. You don't even know what you are capable of and willing to do. When you do it, you better make it count. Make it worthwhile."

Tina drops off more shots, she lights them and we drink them. I am definitely feeling it now. I haven't eaten in a while and this stuff is rocket fuel, but I think it's going down smoother. I have some weird thoughts. I don't think Sev asked me here to get info, even though he was asking me a lot of questions. He's carrying a lot of baggage, and he's doing most of the talking. Could I really be the first guy he told that stuff to?

It feels good to be talking to Sev about all this personal shit. I have to admit I like him. I admire the way he always has control of the place. People do what he says because they respect him, not because he's the boss. In some warped way I think I'm helping him not be invisible. I wish I could have that effect on my mother.

CHAPTER 6

The next few hours at H's place are pretty interesting. There's a lot to Sev and this whole industry row. It's more than a summer job, and there's something to be gained here—although that's what George probably thought, and he ended up losing his head. These boys are playing for high stakes. It's hard to know how to proceed.

At some point in my drunken stupor, I agree to participate in the last two fights of the summer. Sev offers me two things. First, I can use some time during the day to work out and train. Second, Sev offers to take me under his wing, teach me the business. Learn stuff inside the factory and the union. That's the part I can't refuse.

The way I see it, any situation can be my ticket. Some might look at this as a shitty summer job, but maybe it's more than that. Maybe there's a ton of money to be made here somewhere. I saw an infomercial once about some starving junior high science teacher who invented Savage Tan suntan oil. Now he's driving something with 600 horsepower. This guy Balducci who got me the job here is pretty fucking loaded too, and I don't see him as the type to split atoms or invent a new artificial heart. The point is that I could be sitting on something huge. You never know. If I'm here, why not make the most of it?

Eventually I stumble out of the bar and make it to the bus stop. The sun is down now, but it's still north of 90 degrees. Maybe it is really 50 degrees but it feels like 90 because my damn stomach is burning from that crap I was drinking with Sev. Still, I feel kinda good, too, like I am finally going somewhere worth going.

So now I'm getting paid to get in shape and learn the business. It seems reasonable to me. If I avoid getting my head kicked in, then it's win-win.

This week is the best yet.   I'm on a pretty good system. My hours are 9 to five (the gravy shift) with an occasional hour of overtime. No more Industrial Road sunrises. I'm always rotating around to different areas, helping in some and just observing in others. In preparation for the upcoming fights, I work out between 10 a.m. to 11:30 a.m. everyday. I do a bunch of pushups and sit-ups and a ton of punching with 3-pound tongues in my hand. On Tuesday and Thursday I do a lot of leg work. You know, squats and lunges.

The guys get a kick out of helping me. While I'm doing pushups, sometimes they give me target numbers to shoot for and count out as I am going. Felipe brings in his stopwatch and times me while I am punching with the cow tongues in my hands. Since George was killed, Felipe runs the Tongue Room.

Some of the guys from the Tongue Room even train with me. They want to get into better shape, so these six or sometimes seven guys get in a row and we just start going. Johnny's boombox blasts some hard-core rap, and we grab some cow tongues and launch punches: left, right, left, right, left. All in unison, all to the beat. Just like in the hip health clubs. Maybe they should put Cardio-Cow-Tongue-Boxing on their program list. Yeah, I think I'll drop that idea in the suggestion box.

When I finish my fight training for the day, it's back to work. Home base today is the Pastrami Room. These big square slices of beef the size of bedroom pillows are soaking in a vat filled with some kind of solution. I'm watching Miguel at the first station stab at them with a pitchfork, lift the beef out of the solution and then drop it on a large metal tray that can hold about 10 of these slabs of beef neatly spread out to cover

all the space on the tray. The eight people at Station One start
flinging a bunch of spices on the beef. When all 10 pieces are
spiced, another metal tray is locked into the 6-foot guardrails
and dropped down on the 10 slabs of beef that were just spiced.
Ten more slabs are spiced up and another tray is put on top.
This is how a Pastrami Tower is built at Station One, and there
are 12 stations in the Pastrami Room. Throughout the day,
thousands of towers are created. It looks like a fucking medi-
eval city or something.

  The guy at Pastrami Station Two lets out a big sneeze.
He's courteous enough to his co-worker to catch all the spray in
his hands but goes on flinging the spices on the beef. Remind
me not to eat Reuben sandwiches anymore. As I look closer,
I notice the sneezer is Hector Pinto. He must have been transferred here for a while since his injury on the Butcher Block.

  I watch as the Pastrami Towers are sent to be cooked.
They are then packaged in airtight plastic packages and boxed.
I even follow them to the warehouse. I watch the merchandise
go to the warehouse because every time I'm there, I notice a
portion being taken out and separated; some packages never
actually make it into the warehouse. For every ten boxes, one
box gets separated. No one seems to mind or ask and I'm not
going to, either. But I know something really crooked is going
on here.

  I've burned enough brain cells on pastrami allotment,
so it's basketball time. I'm back to playing hoops at Hempstead Park, and my knee seems to be holding up pretty good.
Maybe one day I should put basketball behind me, but I just
can't seem to get it out of my system. I even rationalize that
playing b-ball will help me train for the boxing matches. Nothing beats basketball for a real cardio workout.

  What's really amazing is that Loot and Carey get all
three of us onto a pretty hot team for the South Shore Clas-

sic. It is a big deal. The tournament lasts three weeks, and
I remember as a kid I never missed a game. But the Classic
isn't for just anyone. It draws some of the best talent around,
including college players from some big-time programs. All
the teams have sponsors, and you have to be invited to play.

I'm joining our team for the South Shore Classic in the
quarterfinals. Rosters can add and subtract players at any time
because the organizers know the really big-time talent is not
going to commit for an entire three-week clip. So you never
know who could show up for the finals. That's why Loot can
add me to the roster on such late notice. Besides being the cap-
tain of the team, he's basically the Mayor of Hempstead Park.
It's all he's ever aspired to do, and in a way I'm jealous. Loot
is probably the happiest guy I ever met.

Loot's real name is Jordan Hightower, but "Loot" works
great for the South Shore Classic. Hightower gave himself the
name Loot because as one of the all-time great trash talkers,
he claims to be the "money player." The guy who announces
all the game's action over the PA system loves nicknames like
Loot. This guy is nuts. If you don't have a nickname like Loot
does, odds are you will by the end of the game. The announcer
rarely sits and it's not at all out of the ordinary for him to do his
play-by-play standing on top of the scorer's table, sometimes
even on the court. The crowd loves him. They call him the
Mouth of the South, Mouth for short.

I'm glad Mouth likes Loot, because he tends to help us
out. Today we need the help. Our team, the Buzzards (named
for our sponsor, Buzzard's Bay Bar and Grill on Fulton Avenue), has a particularly tough match-up. Their team has a
6'10", 285-pound player that the Mouth has simply dubbed
"The Building." The team's good, but pretty much it's The
Building and everyone else.

Mouth is in his glory tonight. He is drawing on every
street-ball taunt he has accumulated over his illustrious ca-

reer. My other great friend, Carey, who Mouth has nicknamed
Turbo, has two guys on him and is forced to make a bad shot
that clanks hard against the front rim. Mouth, with his cordless
microphone, jumps up on the scorer's table and yells, "C'mon,
Turbo, you got to give up the rock! Man, you got Loot filling
the lane and you throw up that gunk. Damn, the only way to
get a pass from Turbo is to put a damn net around your neck so
he'll think you're the basket."

Howls erupt from the crowd. It's pretty funny but
encouraging. Loot threads a beautiful pass right into my hands
on a fast break; when I lay this in, we'll only be down eight. I
cross the foul line and start my last step. Before my knee injury, I would slam this bitch, but I better just lay it in. As I roll
it off my hand, The Building blasts in from nowhere and swats
my shot 12 feet into the crowd. The Mouth must be drooling
now.

The crowd simultaneously lets out an "Ahhhhhh!"
Mouth runs on the court and actually smacks me on the butt.
"Get that shit out of my kitchen! Damn, The Building just fell
on you. He blocked that garbage with his elbow." There's no
end in sight; he's on my case now.   Mouth calls me The White
Knight because there aren't many white guys playing at this
event, or even in the audience. Mouth says, "Damn, Knight,
how you gonna get over that? The Building just took your man-
hood!"

I hate to admit it, but Mouth might be right. I hit a few
outside shots, but I can't do any slashing. Any time I'm inside,
the big ugly Building is there. We're gonna lose this game.
The Building is too dominating, and it's going to kill Loot. He
lives for this. For me, I'm just happy to be here. It's a perfect
summer night and I'm doing something I always wanted to do.
There are some faces in the crowd that I recognize, people I
haven't seen in a while.

Loot is pushing the ball up court. There's a minute and

a half left in the game, and we're down nine points now. Loot pulls up at the arc and lets a three-pointer go. It's a nice-looking shot, but it has a bit too much spin on it and bounces off the back part of the rim. The Building leaps over us mere mortals and pulls down yet another rebound. Loot is screaming for us to intentionally foul in an attempt to stop the clock. But it's too late: the ball flies up court and the other team spreads out to run the clock down. Carey finally catches one of their guys and fouls him, but we are down nine with one minute and 10 seconds to go. Their player is on the foul line, but I'm not concentrating on him. Like a fucking idiot, I'm scanning the faces in the crowd again, hoping against hope that C.W., for old time's sake, has shown up to watch me play.

"C'mon, Kevin! Get your head out your ass! We can still pull this off," Loot shouts. I wonder if they hit that foul shot; I was really spacing out. No, we're still down nine points, but he makes the second shot. Loot inbounds to me, I push it up court and pass it to Carey, who lets go with another three pointer that splashes in, nothing but net, but we have only 45 seconds left and we're down seven. Everything now is more or less for show. The final score is 98-91. The Building scored 40 points and blocked 11 shots.

The spectators leave the bleachers and head onto the court. Both teams meet in the center and shake hands. A couple of hugs are exchanged. Everyone's leaving now, but I barely notice; I'm still thinking of C.W. and wishing that, if it had to end, that I had left her. That seems more natural than her leaving me. And less painful.

CHAPTER 7

I pull into Kosher World and immediately start taking some heat. I'm in a jacket and tie and some of the guys find this quite amusing. Bino is not one of them. I'm sure he's a bit jealous because Sev's asking me to join in on the union meeting today. It surprises me that they'll let someone like me into the meeting, but Sev told me if he wants someone there, no one's gonna say anything. He says, "The meeting is a joke anyway, so who gives a crap if anyone has something to say about it?"

The Kosher World management will be at the meeting, along with Sev, Sal, Frank and Wally Strewgats, the shop steward. The shop steward is supposed to make sure the union is being looked after. You know, fight for some rights. Wally doesn't really do any championing for union causes, though. I haven't found a Kosher World worker that likes or respects him, but he manages to win the election each year. I know it's not his talent or work ethic that gets him elected. It must be something to do with the fact that no one will run against him. Bucking the system in place is not really a viable option. I'm going to find out why, but it's pretty clear there are health problems involved.

It seems Sev has some freedom to do things just because everyone knows what a shit-show this would be without him. Sev makes the place run, but we all know it could be much better. There's a ton of frustration. Management is not getting the profit margins and the union is not getting raises and benefits, yet all the tools are here for a successful operation. All the other crooked crap that's going on behind the scenes is handcuffing everyone from making money and even gaining benefits.

Sev tells me how much he hates this particular meeting. It's supposed to deal with the same issues that have been raised for the last 20 years, yet nothing will get resolved. Everyone in the room knows what the problems are, but no one will address them. So the company and union will carry on, status quo.

The meeting might be worthless but it should be interesting to learn what goes on. Also, the raw surprise when Jimmy Balducci sees me with the union guys should be worth the effort right there. I haven't spoken to Mr. Balducci or his son Rich since he got me the job here. Every now and then I see Balducci from the distance, but I never approach him. Knowing one of the big shots might attract some resentment, and I'm all for limiting resentment.

The discussion comes to order in the break room around a large table. Balducci, sitting at one end, looks at me and says, "Now you're bringing in the heavy guns. You guys are shameless. I can't say 'no' to this kid. He's practically family."

Wally Strewgats says, "In that case, can we expect a 10 percent pay increase from management this year, Mr. Balducci?"

Balducci looks at Strewgats and says, "No." He pauses for a second and adds, "Holy shit! That was easier than I thought." Then Balducci lets out a huge, exaggerated belly laugh.

We all politely join in on the laugh.

The meeting is well choreographed and all the dancers follow their proper steps. First the pay raises are shot down. Health benefits get nixed next. Then Wally asks for COLA benefits. The fact that I was new to the scene added a little flavor for them. Wally says, "Now Kevin, it's not that we are thirsty. COLA stands for cost of living adjustments." Wally waits for some laughs. He smirks and looks around the table but his comments are met by the abyss.

Balducci basically speaks his well-rehearsed line in monotone. "Fellas, you know I want to help you out. Why wouldn't I? The numbers are what they are and the cost to produce is outpacing production. Get me more efficient production. Bring that to the table and I can play ball with the benefits."

Wally pleads, "C'mon! We need more than the usual one percent adjustment. We're falling behind."

"Wally, you know what's happening all around this area. I can fire off the names of several unions that got crushed this year. Management just upped and moved the whole operation to where you can't even smell a union. They closed the whole freakin' factory and left everyone high and dry. It's actually better to start from scratch than to be held hostage by the unions. I'm telling you something, cross my heart: we've been approached to move to Indianapolis. How 'bout them apples? You don't want to see 1,800 people without their jobs. Do you?"

"Mr. Balducci, don't you think you're playing a little harder here than usual? You may cause a panic," Wally says.

"That's not the intention. I'm telling you like I see it. Right now, I can offer a one-percent cost-of-living increase and maybe I can get an extra sick day added. Don't kid yourself. Management had to deal with two strikes and one job action in the last 15 years, so don't talk to me about hardball. You do what you got to do, but if you try to demand anything above that, I might be watching the Indianapolis 500 live and you may be drinking Mad Dog out of a paper bag while looking for a cardboard box to keep out the rain."

"Okay, Mr. Balducci, we understand your position," Wally mutters. "I'll talk to the troops and circle back with you."

"Good. I look forward to getting it wrapped up so we

can look ahead."

Everyone stands up and shakes hands. When I shake Mr. Balducci's hand, he holds on and pulls me off to the side. Balducci looks at me squarely and says, "Good to see you. How you holding up?"

"Fine. It's a great job. I can't thank you enough for getting me in here," I say.

"Are the guys treating you well?" Balducci asks.

"Yeah, perfect. It's really been great."

"Shut the fuck up. I heard all about it."

"Everything?" I ask.

"Yeah, I really know everything. Including how you kicked ass in the Industrial Road bouts. Nice job. Look, I've been watching, and you're not just a line worker. On your own you managed to get in with management and union leaders. You're a smart kid, always were. You were great to my boy at Remington Academy, and I'm not sure how he would have done there if you didn't look after him. Why not start toning down the macho crap and start relying more on your brain? Let your head start carrying the load."

"You always make a lot of sense. I'm trying."

"Try a little harder, except tomorrow. I know you're fighting again tomorrow, and I'm putting a lot of cash on you. I can't be there, because I can't know about it. But I figure since I got you in here, I might as well make a few bucks."

We shake hands again and say goodbye. When I get outside I notice Sal, Frank and Sev talking. Wally must be back in Wally-World. Sal and Frank are trying to talk Sev into stopping by H's place for a quick lunch and a few "rinses" to make the day go a little better. Sev's not really in the mood, though. A meeting like we just had must be hard for Sev to swallow. It's like this place is draining and stealing souls. Balducci wants more production before he'll fork over benefits. Yet there is more production than they're seeing. Every single day so many boxes just up and disappear. That extra nut would add a lot to both company profits and ammo for union benefits. I imagine Sev can't help caring. For Sev, professionally and personally, that lost potential must make him feel helpless. A meeting like we just had will magnify that feeling.

CHAPTER 8

The next match goes real well. My opponent telegraphs
his punches. He's shorter, lighter, slower and dumber than
Butch. Maybe I have delusions of grandeur, but this guy is
easy. I see his punches from a mile away. Whenever you start
a match, there's always a "feeling out" period, you know, a
little testing. I'm flinging out some test jabs to get going, and
they're actually landing. Christ, has anyone ever taught this
guy to block?

My trainer for the club fights in college, Tagasumi Wui,
always preached "brocking." "You must brock punch. Concentrate on the four B's. No booze, no broad, no bongs and
always brock. I get girl call me up: 'my boyfriend so upset
you no teach him to brock. He no make love to me anymore.'
I get mother call me up: 'You bad trainer. My son so ugly
now. Why you no teach him to brock?' But that is what I teach
you here, and you must listen to how to brock, so I get no bad
phone call!"

It made sense to me then and would have made sense
to this clown I'm fighting. I drop him in under four minutes. I
spent all that time getting in shape and getting some wind back
and it didn't even matter. I hardly have a sweat going.

I'm surprised how short this lasted and I'm actually
a little disappointed, which is strange. I always say I do this
kinda stuff just for the money, but clearly I've got some other
issues driving me.

At least I can enjoy my win tonight. The last time I
fought I was too freakin' exhausted. There's a pretty good
crowd at the Locomotive Breath. Plenty of guys are buying me
drinks, even some guys from some of the other factories. I'm

having a damn good time. I'm even starting to like the classic rock blaring through the place.

A bunch of guys from Kosher World with their arms around each other's shoulders are singing Van Morrison's Brown-Eyed Girl. They are really lit. It's all good, but something's very weird about hard-ass factory workers belting out the chorus, going "Sha-na-na-na-na lah-tee-da."

H calls to me from the bar and offers me a brew on the house. He hands me the beer and looks at the factory workers, still singing. He says, "You want to know why this song is so righteous, Kevin?"

"Lay it on me, H. Give me something from the rock 'n' roll pulpit."

"Listen up, son." H has obviously been having a few himself tonight. "Everyone has that brown-eyed girl in his past. Everyone's got one. She don't have to have brown eyes, mind you. It could be blue eyes or bloodshot eyes, but you know, she's the girl that got away, the one you miss. She makes you think of another place, and for some reason, you like that place better."

With that profound thought, H lets out a huge belch. The man might look like a wet dog, and that burp certainly smells worse than any wet dog, but I have to admit the guy makes sense. Hell, I'm only 21 and I got one of those girls already. I guess C.W. Wellington is my brown-eyed girl. It's a good thing the song is ending; I kinda feel like joining the fellas in singing now.

I leave the bar at around 10 p.m. I might be on the gravy shift but I still have to get some sleep. I left my important crap like my keys and wallet in the Kosher World locker room. I grab my stuff from the locker and head toward the back exit to the car. I didn't want to deal with the bus after the fight tonight, so I borrowed my mother's car today. Then I see some guys moving something. It's a strange time of night to see things being loaded on a truck. That is, unless it's the merchandise that's always being separated. In that case, it makes perfect sense.

As I watch, a ton of stuff is loaded onto independent trucks. It's taking a while and these guys are moving like it's broad daylight, nothing sinister, just business as usual. I even recognize some of them as guys from Kosher World. Nobody I know personally, but guys I've seen around.

When they finish, the supervisor takes out a wad of cash and begins dispensing it among the workers. I go out to my car unnoticed, pull out of the lot and wait. After waiting for 15 minutes, I notice the independent trucks pull out and head for the Long Island Expressway. I'm following them.

The trucks are on the L.I.E. for just a few minutes. I'm behind a few cars. The trucks get off at the Springfield exit and so do I. We start making some quick turns. I don't really know the streets; I just know I am somewhere in Bayside, Queens, or maybe Flushing. We pull into a neighborhood strip mall that is empty at this time of night.

I don't want to follow them into the parking lot; it would be obvious, as the place is deserted. I park on the street by a meter. I slowly walk around the back to get a view but I'm careful not to be spotted.

They don't waste any time. When I get back there, the stuff's already being unloaded. There are two guys, one wearing a hooded sweatshirt and the other a pullover sweatshirt and a wool hat. The meat is going into a freezer here. This isn't that big a store; it looks like a normal-size local meat market. They've been at this awhile. Are there more stops for this truck? The independent truck is packed with enough food for 20 of these stores. I need to get closer to see what's going on. I am amazed that they are cleaning this truck out, all for this store.

"Yo," a voice from behind says.

I turn around and take a punch square in my nose.
Blood spurts and my eyes start tearing. Before I have any
chance to react, two more punches hit my face. Christ, I go a
whole fight at the Industrial Road bouts without a scratch tonight and this guy starts pounding me. Actually, there is more
than one. As I lie on the ground I feel some kicks in my ribs
and I know it's got to be more than two feet hitting me. They
are barking something at me but I'm not all here right now; I
can't make out what they're saying.

They drag me toward the meat market. When I struggle
and try to break free, I get punched in the head and kneed in
my stomach. This is bad.

They bring me inside. Two guys are holding me down
while the guy in the hooded sweatshirt starts taping my hands
together with packaging tape. Then he begins taping my ankles
together. I am lying here helpless. I got to get my shit together. I feel myself start blacking out. I got to hold on.

I am so uncomfortable from the cold. I can taste my
blood. I see the Kosher World logo all around me. This is the
freezer inside the meat market. Shit, can I feel any worse than
this? I'm blacking out again.

I'm not in the freezer anymore. This is the back of the
meat market. I hear someone talking to me; but what's he saying? I recognize him. It's the same guy who was staring at me
outside Kosher World a couple of weeks back. He's wearing
the same light blue baggy warm-up suit and big gold chains.
He still has a scraggly, blondish beard. I can't understand this
guy because his English sucks. He's got some sort of Russian
accent. But he's trying to sound like a hip-hop guy.

"What up, Dawg? You not happy with your cut from
the bout tonight? Looking to get in on some of my action?"

I look at him and try to shrug like I don't understand.
I'm not even sure I can shrug. I'm starting to wake up a bit,

though I can't fuckin' move.

Blue Warm-up Suit stares at me for a minute and looks over at one of the guys that worked me over and says, "Yo, Hammer, you didn't have to wait for me to get here. You know what we got to do here. Hey, you got any ground beef?"

Hooded Sweatshirt says, "Yeah, plenty. You want some?"

"For sure, Dawg, and a few T-bones," says Warm-up Suit.

Hooded Sweatshirt heads toward the front of the store and disappears. I have enough sense right now to be scared shitless. What the fuck was I thinking? Why was this so important to me? It's just a damn summer job.

Hooded Sweatshirt returns with two trays. One has some T-bone steaks and the other some hamburger meat.

"Thanks, Dawg," Warm-up Suit says. I guess everybody is Dawg to him. "Now go wrap him up," he says as he points at me.

I'm on my back. Wool Cap sits on my hands and stares at me with this intense, demonic look. Hooded Sweatshirt starts wrapping my forehead with the cellophane. He circles around my forehead and continues over my eyes. I am trying to struggle but I don't have enough in me. He continues circling the cellophane over my nose. He keeps going. Now over my mouth. I am already having trouble breathing. He continues wrapping all the way down my neck.

My vision is blurred from the cellophane. I can't make out their faces anymore but I can see them laughing at me. They're not bluffing. This isn't a scare. This can't be it. Not like this. I am trying to breathe. I open my mouth wide and suck, but all I am doing is creating suction. The plastic is getting tighter. I can taste blood. I am losing air. I try not to breathe, but soon my body won't let me resist and involuntarily, my mouth opens and I suck for air. There is no air. I feel my eyes beginning to bulge. Oh God, not like this. Please, I don't want to end up in Lily's locker.

The more worked up I get, the harder it is to breathe. But how the fuck do I not get worked up? My heart is throbbing; it's ready to burst out of my shirt. They're all just laughing at me; their voices are muted, but I can hear them pretty well.

It won't be long now.

Another figure walks over to Hooded Sweatshirt, Wool Cap and Warm-up Suit and says, "What's taking you guys so long tonight? You should have been outta here an hour and a half ago."

I recognize the voice. It's Jimmy Balducci. Thank God, please save me! I'm starting to black out.

"Zorry, Mr. Ball-du-zi," says Warm-up Suit. "Some ash-hole broke in on us and was watching us."

Balducci looks down at me squirming and says. "Pretty fuckin' cool, the fuckin' guy is turning purple. How long he been like this?"

"I dunno, pretty long time. He's a stubborn son of a bitch," says Hooded Sweatshirt.

Balducci puts his face right up to mine. Balducci starts laughing. "What the fuck you fighting for? Are you waiting for a miracle?"

"That is what he does, Mr. Ball-du-zi, he fights. You know, at the fights in the courtyard. He fights for Kosher World in the bouts this night. Tomorrow he becomes hotdog meat." Warm-up Suit laughs.

Ballducci stops laughing and puts his face down to mine again. He's in on this. I can't believe it. "Are you out of your fuckin' mind? Get him some air, pronto. Shit, I'll kill you, Zog!" Balducci shouts.

My mouth is wide open from my futile attempt to get air. Balducci takes a pen, holds my head steady and tries to puncture a hole for me to breath through. There are too many layers of plastic and he can't break through. On the third try he comes down hard and finally a pop fills the room. The others come over with a knife and start cutting through all the cellophane.

I'm gasping so hard for air they are having trouble cutting through. I can't help it. I am making honking sounds. There's not enough air for me. It's too late. I need more air. I am making sounds I've never heard from any human being or animal. So much pain and it won't stop.

"Kevin, can you hear me?"

Nothing but gasps and coughs. I can't say anything. All the cellophane is finally unwrapped. I am lying on my back trying to breathe as my body spasms wildly for a fix of air. The spasms start slowing down and my breathing starts to regulate.

Hooded Sweatshirt comes over with a cup of water. I can't drink it, but I wish I could. I should fuck this guy up, but I'm so grateful to get air that my head is calm. I'm not sure if I'm holding back tears from when my nose got whomped or if I'm just appreciating being alive. Either way, I don't have enough strength to get him back. I take the water and figure I'll be able to drink it soon enough.

Balducci is sitting next to me and watching. He doesn't really look too connected, like his mind is elsewhere. Here's a guy I've known for six years. Donates money to the school, nice to his kids and treats me great. I'm thinking, Lucy, you got some splanin' to do. Then again, is there any reason he needs to explain anything to me? If he doesn't want me to know anything, then he could just repackage me in cellophane. That's probably what's going through his mind right now.

Once my breathing is almost normal again, Balducci informs me that we need to talk and instructs me to follow him in his car. I'm not sure if I am happy about this, but I know that pretending this thing never happened is probably not an option.

Driving isn't easy but I manage somehow. We stop at a diner in Bayside. Ballducci orders a cup of coffee and a mush-room-and-cheese omelet. I'm not that hungry so I just order some waffles, sausage and juice. Balducci isn't saying much. I'm not sure if he feels the need to explain the situation or if he's just going to tear me a new asshole. The expression on his face isn't giving anything away. I wish he would talk.

Here we are, just two friends enjoying their meals. Bal-ducci must be pushing 55, but he looks good. His hair is thin on top. In one sense that makes him look better, almost ap-proachable. But that's consistent with him. He seems to walk the line real well. He has a tough but smooth style. It's like, who would screw with him? Then again, nobody has the desire to screw with him.

Balducci finally breaks the silence. "Anyone fuckin' else, I mean anyone else and it's Sayonara Sammy. I got no choice. I got people to answer to also." It's funny, Jimmy is usually a lot smoother than this. I seem to be bringing out a side of him I've never seen. It's probably a side he keeps at bay, especially in front of Remington Academy people. Bal-ducci continues. "You really helped me with my son when he was at school. He was getting eaten alive there before you started helping him out. Go figure. It's embarrassing having a kid at a fag school, yet alone being pushed around. Imagine what would happen to him if he was doing work around a place like this. Forget it. He's not made like you or me, and I can't make him be that way. Either you got it inside or you don't. I got him hooked up in a Wall Street firm. He's got an intern-ship, doing high-yield bonds. I got a few connections with some companies, so it's going to work out nicely. Now Kevin, about you... you ready to do some real work?"

I don't know how to respond. The question was kinda vague. The last thing I want to do is give the wrong answer.

"Look Kevin, I was going to talk with you when you

got done with school. You know, let you wallow in the real world a little bit and then bring you in with our group. I guess your stunt today kinda accelerated the process a bit. It's not like we can pretend nothing went on here. I always liked you, and you handle yourself real well. Don't get me wrong, you got a lot to learn and you got a knack for getting fucked up. But on the other hand, man, you got so much potential."

"Jimmy, what can I do for you?"

"Well, there's some serious money out there, and I've found plenty of ways of getting it. The better people I have, the more I can get. It's that simple. You got the balls and the desire. I think you got the smarts, but you need some seasoning. It's like you're smart and you're a moron at the same time. You followed the merchandise; you figured something out, good for you. But you followed the merchandise, you fucking moron!"

I look at Jimmy and nod.

"Kevin, what do you think you saw here tonight?"

"I don't know. I saw where all the boxes that were being separated got transferred to, that's it. I thought I was helping out. You know, finding out where the stuff was going. I thought you and Sev would be psyched."

"What you saw is a beautiful thing, an original. I own that store you were stalking, that meat market. It's just a typical store where moms get the shit to make meatloaf. There's nothing glamorous, nothing sexy. I do have one edge. I get my stuff at a really good price. Which is zero." Jimmy gets so excited that some omelet falls from his mouth. "It's hard for me to imagine how anybody can pay for shit when they can get it for free. But some poor slob a couple of blocks away is waking up at sunrise and selling a glob of chopped meat for six bucks that he paid five bucks for. Throw in rent and electricity and that dumb asshole can't even afford to eat at his own store."

"Jimmy, not to be a wiseass, but haven't people been selling hot stuff since stuff was invented?"

Jimmy looks a little annoyed. "That's the beauty; this ain't hot. I pay for it. I just pay zero for it. If you get something hot, it's stolen. Then you got to sell it fast and cheap. Not me. I take my time and sell it full retail. I love the markup," he says.

I'm thinking that this guy is telling me too much information, and I don't think that's an accident. But it's not really a secret anymore either. The fact that an hour ago his guys were sending me to hotdog heaven kinda leads one to the conclusion that something's not kosher in Kosher World. That being said, I think either I'm in or I'm out, and out probably means body parts filling Lily's locker.

"Jimmy, I'm a big fan of markups, too." Jimmy smirks and takes a sip of his coffee. "Doesn't Kosher World mind selling shit for zero?" I ask.

"Kosher World has to live with a deal cut a long time ago. They were getting low on cash and taking it in the ass from the union. They were pretty close to shutting down. They came to us looking for help. Funny thing is, we were causing the union problems. Anyway, not only were we able to get them a favorable loan, but we put the union problem on the shelf. They were a lot smaller back then. Holy shit, the company got big. I was able to buy in as a partner when we loaned them the money. Guess how much it cost me to buy in?"

"Probably the same as you're paying for the merchandise," I answer.

"Now you're getting the hang of what a good deal is. There's a lot of money and clout backing us."

"Yeah, but who is the 'us'?" I ask.

"Don't worry about that now. As far as you're concerned, it stops with me. Just know that we got control of every union on Industrial Road and a ton of others. You'd be surprised by how well we stay under the radar. We got control of the books and that's why, with some creativity, we pay zero. We're not pigs. We take our pound of flesh and let the feds go after Madoff and Enron and we stay low. There's a trail that says otherwise, but at the end of the day, we buy for free. This meat store isn't the only retail store we got. Shit, we're in the process of building our own mall and filling it with all our retail operations. We figure consolidation will help with some of the expenses. One must be prudent. We still need to show positive growth, and as they say in the business world, if you're not going forward you're going backwards."

Is this the ticket I was looking for? Jimmy has managed a good life, and he's right in the heart of the whole Remington Academy scene, even though his family didn't come over on the Mayflower. This whole business is dirty, no doubt about that. But do I have a choice? Balducci's giving me a chance to save my ass; that's what this is about. That's what he's waiting for. "Jimmy, what can I do for you? How do I get in?"

Jimmy pauses, drinks some juice and acts like I just came up with a unique idea. "We'll get you involved slowly. I might know you, but some of the others aren't going to trust you. Believe me, if you're not on board, we'll find out. Plenty of people are cooperating and this whole thing is insulated airtight. Kinda like breathing through eight layers of cellophane." Balducci lets out a big belly laugh and I politely smile and nod. "The truth is there are people involved you couldn't imagine. Anyone finds out anything that I told you and it would be out of my hands. Understand?" I nod. "If the word starts getting out, we will find out. You can't dent this machine."

"Jimmy, I'm on board."

"I know, you're a good man, I just had to say it. But it's real."

"What about college?" I ask.

"You go back to school next month like you're sup-posed to. When I need you, I'll get hold of you. Getting your degree wouldn't kill you. Plenty of us got one."

Jimmy signals for the check. When it arrives he drops $50 for a $15 tab. It's a pretty nice tip. I wonder if he's trying to impress the waitress or me.

CHAPTER 9

Monday comes quick and my face isn't as resilient as I'd hoped. The guys from Balducci's meat market really banged me up. I have a shiner that's probably at its peak for drawing attention. It's still swollen but the dark black-purple color has faded into a greenish tone.

The real trouble for me here at Kosher World is that everyone saw me spank this guy on Friday. He didn't touch me, so how'd I get the black eye? After what happened on Friday, I should stay low. It's really one of those times I should use my head and keep to myself, but I know I'm going to draw some attention.

Sal and Frank greet me when I walk in. They, of course, immediately spot my swollen eye and start looking me over. It's weird. Normally these guys will rag on me, but they're not. They're kinda just biting their tongue.

Lately I've been having breakfast with Sal, Frank, Ramon and Sev. They go over the previous day's production and map out targets for the upcoming day. I sit down next to Sal and Frank. Ramon walks over and sits across from me. Although they don't mention my black eye, they are pretty complimentary about the fight on Friday.

Sev walks over and unwraps a bacon, egg and cheese sandwich that he bought from the silver truck outside. He's got a jumbo coffee and dumps four packs of sugar into his cup. If the sugar and caffeine aren't enough to get his system going, maybe I should offer him some jumper cables from my mother's car. Before Sev sits down he hands me a spreadsheet and says, "Yo, Kevin, can you check on how much we got out of the hotdog room last night? The numbers can't be right."

"Sure, Sev." No one is talking and they're all looking at me. "Oh, you mean right now?"

"Yeah, I need the numbers."

"Okay Sev, I'll be back in a few minutes." I leave my cereal and head over to the hotdog room.

Plenty of the guys are having a good time with me, but for the most part this whole ass-whooping I took is helping me out. Some guys in the smokehouse tell me that they heard I got into a fight in a Forest Hills bar after winning my bout on Friday and that it happened after getting wasted at the Locomotive Breath. They think I'm some sick fuck. I just tell them that I won't talk about it and don't repeat that story if any cops ask any questions. And they're like, "Holy shit! You must have fucked that guy up!" On one hand I want to stay low but on the other much more important hand, I can't miss an opportunity to increase my status.

The hotdog room is in full swing. They started at 1 a.m. I figure the numbers can get screwed up pretty easy in here. At some point during the day, the big hotdog conveyer belt stops dead. They change the Kosher World packaging and insert another label into the machine. Magically out come the same hotdogs, except the packaging says Goldstein's Finest. They sell the same damn hotdogs at 40 percent less. It's a riot. Anyway, they probably got the numbers all confused, and Sev wants me to straighten it out.

Carl Gurdon is in charge of the hotdog room. Carl's a thin guy, about 6'4". Maybe he's in his late 50s, but it's hard to tell. He's got that Lurch from "The Addam's Family" look that makes him seem older than he is. His choppy German accent from the mother country doesn't help him fit in either. Carl takes a lot of shit for being a "Nazi" playing with ovens in Kosher World. Carl always corners me in the cafeteria and tries to talk to me. He's always trying to get me to help him straighten up his son.

I avoid the guy like gonorrhea, but sometimes he sneaks up and pins me. Old Carl gets an inch from my face and starts ranting. "My son was out all last night, he dropped out of school, and he won't get a job. Look at you…you work, you go to the school. Can't you help him?"

"Carl, people take different paths. School's not for everyone," I assure him.

"Yes, but he does drugs, he smokes cocaine. I fucking work my ass off in this factory and that kid just lays around and smokes the junk."

I'm thinking to myself, Carl, your problems with this kid are just starting, but I say, "Yeah, it's tough. Let me think about it a little, Carl."

Now I have to speak with Carl, but I'm determined to keep this conversation to the absolute minimum. I'm just not going to get roped in today. Carl sees me walk in and beelines right up to me. I can see he wants to unload, so I act fast. I blurt out, "Carl, I'm in a bit of a hurry and Sev asked me to double-check these numbers from last night. He thinks there may be an error."

Carl takes the spreadsheet from my hand and examines the stats for a minute and then says, "Same numbers as always, no error. I do this room for seven and a half years and I know the numbers. No error."

I ask him if he's sure, and he is. I take the spreadsheet back from him and say, "Okay, thanks Carl." I give a hard look at the spreadsheet, and I'm thinking Carl's probably right. The numbers are in the same zone as any shift.

I'm confused. Why did Sev have me check these numbers? I'm walking away when Carl barks, "Kevin, I need to talk with you about my son."

"Sorry, Carl, I can't make it today. Sev has my ass all over the place and I'm already behind."

"Yes, but yesterday the police take my son. They arrest

him. I need to know what to do. Please."

I'm almost at the door when I stop. I turn and look
at Carl with his gaunt pale complexion and wrinkled face.
Something about a father worried shitless angers and touches
me in a strange way. Carl is a weird guy, but I'm actually jealous of his kid. It's nice to have a father worried beyond belief
about you. What a cock, to have a father and push him off the
deep end. "Carl, I'll come back later and we'll see what we
can do."

The day goes by. I don't get over to Carl like I prom-
ised and I feel pretty shitty about it. First thing in the morning,
I call a friend who is interning for a lawyer who specializes in
drug cases. He gives me his boss's name and number. I bring
it over to Carl and tell him I'll check in with him and see how I
can help.

Monitoring Carl's numbers was a bullshit move; they
were fine. But that was the first of several expeditions. Sev
sends me on more of these wild goose chases to check on
numbers he knows are right. Sev isn't around much at all these
days and when I do see him, it's all short answers to my questions. He's not pulling me into meetings any more or explaining different things. He definitely has me on ice. I didn't say
anything or do anything to get him heated, and even if I did,
he's never hesitated to let me know before. What the fuck is
his problem?

The cold shoulder has been going on for a week now,
with no end in sight. In my head I'm saying that Sev can screw
himself. I'm here for three more weeks and then it's back to
school. I say it to myself, but I don't really buy it. I like Sev
and I miss spending time with him. Watching him operate is
the one real pleasure I have in this place. I wonder if there's an
exit to Sev's doghouse.

I buy lunch from the sandwich truck. I'm sitting down

in the cafeteria when Bino blesses me with his pasty face. He's standing right across from me. As soon as I unwrap the plastic I get a whiff of the turkey sandwich and there's a 50-50 chance this thing is rank. It's always a coin toss with the truck. I'm laughing to myself that I got this pale white turkey with a rotten smell and Bino is right here looking at me. The similarities are remarkable.

"Yo, Balducci wants to talk to you," Bino barks at me. "And be careful with that sandwich. Sometimes the plastic wrap can be dangerous."

"Hey, Bino, you delivered your message like a good boy. You did a real good job. Now go buy some sun block and fuck off."

Bino smirks and starts walking out, but as he leaves he says, "Pretty touchy, kid. I was just looking out for you. Last thing anyone here wants is to see you get hurt."

It's about a 10-minute walk to Balducci's office. Management offices are in a two-story building that is attached to the factory but separated by the huge warehouse. It's right next door, but there's no shortcut.

Balducci's door opens up. He is shaking hands and gently guiding a very large man toward the exit. The big man stops abruptly and says, "You'll remember to call me about this idea?"

"Of course, Petro, I'll call later this week." Balducci practically shoves his guest toward the exit. When the big guy is gone, Balducci looks at me and motions me into the office. He looks toward the exit. "That's Petro. He's what the founders of Kosher World would call a real putz."

I sit on the other side of his huge oak desk. It almost looks like the headmaster's desk at Remington Academy. The factory is hardcore industrial, but this is a civilized office. Balducci lights a cigar and stares at it for a few seconds in appreciation. I'm not sure if he appreciates the cigar or how he got it—he only smokes Cubans—or the fact that he couldn't care less about the laws against smoking indoors. Mostly, I think he is staring in appreciation of his own righteous indignation.

"Thanks for coming over here, Kevin. Listen, there's something you can do for us. I know I said it may be a while, but I need something now. Ready?"

"Name it."

"It's real easy. Your last fight in the Industrial Road bouts is next Friday, and I want you to lay down for me."

He's not kidding. He wants to bet some wood against me and I've got to throw the fight. This sucks. Right now the guys love me. They've made a few extra bucks, and in a small, weird way I help give some pride to Kosher World. I don't even know how to flop. Shit, I'll do anything for a few bucks, but I don't want to screw the guys. They've been talking about betting their whole month's pay on me. I've gotten a lot of respect with the bookmakers now. I'm actually the favorite next week. The guys are gonna be bummed. Sev will be bummed.

Balducci looks at me and I think he's surprised I didn't snap an answer back at him. "There's no problem here, is there, Kevin?"

Well, I'm not going to say 'no' to Balducci. I remember what it's like not to breathe. "No problem, Jimmy. Consider it done." I guess I just got on the train to Douchebagville.

Every time someone slaps me on the back, every time someone tells me how they're going to spend their winnings next Friday, it feels like needles sticking into me. It feels worse than if all of a sudden I woke up and looked just like Bino, if you can imagine that.

I like what I got going here, but now I'm heading back to the proverbial Tongue Room again. Man, this sucks. At least I'll be done here soon. It'll be like a drive-by shooting. Fuck these guys and disappear. But what happens when Balducci needs me down the road? No doubt I'll have to deal with Kosher World again. It's Balducci's HQ. Man, I don't want to face these guys after flopping on their dime.

On the other hand, I don't want to end up as hamburger meat. Haven't I always said that I'll do whatever it takes to get ahead? Now it's time to shit or get off the corned beef. Fuck it. Kosher World guys don't have any money and never will. So they end up with a few less shekels. So what? I never asked them to give me the red carpet treatment. Everything will be just fine. The guys won't have an undefeated fighter to crow about at H's place, and I'll be on my way to the good life. So be it.

I say it to myself. I keep saying it to myself. But I've always imagined getting my breaks on my terms. I didn't think it would be at the expense of factory workers. It shouldn't happen at the expense of my integrity. But integrity is over-rated. It's not that big a deal. It's just a fight and some money. Why does it bother me so much?

CHAPTER 10

Sev switched me over to the late shift again. I start tomorrow, 9 p.m. to 9 a.m., and this blows. Before, he just had me on the outside of things, just keeping me away, and now he's busting my chops all over again. I want to straighten things out with Sev, but what's the difference? In three days when I throw the fight, I'm going to be dogshit anyway. I'll just take my shifts, do my time and then move on. It's not like I have a ton of choices. But throwing this fight is really gnawing at me, and it shouldn't. Should it?

I go out of my way to find Sev before I leave. I want to see his reaction to me. But when I find him, he looks at me and it's nothing. When Sev shoots his angry glare at someone, the effects are immeasurable. As far as a mile away, children are crying for their mothers and German Shepherds are trying to crawl underneath beds. But the look that hurts me the most is this empty stare. It says I don't give a shit.

It's not like I have anything to lose. It's time to have a chat with Sev. This is enough already. "Sev, what's with the all-night shift? I thought we had a deal. I do the Industrial Road fights and I don't have the all-night shifts anymore."

He looks at me and graciously acknowledges my presence, so I now feel that I have a pulse. "Kevin, you got the balls to talk to me about the Industrial Road fights?"

I'm not sure why he said that to me, and he said it in a strange way.

Sev stops looking at me. Instead, he looks over me. He says, "Tell me, Sugar Ray, how much should I bet on you this Friday? Should I load the boat? Maybe I should get my relatives to bet on you also?"

I can't believe Sev knows that I'm going to dive. "Man, nothing gets by you here." There's no sense in playing like I don't understand. "I don't want to do it, Sev, I really don't."

"I told you awhile back. You're gonna have some choices, some roads are going to fork. You picked a road, now live with it."

"C'mon Sev, it's just a fight and…."

"First off, it's more than just a fight. It always was. Second, everything I did with you was a waste of time. You sold out to the soul snipers. Go live your life and make your mega bucks and have some laughs, while you can."

"C'mon, man, how can you lay that on me? You said when you were my age you were taking people out in Special Operations for…."

"Hey, asshole, I thought I was working for the U.S. government. I got duped. Is there any doubt in your mind who you're working for? I got an idea. Why don't you ask George Skolinsky who you're working for?"

"Sev, every time I ask you about George, you change the subject. Why did he get whacked?"

Sev's eyes are flaring like lightning. "You don't demand that shit from me! What were you doing following everyone around that night? How much further up Balducci's ass you want to get?"

"Sev, I went out there because I thought I was doing something for you."

I tell him how I knew he was bummed because production was down and Balducci was thinking about closing the place. So I decided to figure out where all the extra merchandise is going. I'm thinking if I can figure this out, production goes up and they can throw something back to the fellas. "Who the hell thought Balducci was stealing from himself? I just wanted to help you. I'm not lying. Why would I?"

He digests this information. "Yeah, makes sense, I guess." Sev's cheeks puff up with air and he blows out a sigh that seems to release the venom he was holding toward me for the last few days. "George was working for Balducci in his side business. Small jobs that didn't take a lot of time, like collections and being a messenger. Some of the messenger stuff was delivering drugs. George got in over his head. Does that sound familiar?"

"Go on," I say.

"Problem is, some of the few police that Balducci doesn't control pinch George with a fair amount of Balducci's heroin, enough to put George away for awhile...unless, of course, he cooperates with the police." He says that George, a family guy, will do anything to stay out of jail and keep from embarrassing his family.

"So George starts wearing a wire and gets the cops some information. But the fuckin' guy is so sweaty and jumpy Balducci's guys catch on. They can spot this shit a mile away." Sev sees me thinking, then says, "Hope you enjoy your new career."

The man is shedding some new light here. "I've changed my mind. Screw it Sev, you're right. I'm not gonna work for these goons, and I'm definitely not going to throw any fight." Just saying that was an unbelievable relief.

Sev is smiling, almost laughing. It ain't a proud-papa smile, either; he's laughing like I'm some kind of dick. "Did you tell Jimmy you would work for him?"

"Yeah, but I'm not going to do it. Jimmy will let me out. We go way back."

"Yeah, Jimmy's a great guy," Sev mutters. "He bailed you out at the meat market when Zog was wrapping you up in plastic. You really think he's going to let you go back to your frat parties now, after what you saw? You throw the fight and we'll figure something out after that."

"No Sev, that shit stops now. I'm not going to dive. I'll just fucking get hurt before the fight. Shit happens."

Sev tells me my plan won't work, that the fight and the money mean nothing to Balducci. He says Balducci wipes his ass with money that would break the bookmakers. This whole fight flop is all about testing me, he says. It's the first test of my loyalty, to prove that I'm on board.

"Well, I'm not going to pass his test," I say.

"Listen, you don't have a choice. There really is only one answer at this point, and I guarantee you the answer is not 'no thanks.'" Sev looks like a storm cloud, he's so serious. If you don't play ball, you're in deep shit." I mumble some response about walking away from the whole mess but Sev isn't buying it. "Look, we'll talk more about this later. You're fucked up right now."

Something occurs to me. "Do you work for these guys?"

He shakes his head. "Naw, they leave me alone. I don't make waves and I keep the place running. They talked to me once about it, but I didn't take their bait."

I'm not buying that one. "C'mon, Sev, they just left you alone?"

"The place runs better with me here and I don't make waves. End of story."

CHAPTER 11

I have one more day until my showdown at the Industrial Road bouts. There's a lot of buzz in the factory. The guys are amped for it. I know Sev wants to talk to me today. He's expecting to meet up with me at closing time, only this time it's me who is avoiding him. I know what I've got to do now.

I spend the day telling everyone to load up on me and I'm feeling real good. Then I skip out early. What are they gonna do, fire me?

Better yet, I'm gonna take the day off tomorrow and sidestep Sev all together. I leave him a note saying, "See ya at the fight, and don't forget to bet on the good guy."

Then I go outside, take a breath of relatively fresh summer air and take the top down on my new Saab convertible. Okay, the Saab is used, very used, but it's new to me and it's mine. I made enough money this summer between the factory and the fights to help my mother with expenses and get a car. The Saab drained me, but after the fight tomorrow I'll have enough cash for school and won't have to work anymore odd jobs, at least for a while. They take their toll on a man.

I drive to Westchester to see a friend but he isn't home; I don't know much about the place, so I just cruise around for a while. I get so lost I think I may actually miss my last fight tonight. Eventually I find the Whitestone Bridge which gets me to familiar territory. I'm laughing to myself because there are a ton of text messages and missed calls from Sev.

I finally park the car at the Moonbeam Cheese Factory as the first fight is beginning. I'm scheduled to fight the second bout of the night. The cheese factory doesn't have the same courtyard as Kosher World, so they basically turned the parking lot into an arena. It's even more crowded than the courtyard at Kosher World. The bookmakers are going nuts. There's a lot of activity here tonight. I'm not 10 feet from the car when I am swarmed by the Kosher World guys. "Holy shit, Kevin! Where you been?"

"Doesn't matter where I been. It matters where I am, right fellas?"

Felipe yells, "That's what I'm talking about!" Then he pulls me aside and asks if I've seen Sev. I shake my head. "Man, he's been after you all day. You don't owe him money, do you?"

I shrug my shoulders like I don't know what's up. "I can't worry about Sev now. I got a fight to get ready for." In the meantime the crowd lets out a huge roar as the bout going on heats up. I push my way through to get a look at the action. In the ring two fat guys are hammering the hell out of each other with all the grace of mating elephants. The fatter one is bleeding all over his face and I can't imagine how he can see. But he's a gamer. Just when you think he's going down, he lands a great punch that catches his opponent square on his mouth.

The slimmer one reels back three steps. He's both surprised and really pissed. He charges in and there's no doubt from anyone that he's getting it done now. He lands a few more punches and the fatter guy drops to his knees. The slimmer guy knows how helpless his rival is. He could just push him over to end this but instead opts to kick him right in the face. Man, that's cold.

There's a break in the action for everyone to collect money and to place bets on my fight. I'm on deck. I got to get my head right. I need to get into my own zone, so I start stretching out for a few minutes and then throw some punches in the air to loosen up. After a few minutes I'm starting to feel good. I take a brief break to catch my breath, and when I look

up I see Sev and he's staring at me. Shit, he is pissed. Really
pissed. I'm thinking, *Lighten up, Sev.*

I make my way into the circle. Tonight I'm fighting a
short, stocky guy named Vic Catino. Vic is already in there.
Vic isn't much older than me. He's been in a few Industrial
Road bouts and won some, lost others. The word is that he's
got a lot of heart and is as tough as nails. But he's not that athletic and that's why he has a mediocre record. I question how
smart he's gotta be. After all, fighting is the last sport you want
to have a .500 record in. It's not like a baseball game, when
you lose and shake hands and move on to the next game. You
lose in a fight and you got some other issues. You would think
a guy could figure that out.

I take my shirt off and start flinging punches in the air
again when three cops barge into the ring area. Where the fuck
did they come from?

"Okay, everyone stay put and don't move," the larger
cop says. "Everybody be cool, or we'll take the whole lot of
you in."

It gets pretty quiet. I never thought about the police in
this equation, but I guess these bouts are probably not on any
approved recreation list the cops might have. The taller guy is
a 6'2" slender black man with tight curly hair that is more gray
than black. This cop must be in his late 50s or early 60s. He
definitely seems to be the leader, though. The other two cops
are much younger.

The lead cop barks, "So you guys think you're gonna
be doing some fighting here tonight. I don't think so...."

Bino walks into the middle of the fight area, joining me,
three police officers and my should-be opponent, Vic Catino.
Bino stares at the head cop and says, "I don't think you know
what you're dealing with here, Dick Tracy." Bino starts dripping some attitude at the cop and says, "Look, this stuff has
been okayed. Just do your homework. Why don't you guys

just kind of vanish? Trust me, in the long run it's gonna be a
lot less of a hassle for you."

        The head cop looks Bino up and down. He notices
Bino's fire-red hair and powder pale skin and then looks again,
as if he needs to confirm that the data is registering in his brain
correctly. The cop makes a quick and deliberate move I will
never forget. "Yo, Red, you got a bad attitude," he says. Then
he snaps his arm and thrusts out the hard part of his palm, hitting Bino square on the bottom part of his nose. I can hear the
bone shattering; blood is flying everywhere. I've done a fair
amount of boxing before and I've also seen my share of broken
noses, but nothing like this. It's an awesome display of raw
damage in a compact format.

        Bino falls on the ground wailing like a bitch. His hands
cover his face but a ton of blood is dripping through his fingers.
The cop looks at him and says, "Quiet down. You're giving me
a headache." But Bino just goes on screaming. He's yelling
something about there are witnesses here and something about
how they don't know who he is, but it's mostly just aahh my
nose, help, my nose.

        The cop screams, "Shut the fuck up! I'm trying to get
something done over here. Do I need to rip out your vocal
cords?" That seems to work, and Bino brings it down to a
whimper.

        The cop walks over to me and says, "You one of the
fighters?"

        I nod my head. So here I am being all cooperative and
everything and this cop snaps an uppercut into my stomach.
Even if I were ready for the shot, it would do damage, but the
fact that it surprises me causes all sorts of havoc with my body.
I drop to my knees, wheezing for air. That was a sick punch.
I'm on the ground and still trying to get some air while the
cop takes his foot and pushes me over onto my stomach. I am
totally defenseless. He drops down and sticks his knee in the

back of my neck. The cop grabs my hands, puts them behind
my back and slaps handcuffs on me. He grabs a handful of my
hair and begins lifting me to my feet. When I am standing, I
notice that Vic Catino is also in handcuffs, but it doesn't look
like he was hit. Bino's in cuffs too, and man, he looks like he
just lost a cherry pie-eating contest.

The lead cop instructs the other two officers to take
Bino and Vic in their car; he will take me in his car. How
lucky for me to be able to spend even more quality time with
this guy. The cops push us through the now-quiet crowd and
toward the police cars that are parked near the back of the
lot. As we progress toward the cars I notice everyone staring,
including Zog the Cellophane King. He knows he should be
doing something here, but he has no idea what the fuck to do. I
know he wants to be effective but not look like his pal Bino, so
he just stays quiet and watches us being dragged away.

The head cop pushes me into his squad car and I kinda
feel cheated. In all the police shows, the cop always reads you
your rights and puts his hand on your head to guide you into
the car, making sure you don't bang your head. But this guy
just shoves me and my head slams into the roof as I'm on my
way in. Damn, where's the protocol?

The cop screeches out of the area in a clear effort to
put on a show. He gets onto the Long Island Expressway and
drives for a while, then suddenly pulls off near Hunts Point.
We pass a bunch of factories that are similar to the ones on
Industrial Road. We go deeper and then past rows and rows of
warehouses. Some look like they are barely standing and some
are empty shells, leftovers from a fire, maybe. Whatever the
case, there's no way we're going to a police station.

Eventually we pull into an empty warehouse that looks
as if it's been vacant for years. The good news is I'm not about
to get butt-fucked in some jail cell tonight. The bad news is, I
might get butt-fucked in a deserted warehouse.

The cop slows down and makes a left turn into the parking lot of one of these warehouses. He then drives around back to the loading docks. A police car and an SUV are already parked in the bay of the loading docks, well hidden from the rest of the world. The two younger cops who broke up the bouts tonight are sitting in the front seat of this other police car. They are staring at me as we slowly park next to them, and there's no sign of Bino or Vic.

Inside the warehouse it's pretty dark. I suspect this place isn't exactly up to speed on the electricity bills. We walk around a bend to an area with a few chairs and a table. On the table is a glowing electric lantern; some moths are banging into the glass, attempting to find their little piece of paradise. There are a few more battery-operated lanterns hanging from nails on the walls, offering barely enough light to see. And what I see is pretty interesting. Sev is seated at the table waiting for us. In this light and from this distance I can't really make out his face, but his figure is pretty unmistakable.

"How'd it go, Curtis?" Sev asks the lead cop.

"It was pretty easy, like you said. We were in and out," the cop replies. "Except for that alien-looking redhead. Sneezing is gonna hurt him for a while."

"Fuckin' Bino. Still, I appreciate it," Sev says.

Curtis smiles. "Gotta get these cop cars back. Let's talk later this week." Curtis walks over and softly punches Sev in the chest. "Damn, it's good to see you again."

"Thanks for the favor, man."

My new pal Curtis, the almost cop, leaves. When I turn around to my old pal Sev, I am met by his huge hand that wraps around my throat, with quite a lot of pressure, I might add. Sev screams, "Are you out of your fucking mind? What the fuck is wrong with you? You into suicide? Are you that crazy or are you just that fucking stupid?"

I'm thinking, damn, I can't keep up with all these questions, and even if I could, he's choking me, so how the fuck can I answer him? Eventually Sev lets go of my neck. I cough for a little while and look up and sputter, "What gives, man?"

"What gives? What gives?" Sev's eyes are bulging and I see a vein in his neck dancing and flexing. I'm thinking that I may have found a whole new level on Sev's snap-o-meter. This shit is ugly. "Man, you leave me a note saying bet on the good guy and then you fucking disappear. You don't even return my phone calls. I got to chase you fucking down, and you just disappear."

"Sev, I have it under control. I'm taking care of it."

"You were going to fuck Jimmy Balducci, make him look like an asshole and then die. You don't think you will, but I've seen guys do less and then take a cap."

"Sev, I didn't have a choice. I thought about all my options and believe it or not, this one made the most sense."

"I can't wait to hear this fucked-up logic. Let me hear this shit," Sev commands.

"Look Sev, first off, think about what you told me. We were talking about the fights and me throwing this fight for Balducci. Remember what you said about the fight flop being a test? That I had to prove I'm on board, and then there would be more tests, harder tests?" Sev nods; he remembers everything. "I thought about what you said long and hard. It's all I could think about. Obviously, Balducci ain't the great guy I thought he was when I started to work here. He had this plan for me all along. I understand. They get you in deeper and deeper until you have no choice but to be on board." Sev is listening, his eyes motionless, locked on me. "The one thing I've been hearing is that once you're in, forget about getting out. So how am I supposed to not get in and stay healthy? I saw some stuff at the meat market when Zog wrapped me up in cellophane. I know some stuff I shouldn't know. I don't want in on this shit. I'm not looking to be a wiseguy. I work for him, shit, my life's over anyway."

Sev interrupts, "Yeah, we all know the problem. I still don't know what the fuckin' solution is."

"Look Sev, there are two things you said to me that just kept coming back to me and wouldn't go away. Balducci's gonna test me and Balducci's got people he's got to answer to. You said it, right?"

"Yeah, I said that. Go on."

"Well, nobody above Balducci knows shit about me. Hell, I bet no one even equal to Balducci knows shit about me. Why would Balducci even mention me before I went through all his tests? The best shot I have is to break away from Balducci before anyone above him is on board, you know, before anyone upstairs from him signs off on me. Then I'm their responsibility, too. You see, I have a shot if I make Balducci look like a dick to people under him, but make him look bad to people above him, no way. It's now or never, now or never."

Sev cocks his head and gives me a bewildered and amazed glance, like he's watching a train wreck. "That's what you got? You're betting because people above Balducci don't get wind of this slap in the face that you can slide? Don't you think he's gotta make sure the people below him don't ever think about turning on him? You know, set an example."

"I'm an outsider," I say, "a family friend. No one else can claim that. I'm in uncharted territory." Sev gives me another train-wreck look. "I'm not saying it's a foolproof idea," I continue. "Hell, I'm not even saying it's a good move."

"So why the fuck do it?" Sev asks. "Shit, in the Marines you look at risk-reward profiles. You ever think about your odds of surviving this stunt?"

"Hell yeah," I said, proud to have an answer. "Forty percent chance I get whacked. Fifty-nine point five percent shot I get beaten so bad I can't even get a piss hard-on anymore. Zero point five percent chance you bail me out. Who were those guys that kicked our asses and dragged me here? Are they really cops?"

Sev glances away and says, "They ain't cops. I used to work with them." I know he doesn't mean Kosher World. "We served together in a few different countries. Curtis saved my ass in Biafra and I saved his ass in the Congo."

"Didn't you disappear from those guys you were with in the Army?"

"First off, it was the Marines, but the CIA grabbed us from the Marines, and second, once the CIA is involved you can never really disappear. So while you're worried about getting stuck with Jimmy Balducci for life, the U.S. government is a lot worse. At least you can have some laughs with Balducci. The government doesn't have much of a sense of humor."

"I don't know. Your boy Curtis seemed to be having a ball with me and Bino tonight."

Sev laughs and looks down at his feet. "Let me tell you, Kevin, Curtis knows how to get the job done. He got in and out of there with little chance of disruption."

"The other cops took Bino and Vic. Where are they?"

"They dropped the other fighter off in Flushing somewhere, then they dropped Bino about a 10-minute walk to a hospital in Forest Hills. But they were both told to relay a message. No more fights, unless the cops get some more kick-back money."

"What's the point if they're not really cops?"

"It's just a red herring. First, Balducci's organization will get all pissed off at the cops for looking for more money. When they realize it wasn't the cops, they're really gonna freak out. They're gonna start thinking someone else is trying to cut in on all this union action. These stiffs are gonna go nuts at how easy it was for Curtis and his boys to walk in and wreak havoc. They'll start pointing fingers and getting all paranoid with each other. It'll be a real shit show. I love it."

"I get it. They can think anything they want as long as they don't know you had anything to do with it."

"Yeah, you got it.   It's the way they taught us."

I smile and say, "That's a great plan, a win-win situation." Then with a chuckle I add, "Except for Bino."

"Not so fast. It's not so win-win for me," Sev mutters. "Yesterday I was invisible. Today I'm not. Curtis has a lot of pull, but you don't procure police cars and staff and make this happen all by yourself. Especially in one day. I shit you not, I'm a lot more vulnerable now."

"Damn, Sev, I'm sorry." This was supposed to be just a summer job. How did I let this get to here? How do things get this far? "I don't want to get you fucked up."

"Look, kid, you didn't ask me. I did this. So far, your mistakes are your own. I'm telling you, if you can do anything, if you can learn anything, make sure your mistakes are your own. Look, I let you go into those fights at the Industrial Road bouts and I brought you along to those union meetings. I was trying to help you out, but I ended up dumping gas on the fire. I liked the way you were handling yourself, but in the end you wound up facing down Jimmy Balducci. I could have stopped this."

"I don't know Sev. You didn't let me do anything I didn't want to. I was enjoying fitting in and being something here. Why you being so tough on yourself?"

"I've been here before. I could have stopped this from developing, and I should have. Let your mistakes be your own. That's a hard one to learn. Let your mistakes be your own."

Sev is just kind of staring off into space. I had enough of this hidden bullshit. "What mistake? Don't hold out on me. Would you please come clean?"

Sev pauses, then speaks, and his voice is soft. "I made a bad judgment in my past that affected people real bad and I have trouble living with it," he says. He tells me that back in

1981, in El Salvador, he got orders to train a special group, the first unit of its kind to complete its training under the supervision of United States military advisors. The government said the El Salvadorans need help defending themselves in counterinsurgency warfare, but it was all Cold War bullshit. So Sev and his buddies taught these guys how to shoot and how to fight. "We gave them a real fighter's edge. We got their teeth sharp, know what I mean?"

Sev says that, despite their training, these guys have their own ideas. They are supposed to stop guerrilla warfare but they can't find the guerrillas, so they figure if they get the families of the guerrillas, they'll fish them out. "The cocksuckers we train go into a village on their first mission, their first motha-fuckin' mission...." Sev pauses, his face darker than usual. It's at least a minute before he continues. "They wipe out a whole town. Torture and kill the men. Then they slaughter the women, and they finish the day by holing up the kids in a damn church and gunning them down. One hundred and eighty people dead, 180 fucking people dead. And I trained the guys who killed them. So I'm telling you, let your mistakes be your own."

"Shit, you were doing the job they told you to do. That's how they train you, to follow orders."

"Yeah well, I should have been more than a Marine, more than a CIA agent. I should have been a person, a human being," Sev says. "Look, you were really fucked up with your stunt tonight. But you were better than me. You were gonna face down the man and take your medicine. I'm ragging on you, but that's what I should have done back then. Instead I've been looking over my shoulder and working this shit job. Everyone else involved in that little 'training mission' is worm food. Curtis and a few other friends helped me get by. Whenever I think things are getting normal, something always snaps me back to reality. I know if I went out and got a wife and some kids, somewhere along the way they would be paying for my mistakes."

It's too bad Sev felt he couldn't have a family. He'd be pretty damn good at it. "Sev, you stuck your neck out for me today. You got other people to do the same. I really appreciate it. No one does that shit for me. Thanks."

"Don't worry about it." Sev says. "The important thing is for you to be consistent with Bino and that guy Vic when you talk to Balducci. Just tell him some cop roughed you up and dropped you somewhere in Queens. He told you to tell the man 'no more fights until they get their money.' Then tell Balducci you asked the cop what man he was talking about. Then tell him that the cop punched you again and called you a wiseass. That's going to tie out with Bino. You got it?"

"Yeah, I can do that."

Sev told me to stay low, that I'd be done in a week or two anyway. We'd bought some time, but we hadn't solved the problem yet. "Balducci is going to be nuts for a while figuring out which cops are out of control."

I can't believe that Balducci has control of the whole police force, but Sev says he does. The big guys in the force get money and everyone else is just plain scared shitless. He says it's been that way pretty much forever. "The cops aren't bad guys. Most of the time they do their job. They just know at certain times they got to look the other way. They got no choice; it's not just about losing their job. And it's not just the cops. They got cops, politicians, newspapers and every other angle to insulate themselves."

"C'mon, didn't this stuff stop years ago? Didn't Giuliani chase the Mafia out of New York City?"

"Fuck, that shit is tame compared to this crap, kid. Forget The Sopranos. Balducci used to be part of that wiseguy crap, but he was one of the few guys who could merge into this new corporation. Give him credit; he managed to reinvent himself. And this isn't an Italian thing. They take all races and religions, just as long as you don't got a heart or soul."

"Anybody try to do something about this recently?" I ask.

"Yeah, plenty. George Skolinsky was the most recent. But that shit happens all the time. They consider it a 'minor irregularity.' When they took George's head off, business just went on as usual."

I ask him when the last time was that anyone came close to getting in their way.

Sev lets out a long sigh. "Ten years ago there was one real good shot at bringing down this whole thing. Some major guys from the Corporation were about to get nailed. There was a pretty determined detective and a real hotshot district attorney who had these guys dead-to-right. They had it all: taped conversations, photos and unknown hidden witnesses.

"Then some info got leaked to them and they started scrambling like motha-fuckers. They tortured the fuck out of the detective to make him sing. The word I got was that they used a blowtorch on different parts of his body until they got what they wanted. But I wasn't there so what the fuck do I know? Anyway, they found out who the hidden witnesses were and I'm sure they don't exist anymore."

"What about the hotshot DA?"

Sev cocks his head and says, "They already had the situation under control and were just looking to set an example by that time. You know, get the word out that nobody should try this shit. Balducci sends Zog and Bino out to set that example."

"Bino whacks people?" I ask, stunned by the idea.

"Not really. Remember, this was about 10 years ago, so Bino was just kinda getting started around here. They sent him out to ride shotgun and assist Zog. Of course, Zog didn't need anyone to assist him. The guy jacks off to doing this shit.

It was really just a final way to suck Bino into the point of no return. You can't walk away after you're an accessory to a high-profile killing, right?"

"That's where I was heading, wasn't it?"

"No doubt. Those stars were lining up. Anyway, Zog and Bino make their statement. Right there in broad daylight, they drive over the DA when the guy was crossing the street. It was right in the middle of town. But here's the thing: the guy was walking with his daughter. She had to be like 5 years old."

For a moment, I go blind. My vision just disappears. In my mind's eye I see Karen, the doll, lying on a chair in the barbershop. Then I can see again, and Karen is gone. Shit, no, my mind is screaming. My stomach is in knots and my head gets foggy. My knees are losing tension and Sev has no idea what's happening. He just continues, completely unaware that he is telling me my story. I gain just enough composure to say, "Long Island." I look at Sev and say it again. "Long Island. It happened in Manhasset on Long Island, right?"

Sev looks at me in an inquisitive way. "Yeah, it did, but it's pretty weird you would know. Taking out a prosecutor would normally make TV and front pages, yet this thing just got whispers. How do you know about it?"

I'm losing it. The knots in my stomach are now waves of nausea and I can't control them. For the second time in my Kosher World career, I am blowing chunks. This time with no warning or, as I'm sure Sev is thinking, without any rhyme or reason. Whatever the case, the contents of my stomach echo on impact in this huge abandoned warehouse. My throat is burning from stomach acid.

Sev knew I didn't have a father but I guess I never told him how he died. No reason my sister would come up in conversation either. I'd like to tell him now but I got to think this through.

Sev is looking at me real weird and I can't blame him.

When I'm able to speak, I say, "That guy Curtis really tagged me in my gut.   My stomach's been fucked up since he got me."

Sev tilts his head and looks at me. Sev's no dope, and he knows it's not likely someone will heave an hour or so after getting hit. But what the fuck, I did heave, so let him come up with a better explanation. The only thing I know is I gotta get out of here; my head is really screwed up right now.

CHAPTER 12

The day after what should have been my last fight I was summoned into Balducci's office. My story tied out with Bino, Vic Cantino and the rest of them, but it's hard looking at Balducci now. When I speak to Balducci I make sure to sound real nervous. I have no desire to look like a golden boy to him anymore. It's a little late for this now, but I want him to start getting worried about bringing me into the group. I bitch to Balducci that I thought I was getting arrested, I don't want a rap sheet, it's so fucked up, blah, blah, blah. Let him start doubting I have the heart for his little club.

I don't think it much matters though. I'm not on Balducci's radar screen right now. It was just like Sev said: Balducci is having convulsions over who broke up the fights. Right now he thinks it's a new group of cops with their hands out for kickbacks. When he realizes it's not the cops he's gonna really lose it. Anyone who could strike as quickly and effectively as Curtis will be a real threat.

I decide to bag my last week at Kosher World even though I really need the cash. There's no way I can deal with these guys now. I was counting on winning a lot of money at my last fight to get me through my last year of college, and I'd bet big on myself to win. Now I've won nothing and I have to figure out how to get my big bet back. But all that isn't even on my short list. Now that I know who was driving that car, number one on that list is a house in Queens.

For the fifth morning in a row I drive to 42 Prescott Lane in Howard Beach, Queens, park and wait. And wait. The first day I was here, Zog came out with some skanky-looking bimbo. The two of them practically left a slug trail on the streets. The third day Zog was alone, but there were people on the streets around him.

It's 10 a.m. and raining and I'm still waiting. I touch the deadly contents of my jacket pocket and remind myself that I have to be cool. I can't screw this up. I don't want to draw attention to my car so I keep the windshield wipers off despite the drizzle. Then I notice that Zog's door seems to be opening. Someone with a light blue warm-up suit, rotund figure and scraggly beard comes out. I can't make out the face yet, but there's no doubt who it is. This is perfect. He's alone and there's no one around. The rain is keeping everyone inside.

I quietly exit the car and approach Zog as he walks from his house. He is deep in thought, probably about drowning a puppy or something. I get closer and closer but he still doesn't see me. When Zog does finally catch me in his peripheral vision, he jolts a bit from the surprise.

"Hey," I say to him.

Zog stops in his tracks and doesn't respond. He looks at me but doesn't answer my greeting. I can just imagine his vast brain running all sorts of scenarios and variations and trying to conclude what the fuck I am doing in front of his house. After letting him stew on the situation for a moment, I say, "We need to take a ride. Balducci sent me here to pick you up. He told me to get you because we know who screwed up the Industrial Road bouts. He knows what they are looking for, and Balducci has no intentions of playing ball. He wants the problem to disappear and he wants us to do it."

Zog squints and says, "Mr. Ball-duzzi never told me any of this."

I tell him that Balducci is being real careful to cover his tracks and to put space between the troops and management. Things are moving fast, I say. Balducci depends on him. Trusts him. Zog opens up a toothy grin. "My car's down the block," I say. Let's go."

"Why do we take your car? Why not mine?"

I tell him that I could give a flying fuck whose car we take, but I know that Balducci is steaming today. No one's doing anything right, he says. We're supposed to meet him at Hunts Point, and he doesn't think Zog can find the place. I say that this has to go down today without any fuckups. "You want to start changing his plan, fine with me. But I'm telling him you wanted to change the plans."

Zog hesitates and then says to me, "You drive."

A short time later we're on the Long Island Expressway and Zog pulls out his cell phone and starts dialing. Shit, I can't have him talking to anyone. I didn't think about a phone. Fortunately for me, Zog is one of the 12 percent of the world population who is left-handed. When he puts the phone up to his left ear, I grab the phone out of his hand and throw it out of my window, smashing it to pieces. "Balducci told me, make sure no one knows where we are going."

Zog is obviously surprised by my move, but what can he do? He's so flustered that he can hardly get any words out. It's hard enough to deal with his Russian hip-hop accent when he's calm, let alone when he gets heated up. "Fuck you. I call who I want. Dawg, you going to buy me a new phone or we have serious problem."

"Listen up," I snap back. "Before you start getting emotional over a damn phone, just think about if you're supposed to be using a phone now. And don't fucking cry to me about a broken phone. It wasn't too long ago you had me wrapped up in cellophane, counting my last few breaths. I had to get over that, so you can get over a damn phone."

"Next time, just tell me to turn phone off," he mumbles.

My heart is pounding right now. Something can go wrong at any minute. It's not like this is a science. I am about to do something so nuts that I'm almost hoping something happens and stops me. I don't even know what to concentrate on.

Zog interrupts my attempt to concentrate. He looks at me earnestly and says, "Sorry I wrap you up in the cellophane and stop your breathing."

I look at Zog and say in an equally sincere tone, "Sorry I threw your phone out of the window."

Zog nods in approval and says, "It is okay. Now we are even."

My heart is thumping so loud even this fuckin' dope sitting next to me is going to hear it beating over the hip-hop that he insists on playing on my radio. I want to bail, but I'm in too far now. Man, how did this shit get out of hand? I can't concentrate; I got to stay cool.

Zog is engrossed in a song and he's singing along, or trying to. He sounds like a cat being set on fire. My heart is beating faster than the beat of Zog's hip-hop song and my mind keeps racing. I'm sweating bullets as I pull the car into the loading docks of the abandoned warehouse where Sev and I talked after Curtis broke up the fight. There are no other cars or people around, as I suspected. I just hope that Sev and Curtis don't use the place on a regular basis for their cloak-and-dagger bullshit.

We walk in and before Zog can tell we are alone, I grab the piano-wire garrote hidden in my pocket. I jump on Zog's back and wrap the wire around his throat and start choking the shit out of him. He's trying to get me off his back and he starts flailing around like he's Frankenstein or something. He drops down to one knee in an attempt to shake me off his back. This gives me a better angle to apply pressure, which I am happy to do. I remember my conversation with Sev at the bar. "Kid, you are gonna kill someone sometime. You better make it count. You better make it worthwhile."

The piano wire is so sharp it opens up a free-flowing cut around Zog's neck. I keep squeezing. Zog is on his stomach now. "C'mon, bitch. It sucks when you can't get any air, don't it?"

I have my knee in the center of his back and I'm pulling his neck toward me with all my strength. Can I break his back before I choke him to death? I know it's not all Zog; he just finished my father. Balducci and his "I buy for free" fucking corporation is the real problem. Today, the solution starts with the Cellophane King. I can't get my father or sister back, and I doubt I'll get my mother a ticket back from whatever planet she's been living on, but this is a start. If anyone ever bet anything on me, they can bet Balducci and his corporation are going down. I may end up with my head cut off and stuffed in a locker, but I will get my pound of flesh first.

Zog goes limp and I'm pretty sure he's not breathing anymore. It's probably about time to let go of the garrote but I can't seem to stop squeezing and I'm not sure why I won't let go. I can't believe I got up the balls to do this. How 'bout that? I just whacked a guy. My heart has shifted in so many directions. My heart pounds because I was scared to do this, my heart pounds from the exertion of doing this, my heart pounds in retrospect, holy shit, I just did this.

I let go of the wire and Zog's face drops down with a thud against the warehouse floor and the force of the fall rolls him over on his back. His eyes are still open and are bulging from the sockets. His face is a nice shade of slate blue. More than anything I want to smash that face. I start punching it hard, hard enough to hurt my hand but I don't care. Soon his face is a bloody piece of meat. "Do you know what it's like to grow up without a father?" I yell at this dead man, still punching. Now I'm crying, too. "Do you know what a father is to a 10 year-old boy?" I see Balducci's face and punch hard and I punch harder and I feel things breaking on impact.

After a while my rage burns out and I stop punching. My hand is fucking sore. I get up and retrieve some green plastic wrap, packaging tape and an old Oriental rug I've stashed days ago deep in the warehouse. I'm going to need all of it to make this guy disappear. I wrap him up with the green plastic wrap and start taping around his ankles. Then I tape his neck, followed by his arms. "How about that for plastic wrap, you fat fuck? It's even better than cellophane because I don't have to see your face."

I roll out the Oriental rug. Once the carpet is laid out, I drop Zog onto the corner of the rug. I start rolling Zog and the carpet as one, like a cigarette. When he is completely rolled into the carpet, I tape it real good so it can't unravel.

Lifting Zog is a bigger problem than I thought. Zog's a pretty big guy to begin with and the carpet's not that light either. Plus, I guess there really is something to the phrase "dead weight." I have to drag Zog to the entrance and that's not so easy; I'm sweating through my clothes. I stick my head outside to make sure no one is around. There's no one in sight.

I pop the trunk to the Saab and struggle to lift Zog. This fucking guy has no shot to fit into this trunk. What was I thinking? In an attempt to adjust, I drop the front seat and start the long, hard process of squeezing Zog into my backseat. It's kind of a bad time to get pulled over by the cops, so I vow to drive really carefully.

The meticulous drive home takes about 55 minutes, which is about half my usual pace. To say I got a case of paranoia is an understatement. I park the car in our driveway and start hustling. My mother is watching a rerun of Family Feud from the '70s and Richard Dawson practically has his tongue down some 80-year-old grandmother's throat. I call out to Mom as I head to my room but, as always, she doesn't reply. Most of my gear has already been packed, but I have to do some rearranging now. I was going to stuff Zog in the trunk and put all my stuff in the back seat; now that needs to be reversed.

I wash up, and on my way out I kiss my mother on the cheek. "Good-bye, Mom. I'll call you when I get to school."

She looks at me and cocks her head. "Have a good time. What time will you be home?"

"Mom, I'm heading out to State. You know, the university. In Albany."

She looks at me for a moment and answers, "Of course." Then she turns her head and gets back to Richard Dawson.

The tank is full, the car is packed. It better not break down or I am going to lose it, for sure. The ride to Albany takes about three hours, except I need to make a quick stop with my good friend Zog.

By 2:30 a.m., I pull into what's left of Camp Pack-A-Tu, a children's sleep-away camp that's been closed for nearly 10 years. It's a pretty secluded place about a half hour from Albany. The owners were two brothers who had a propensity for getting a little too friendly with the little boys. So between the legal expenses and the fact that there's no discount big enough to convince parents to enroll their children in Camp Fondle You, it was enough to shut the gates for good.

Albany weather can be pretty brutal, but in the fall and spring some of my friends and I used to go to Camp Fondle You and blow off steam. We would swim in the lake, barbecue some dogs and burgers. At night we basically had a race to empty out the beer coolers and smoke all the weed we brought. Those were great times.

Anyway, this place is so special I want to share it with Zog. I'm not sure if he was much of a baseball fan, but I intend to build him a home in what's left of the ball field, past left field. I have a battery-operated lantern and there is a full moon so I can get around easier than I thought. I tie a pick and shovel around the large carpet that engulfs Zog and drag him into the field. I use the tools to carefully remove some of the waist-high grass about 20 yards beyond the home run wall. By 5:15 a.m. I have dug a hole big enough and deep enough to fit Zog. Not knowing what else to do, I take the path of least resistance and just dump Zog, carpet and all, into the hole. By 6:45 a.m. the hole is filled with Zog and the original dirt. I put the weeds back and step on them a little bit, like when I re-placed divots from all those golf rounds I caddied.

I get my pick and shovel and head back to my car. The sun is starting to fight its way into a new day. I turn and look back at the baseball field and I'm thinking I did a pretty good job. The field looks untouched. Not bad for an amateur, I guess. I get the car going and head to school.

Despite what I just went through, it's hard not to feel a slight surge of optimism. There's a new school year; everyone feels they have a clean slate. It's just a matter of time before the reality of what I have to do will overtake me. Just getting by was hard enough before. Now I gotta finish up school and, more important, take down Balducci.

CHAPTER 13

I am majoring in business because of Jimmy Balducci. Okay, that sounds a little strange, but the one thing I have to say about Balducci and his "buy for free" corporation is that it has given me a direction and a focus that frankly I could never have obtained otherwise. Put aside whacking Zog, because we know killing is frowned upon in business ethics; being involved in drug dealing, sports handicapping and bookmaking , which I am now, is probably not good for my resume either.

Yet, for me, things are looking a lot clearer. Well, in some areas things have gotten clearer; in others they're still a little murky. I know I'm fucked up with how much I think about Jimmy Balducci and C.W. Wellington. But I'm working my ass off. I have been able to forge a path that's unique, profitable and has ultimately put me in a position to accomplish what I want to do. What I know I have to do. Which is a lot different than the average poli-sci student stressing over law school.

I've found ways to make money and a lot of it, and I'm not talking about drinking money for college; I'm talking about real-world money. I used to need money to get by around here and to keep up with the crowd, but I didn't really need to be here per se. If I wasn't at school I would figure things out without burning four years in college. But always in the back of my head I knew that, without some sort of promising career, there wouldn't be a shot of getting back in C.W.'s good graces.

Basically, I always had C.W. in mind. It's practically the only reason I got involved in college. There have been some good times and I've learned a few things, but what am I really accomplishing here? Sometimes I catch a good profes-

sor or an interesting topic, and I'm grateful to be here. Sometimes in the classroom, I feel comfortable because it's an even
playing field, but it's that time after class that I feel like I'm a
step behind. Socially, up until recently, it was pretty difficult.
I felt like I belonged here as much as Lily from the Tongue
Room at Kosher World would belong here. But things are better now. Now that I don't give a shit, I can fit in.

I'm so busy that often at the end of the day I'll think to
my self, "Holy shit, I didn't think of C.W. at all today." But
then again, when that happens, I just thought of her. Discov-
ering the guy who wiped out half your family can shift your
focus a bit. So my mind pictures Jimmy Balducci a lot more
often and therefore, there's less C.W. Wellington. My head
must have been given a limited hard drive.

Getting C.W. back was always a long shot, and so was
any major Wall Street career. Being the mature adult that I am,
I've got to be realistic about my priorities. I was always heading further away from C.W.'s world, but now I'm not fighting
it. Hell, she probably thinks of me as often as I think about
Zimbabwe's political situation. Christ, if she or any of our
old friends knew how much I still think of her, it would be so
weird. It's ancient history for everyone else. If I had a father,
I'm sure he would say something philosophical like, "Women
make you do crazy things."

But I don't have a father and the reason is Balducci and
his "corporation." I know I can get close enough to Balducci
to take him out, but that's not really curing the disease. When
my father was the DA, he was trying to take down the corporation, but Balducci got wind of it and they got to him first.
George Skolinsky was a nobody forced to be an informant and
thrown in the middle of the crossfire. Skolinsky was informing
until the corporation caught on. So working with the law got
Skolinsky sliced and diced, and it got my father run over. My
father had a family, Skolinsky had a family and I guess over

the last 15 years the corporation has ruined hundreds or thousands of families. Not that it matters. The fact that it ruined
my family is enough. This shit's got to stop, and working with
the police ain't working. So I'll bring them down another way.
My father started a job and the way I see it, I'm going to finish
it for him.

I'm done working myself up into a jealous frenzy over
how much money the Remington Academy crowd has or what
cars the NY State guys get from their parents. I used to feel
so cheated because my mom and I had to move from plush
Manhasset to Hempstead. Like Hempstead was so bad. Shit, I
was so damn entitled. Now my ambitions have a real purpose
and all bets are off. Just about the only thing I care about is
how to get Balducci's corporation, and I know how I can do
it. It's going to take money and those "businesses" that I had
been previously avoiding. Those odd jobs that, as Cliff might
say, will keep the point of the sword aimed squarely at my
gut. Now that I'm involved in drug dealing and gambling, I've
pretty much sold my soul, but it's all for a cause.

I used to do a bunch of different things and I thought I
was doing them just to get by. It turns out everything you do
can be used if you remember it and exploit it when you need it.
I've found uses for all the work I've done, including my time at
Kosher World. Just noticing the way Sev leads, the way he can
take over a room, is worth more than any class I've taken.

I arrive at my apartment to get some much-needed
sleep. I used to live in a group of dilapidated apartments
located at the top of a hill on Cox Street. These clusters of
apartments provide the barest existence and are less-than-affec-
tionately called Cox Boxes. For the tenants, who are students
trying to get by, there's never any sentimental appreciation for
the place. People hardly even know their neighbors. It's hard
to be social when you can't fit a six-pack and enough friends to
share it with into the place. You're not in the dorms with fresh-

men, but you're not really living in an apartment, either.

That's all behind me now. My buddies and I changed apartments recently when things started going well. Spring Valley Lakes is a four-tower, high-rise apartment complex complete with an amazing health club, tennis courts, clubhouse and restaurant. It's where all the parties are.

Spring Valley Lakes is practically its own ecosystem. The core seems to have developed from the new breed of lawyers being created. Besides NY State's highly-rated law school, there are all sorts of young lawyers spilling out from the Albany State Building. As the capital of the state, there is plenty of politicking that goes on, and therefore, Spring Valley Lakes has also drawn its fair share of lobbyists who need to bully and sway state officials on policy making. Good or bad, you can say what you want about the lobbyists, but the one inarguable fact is those dudes can throw a party.

The group that tends to irk me the most at The Lakes are my peers from N.Y. State. There's a fair share of N.Y. State Gorillas living here, jocks who are not as smart as their name-sakes. The few times in the past that I was able to maneuver into a party at Spring Valley Lakes were always mind-blowing experiences. It amazed me that some father would pay for his little darling to live in one these ridiculously expensive places. I understand a father not wanting Pumpkin to live in a Cox Box, but holy shit, why spoil your kid this much?

At the end of the day, it appears many of the daddies are doing more than indulging their kids; they're setting the table for themselves. Daddy came through with rent, BMW, furniture and plasma TVs for a reason. Don't get me wrong; there are plenty of women who are busting their asses in school. Plenty of girls are getting good grades and studying for their LSATs or MCATs and are determined to make it in corporate America. But those girls ain't living in The Lakes.

The guys are worse. Forget earning a living and forget all the hotties they spent the last four years chasing. Why bother if you can hook up with a porker whose father has a business waiting for you? A lot of these missile-seeking budding socialites live above me, below me and next to me.

Obviously, I don't like them, so why do I want to live among them? That would be a very reasonable question; after all, I don't view myself in the same bucket as them. I'm no angel, that's for sure and I have issues that none of these clowns could even dream about. So I know I shouldn't be judging anyone.

But the main reason I'm at The Lakes is because of Austin Trotter and the fact that I'm a bookie, among other things. First of all, Austin Trotter is a senior who thinks he is God's gift to the world. His dad thinks so too, and had this apartment – my apartment – outfitted for him. Austin also thinks he can gamble, which he can't, at least not very well.

I took over this bookie business awhile ago when a guy named Andy Lyss approached me about running it. It was an up-and-coming business with a full list of clients, but Andy couldn't run it effectively. The biggest problem was that he couldn't collect from guys like Glenn Bessen. Andy couldn't use force because Bessen, who comes from private-jet type hedge fund money, claimed to have influential friends and yada yada. As a bookie, you need to collect, but you are a little limited in your methods. It's not like in the movies where you have big thugs breaking thumbs. You want to make a point but you don't want anyone running to the cops.

I was just getting involved in sports handicapping at the time, which, by the way is legal. I figured what the fuck. Any opportunity to make money. I bought out Andy and in return got his phone numbers, clientele and his willingness to transition his customers into a new voice: me. Glenn Bessen was one of those clients, a real prick, a rude, condescending deadbeat. In the end I had to beat the shit out of him to collect.

I know I said it's not like in the movies, but sometimes either
a situation warrants it or a guy is begging for it. As a bookie,
you have to be able to collect, and setting an example is good
for the business. Turns out he didn't want his influential
friends to know he was an inveterate gambler, and a bad one at
that, because he never ratted me out. Funny thing is, he wanted
to go on playing. He couldn't go a day without a making a
bet. Eventually he reached the end of the line, though; Daddy
must have figured out what was going on. I had to close him
out, and that's how I got this great apartment with the leather
couches, artwork and expensive entertainment system. In exchange I gave him my Cox Box. Fair is fair.

My apartment is on the 24th floor, and even before I
put the key in the door I hear Loot and Carey arguing over
something. I can't make it out yet, but I'm pretty sure it's not a
debate on existentialism. I need my sleep and when these guys
get going, winding them back down is challenging. Don't get
me wrong, I'm lucky they're here, I don't know how I'd get by
if they hadn't moved up from Hempstead. Loot was working
at a dry cleaners and Carey was a busboy, so I didn't ask for a
huge sacrifice in having them come up here. They seem pretty
happy and honestly, I'm more balanced with them around. At
the end of the day, Loot and Carey are the closest thing I really have to family. I got a lot going on now, and I really need
them. Right now though, all I need is sleep. The door opens
to them arguing and the subwoofers whomping along with the
not-so-soothing sound of Whip It Out's hip-hop rampage. The
storming rap music is causing the apartment to shake. I assume
the neighbors have been feeling it for hours.

These morons don't even see me. Loot is in a froth-
ing rage. He's in his bathrobe in front of our 52" plasma TV
and he is bouncing up and down on my black leather couch.
His dark skin and black silk bathrobe nearly blend in with the
couch. Loot continues bouncing and singing the same verse of

a song. He is trying to sing Whip It Out's song but changing the words to: "Biatch, pay me that 200 bucks now!" Usually, Loot's hair is tied tight in cornrows, but when they're untied, like now, his hair is one huge mountainous Afro that could almost tip him over the edge of the couch.

Carey is shaking his head, probably because there is no end in sight to Loot's trash talk. I glance at the TV and see they are playing some combat video game. Next to the couch, on the floor, my friend Ray is spread out on the carpet, passed out next to a nearly empty bottle of Paco Tequila. Most of the other friends I have at Albany State are a little put off by Loot and Carey and their less-than-suburban demeanor, but Ray just likes to get wasted. Carey sees me and shrugs.

I look at Carey and say, "What's up with Loot?"

Carey answers, "Damnedest thing. We were playing since four in the morning when all of last night's action was over. I was up $2000, but he wouldn't let me quit. Finally I get him to agree to a time limit. We agreed to play until 10 this morning so that we can get at least some sleep. He thinks he just won the Super Bowl."

I glance over at Loot and he's still dancing, singing, "Biatch, pay me my 200 bucks."

I turn down the music and face Loot and Carey. "Fellas, I got no zzzz's last night. We burnt it hard but we put up good numbers. We'll do a full accounting later, but I gotta sleep now."

Loot stops dancing, and the place is suddenly peaceful. "Not a problem," he says.

"Hey, can you guys throw Ray on the couch before you go to bed?" I ask.

Carey shrugs. "Yeah, we always do."

I don't bother washing up and plop down in bed. I mush around and try to find the comfortable position that will ease the burden of joints that are throbbing from a lack of sleep. Just as I start drifting off to sleep, my cell phone rings. Fuck, I forgot to shut the damn thing off. There's no way I'm gonna answer this, but when I recognize the number I take the call. "Yeah," I say into the phone.

"Hey, man, I'm ready for more," Barry says. He's one of my best customers. "I need eight boxes of shirts." For some reason, we have developed a code where eight boxes of shirts means eight pounds of pot. I say okay, I'll call him later.

I shut the power off on the phone, flip it closed and then find that comfortable position in bed almost immediately, probably because that last call is helping me ring the register again. As I start to float off toward sleep, somehow I get nostalgic and think of Speed Dial Pizza. How are pot and pizza connected, and not just through the munchies? Well, it wasn't that long ago that I was struggling to get by, and one of the several jobs I had was delivering pizza for Speed Dial Pizza. Yup, Speed Dial Pizza, of all places, got me my first real weed customers.

Speed Dial guaranteed your pizza delivered in 30 minutes from the time you ordered or the customer gets the pizza free. So I'm practically running sprints all night. I'm driving 80 miles an hour in an asinine purple pizza uniform that's soaked through with perspiration for shit wages and sometimes the only tips I got were bong hits. Which combined with the next 80-mile-an-hour delivery was not a brilliant combination. I did get a good view of the stoner landscape, so I came up with a plan to earn bigger bucks and get that much closer to creaming Balducci. See, I knew a dealer in Arizona who had great quality and his price blew away what was here. Locally, I was able to either supply shit to them at a better price and quality or put them out of business. The guys on the pizza circuit were just the start of my clientele. Once I got in, it was easy to carve out my own niche, especially at Spring Valley Lakes. The lobbyists, lawyers and NY State privileged students in this asshole factory make the greatest customers.

At some point I drift off to sleep. I wake up startled by the sight of Zog the Cellophane King standing above me, covered in dirt from the Camp Fondle You baseball field. I'm relieved to realize that it's only a dream. I wake up but then I'm pissed because it's almost four in the afternoon. Then I remember, Carey did wake me, but I rolled back over. Fuck, I'm behind now.

I do some reading for my advertising and marketing class and head out to HQ around 5 p.m. I'll spend a couple of hours at the office and head back to The Lakes for a party that could be productive.

I enter the apartment with a couple of guys I don't recognize. The music is blasting and the air is so thick with the sweet scent of pot you can practically eat it. I'm not even sure who is hosting this party. It's a nice enough apartment and the music is kind of cool. An eclectic new-wave beat is pounding through the room like a train.

There's an interesting tone starting to develop at these parties at The Lakes. A new set of "haves" and "have-nots" are forming. The "haves" include those who are sitting on a job offer or an ugly girl's family business, those heading to law school or lobbyist training grounds. The "have-nots" are those who want that situation. There is a swagger in one group and a feeling of heaviness in the other. With the final semester around the corner, the conversation always moves in that direction when there is a room full of upperclassmen. Me, I don't give a fuck, because I'm the only person in this room who knows where my future is and where I will be when school winds down, and there's a fair chance I won't even be breathing.

Whoever our gracious host is, he has set up a bar in the furthest corner of the room. Nothing too elaborate, it offers a few different brands of vodka, some tequila, some 12-year-old Scotch, a few bottles of wine and some bottles of beer. I drop some ice into a cup and start pouring in some vodka. I can use a couple of Absolutes to help me loosen up a bit. I don't really want to be here tonight. I've got a big, big shipment coming in from my friend Al in Arizona, and I'm getting a little antsy about it.

I start scoping the room and take inventory of who is here, but I don't see many fresh faces. Pretty funny how you walk into school as a freshman and get lost in a flood of 50,000 students. Then each year the cliques develop and grab their members. The stoners down this river, frats and sororities down that stream, real academics follow this trickle and jocks down that brook until everyone has made the school smaller with their own sub-groups. So here I am at a party with practically the same people from the last party. Where are the other 49,900 students? What else can we say to each other at this party that's different from the last?

As expected, I notice a ton of familiar faces. On the unusual-to-see-here-side, I see Rocky Campbell standing by the other wall and talking to some people. This party at The Lakes is probably an experiment for her. Rocky is wearing brown cowboy boots and a tight pair of blue jeans. The pants are on a long winding road that continues up her lengthy, tight figure. The horizon of her low-cut jeans is met by a tight tan tank top. The tan shirt complements her wavy auburn hair, which tumbles sensuously down her back.

I've lost track of how many times I've asked out Rocky Campbell. To no avail, I might add. We share a lot of classes, so I see her practically every day. Talk about tantalizing. Sometimes I feel I'd rather not be around her at all if it means she's going to reject me, even in a nice way.

Ray and his girlfriend Cindy are here, sitting on the sofa and holding court. I lock eyes with Cindy and she breaks away from Ray and moves toward me. Cindy's wearing jeans, expensive black shoes and a tight grey shirt showing a decent amount of belly, but perhaps she shouldn't be showing so much skin. She's been doing a fair amount of partying these past four years and she's gotten noticeably thicker. Both in the stomach and the head. Four years in college and I think she went backwards. She comes up so close to me I can smell her perfume over the stink of the pot. For Cindy, she actually looks fairly serious. Dispensing with a normal greeting, she launches right into her main topic. "Kevin, what are you doing to Ray?"

"Nothing. Why?"

"I think he's hanging out at your place a bit too much," she says, with a sort of affected sigh that fucking irritates me. "I mean, he's wasted way more than usual, and that's saying something. Are you looking out for him?"

"Cindy, I'm trying, but I have to admit, I got my concerns. We should talk more about this some time."

"Right." She looks at me for a few seconds, as if she has noticed something distasteful. "I'll give you a call. And don't be so mean to Ray." She sashays away, only she's bombed and her sash is out of sync with her ay. Two years ago, I used to think she was worth stealing from Ray, but now, not so much.

At this point, I see Rocky Campbell being cornered by a particularly pompous looking guy. No doubt he is explaining how he will be a managing director of Blow Me & Blow Me. It's been a while since Rocky last shot me down, so while this guy is spewing and Rocky is tapping her foot with boredom, I might as well give it another try.

I move closer to her and we briefly make eye contact. Rocky smiles the smile that puts her over the top. Rocky has a smile that stops time. Not because her teeth are bleached white or perfectly straight because frankly, it's neither of those. Her teeth are naturally pretty, and her smile is playful and sharp. Even when she shoots me down when I ask her out, her smile mitigates the damage of rejection.

I casually approach her, but the schmuck she's talking to is really on a roll. I want to get in there, but that would mean breaking the imaginary force-field of the existing conversation. If I barge through this force-field and then go unacknowledged, I'll feel as welcome as the Dali Lama at an NRA meeting; I'll have no idea what to do with myself while I'm standing there. Luckily, even though the schmuck has Rocky cornered, I am able to make eye contact with her again. Before I hit the conversation circumference, Rocky calls out to me, "Kevin, how are things going?"

"Doing okay. How 'bout you?" Before she answers, I slink in and practically put my back into the schmuck's face.

"Kevin, are you going to ask me out again?" She's smiling that killer smile.

"Let's see," I say, pretending to concentrate. "When Dave Mathews was playing at the Pearle Street Arena, you said, 'No thanks.' When the new George Clooney-Kira Knightly movie opened, you couldn't make it. When the Gorillas were playing our archrivals the Syracuse Orange you said, 'Not sure if I'm going to be able to go, but if I do, maybe I'll see you over there.' You know, Rocky, I just might be running out of ammo. Do you think I can handle any more rejection?" I ask.

"I'm a little concerned about your well-being. Maybe you shouldn't have to deal with any more rejection issues," she says.

"Well, doctor, what would you recommend?" I ask.

"Can I see your cell phone?" I give her a confused look. "Cell phone please," she sternly states. So what the fuck, I hand her my cell phone.

Then much to my surprise—and I've got to believe to

the surprise of the schmuck—Rocky Campbell begins input-
ting her contact information into my phone directory. Then she
hands back my phone. She smiles again and says, "If you can,
give me a call this week. I bet we can figure something out
that works."

I take the phone back and glance at the schmuck, who
has no idea what to do. It's hard to leave a conversation you
were just in when you weren't really in the conversation. It's
hard to say goodbye when you haven't been introduced.

I look at Rocky and I say, "Okay, what gives? Not that
I'm complaining, but why now? Is this, some sort of sympathy
thing? Like, oh poor frustrated Kevin. I'll-do-him-a-favor-
out-of-pity kind of thing?"

"No, nothing like that," she replies with half a smile. "I
kinda like the way you asked me again. You know, persisted.
I'm not saying I was testing you. I just find your persistence
sort of...brave. You know, you must have asked me out 10
times, and I always said no, but I bit my lip every time I did it."
She grins in a friendly way and says, "I know it sounds weird,
but that's it." She loses the smile and says, "I'm up for coffee
some time or maybe a few drinks, if you still are."

"Hell, yeah," I say. "I'll call you this week."

"Sounds good. I'm checking out of here now, so I'll
speak to you then." With that, Rocky heads toward the closet
to grab her coat and just like that she's gone. Except not totally
gone because she left her number with me.

I nod to the schmuck and he nods back to me. "Kind of
a weird party," he says.

Yeah, I think, smiling. But weird in a good way.

CHAPTER 14

It's a Tuesday night and that's an important night for us because we do all our accounting then. Tuesdays, during the day, is when we collect; so by nighttime, we know what we actually have in hand. Before we can do anything, I have to send my old friend Ray on his way. He is getting pretty sloppy. That's what he does when he's not around Cindy. Ray and Cindy used to get wasted together, but Cindy is getting pretty spooked. At least that's what she tells me. As much as Cindy used to like getting smashed, she sees school ending soon, and Ray isn't getting that real world joke. So Cindy wants me to reel him in a bit. Like I have the time or the ability to take on that project.

Loot and Carey get a kick out of Ray. In general, the privileged Spring Valley Lakes crowd doesn't really appreciate Loot and Carey. Every person in their elite world has to serve a purpose, and what purpose could two black dudes from Hempstead that aren't even students serve the Spring Valley Lakes' ecosystem? I've got to give Ray credit; he doesn't act that way with me and he doesn't act that way with Loot and Carey. Ray just likes to get baked and he is an equal opportunity partier. But I need to take care of business today and Ray can be a distraction. So we graciously point out where there is a party in the Lakes tonight and kick his wasted-ass out.

Carey, Loot and I finish the Tuesday night math. The sports marketing business is lame this week, but the bookie business is strong. Between college football and the NFL, we crush it. Pro basketball is slightly ahead, but the gravy is a huge shipment of sensimilla weed from Arizona that we turn over very nicely. Our best week yet; we are looking at

$18,000. I'm glad the numbers are good. I suspected this week was better than most, but I'm surprised by how much. You never know until it's all in and counted.

After we do the numbers for the week, I call Sev. To the outsider it might sound weird, but I call Sev about once a week. I admit we don't have a ton to talk about, but the truth is, it feels good. It's hard to explain, but for years I have been a bystander as my roommates and friends called home once or twice a week to check in and bullshit with their folks. I could never have an ongoing long-distance conversation with my mother. When I'm there in person with Mom, sometimes we can connect, but our phone conversations are fragmented and short.

I always envied my friends for that continuous update with home and wondered what it was like; I guess Sev is as close as I get. He doesn't get a ton of calls, other than Kosher World stuff, so I'm pretty sure he appreciates the call as well. We speak about what's going on at Kosher World, the action at Locomotive Breath and every now and then some current events.

But today's call is rough. Sev is really bummed. It's difficult for me to get him talking about what's bothering him, but when I get him going, it just flows. "You remember Hector Pinto?" Sev asks.

"Sure. If it weren't for him, I never would've been able to fight in the Industrial Road bouts."

"That's right." Sev chuckles for the first time tonight. "When he cut off his finger, you made me put you in the fight. Man, you were a crazy mothafucka."

I laugh and say, "I know, but I needed that fight. That one night of work got me off everyone's shit list. So what's going on with Hector?"

"Nothing's going on. He disappeared."

That hit me hard. "What? Do you have any idea what

happened to him?"

"Yeah, unfortunately I do. I saw it coming from a mile away. Hector had a chance to go back to the Dominican Republic and work with his family in some business, but Balducci won't let him quit. There ain't a ton of work down there in the Dominican Republic, but now he has this great opportunity and wants to bring his whole family back home. That was his intention all along, make enough money here or wait till something opened in the Dominican Republic."

"Sounds reasonable," I say. "How can Balducci stop him from going?"

"Balducci's more fucked up than ever. He's trying to get more and more things under his control, but at the same time he feels he lost control. He can't lose control of Kosher World; he's got too much wrapped up here. Reason he made Pinto disappear was to send a message to everyone that Kosher World is your job and don't focus on anything else."

"How do you know Pinto didn't just skip town?"

"His wife and kids are a mess right now. They know something happened and they ain't that good at acting."

I take a deep breath, imagining the worst. "You think he'll do something dramatic, like when he chopped up George?"

"Yup, something creative like that," Sev says, steaming. "That cock Balducci is turning this place into a slave farm. If a guy is not allowed to go work somewhere else, what the fuck do you call it? When does this shit stop?"

"Fuck, Sev, that's unbelievable," I say.

Sev sighs. "That's your mentor. Great fuckin' guy. You still speaking to him?"

"Naw, Sev, I haven't spoken to him in awhile." Which was kind of true. Every now and then around the holidays or when I know his son is in town, I make a point to go out with Richie. We get liquored up somewhere and I crash at his

house. Just like in the old days when we were in high school
together. The only difference now is that when Richie goes to
sleep, I snoop around the house and find information and records about Balducci's businesses. Balducci is definitely more
edgy these days. He doesn't shoot the shit with me like he did
in the past. But one time he said, "You stay loose, kid, I'm
gonna need you soon." I told him I'd be there for him, but I'm
really thinking, *You have no idea what you're gonna need when
I get through with you, asshole.*

The call with Sev is upsetting but it makes me even
more determined to push through with the plan I have. I'm
relieved we have these good numbers, and while money is nice,
even more important, I feel like my idea is gaining traction.
Still, I never thought I would worry about Sev, but he sounded
really bummed. I told him I was going to be in town next
weekend and we should get together for a little while. I even
offered to buy the drinks.

CHAPTER 15

I'm seeing Rocky quite a bit now, nothing too crazy, just studying together or walking around campus or going to some lame party. We talk on the cell a lot, too; the girl gives great phone.

We go out to eat a few times too, including one date at a nice restaurant. The dinner is great. Just to be able to afford expensive food makes it taste much better. I order a nice 2001 Brunello di Montalcino. We have a good laugh from the fact that I even know how to order a bottle of wine, but the truth is, I learned how to do it from C.W. Wellington's father.

Buster Wellington would go through the whole deal, smelling the cork, swishing a small sip of the wine around his cheeks and examining the label. Mr. Wellington would talk wine for as long as anyone would listen, so I got a little bit of a wine degree from my time at the Wellington School for the Insanely Affluent. The thing that always surprised people was that ol' Buster actually had the balls to send shit back every now and then. I'll never know if he really tasted the difference or if it was a power thing. The point is, Buster knows his wine and he knows how to work a room.

The truth is, whether I'm thinking about Rocky or C.W., the last thing I need right now is the distraction of a girl. What I really need to do is focus on Balducci. I need to think about finishing that job every minute of every day. Yet, sometimes things just happen. Rocky Campbell is in my mind now and I can't help it. Frankly, I don't want to help it. But the question isn't why I'm this interested in Rocky. The question really is, why does Rocky care about me?

It's definitely not the money or danger; I can tell she

doesn't give a shit about that stuff. I might be naïve but I
think she really likes hanging out with me. She gets on really
well with Loot and Carey, too, which means a lot. Why is she
interested in me and not some wanna-be lawyer, banker or hotshit lobbyist? It's what all the other girls are looking for. What
does she see in me that no one else does?

I figure I'll really show her what's under the hood and
see if she runs. Shit, why drag it out? If she bails, at least I
could focus completely on Balducci, which is what I should be
doing anyway. But I don't want her running for the hills and
I'm really not sure if I can handle her blowing me off again.
Letting her in on some of this stuff is plain risky; this operation is more than just dope and gambling. It's a lot more, when
you throw Balducci into the mix. Anyone involved with me
is looking at jail time or dead time, and if I really care about
Rocky she should know what's involved. It's got to be her
choice to stick around.

It was easy telling Loot and Carey because we're willing to drive through walls for each other. Don't get me wrong;
they enjoy the money here, but they know what this means to
me and they want to help me get the bad guy. There's plenty
that think I'm a low-life, drug dealing, bookie hood. To some
I'm a guy who's hustling to stay in school. Nobody except
Loot and Carey know about Balducci and what he did to my
father.

Rocky and I are studying in my apartment when a
good-size shipment of Arizona sensimilla pot arrives. It comes
in three boxes that are pretty innocuous. I know this shipment
is being delivered today, but I didn't tell Rocky because I didn't
want her to have any preconceived notions.

I sign for the package, which is a pretty unbelievable
thing if you think about it. Here's 15 pounds of pot being delivered right to my door, and I sign Kevin Davenport like I am
signing for the dry cleaning. I always figure that if I get busted

I can claim I didn't know what was being sent to me. "Officer, I wasn't expecting anything. I got a package and I opened it and there was all this weed. It must have been sent here by accident." Now deep down I know that's not going to hold water, but that's the only mindset you can have. You show me a dealer who thinks he's gonna get caught. I guess I can sign a fictitious name, but why add forgery to the list if I do get busted?

"Weed shipment," I casually say to Rocky. "It looks like I gotta go to work."

"Oh, does that mean you need me out of here?" she answers with casual surprise.

Well, she doesn't seem freaked out by the whole thing. "Loot and Carey are out. Do you mind giving me a hand?" I ask.

"I guess it's okay. What do you need me to do?"

I ask her to go to the kitchen, locate a clear spray bottle, fill it with water and bring it back to me. She complies and returns as I am slicing through all the tape on the box with a knife. "The guys in Arizona did a pretty good job in sealing the box so that there's no place for air to escape. I'm glad they're thorough, but it's a huge pain in the ass getting through all the layers."

Inside there are layers as well; layers and layers of T-shirts that must have been bought at a thrift store or stolen off the back of some kid with bad skin and braces. I mean really lame T-shirts that have pictures of the Incredible Hulk or Harry Potter. Occasionally you might run into a cool college T-shirt or a pro sports team, but for the most part these shirts are only good for disguising pot. We sift through all the shirts.

Hiding the potent smell of herb is a coating of talcum powder generously sprinkled on top of the last plastic cover that separates the pot from all the other nonsense. The powder rests on plastic wrap thicker than the cellophane Zog wrapped around my face. Beneath that layer are airtight bags, each containing a half-pound of pot.

Rocky observes me as I meticulously collect ten half-pound bags from each box. I make three piles: one pile is about 20 worthless T-shirts, and another has three T-shirts that are keepers: Cold Play, San Diego Chargers and Sunrise Surfboards. The third pile is the 30 half-pound bags of pot stacked like bricks. I ask Rocky if she wants any T-shirts, but she passes.

I carefully weigh the pot on my scale to make sure I'm getting what I paid for. "Listen, Rocky, if this is making you uncomfortable in the least…." She says it's not a problem, and I believe her. "Well, I can certainly use the company," I say sincerely. So she's not motoring out of here yet. I've already told her that I move pot, so that's not a surprise, but the sight of 15 pounds of boo can make a strong impression. So far, though, it looks like she appreciates the situation as an amusing curiosity.

The 30 bags weigh in correctly. It looks like I'm in business.

"How are you going to sell these?" Rocky asks.

"That's done already. I got some loyal customers who paid half up front. I sell this for more than double, so if the ridiculous happens and the customer who laid out the money doesn't show, so much the better."

I start spreading out newspaper. In between the kitchen and our three bedrooms the narrow hallway acts as the perfect place to start leveraging. I meticulously spread the newspaper so that none of the wood floor is showing. Rocky wants to know where I get all my customers, so, as I'm spreading the paper, I tell her briefly about my connections. I pick up a few buds and examine them. The buds are almost day-glo green with a few red fibers wrapping around the buds like protective vines. There is hardly a seed in sight. I smell the bud and recognize the pungent odor, and for a moment, I am Buster Wellington examining a bottle of wine.

"Does it meet with your approval?" Rocky asks.

"Indeed it does." With that I flip open my cell phone and when Joel answers, I instruct him to be here in 45 minutes. I look at my watch and say into the phone, "No kidding, Joel, I got somewhere else to go. Be here before 4:20." I hang up the phone, look at Rocky and say, "We've got to hustle now. I got to get this stuff back into those half-pound bags it came in."

"So the stupid question I am compelled to ask is, why did you take it out of the bags in the first place?"

"Not a bad question at all. We are preparing for a unique technique we invented called leveraging. First, we need to break down Mt. St. Dope here." With that I start flattening the big mountain of pot into a thin layer stretching out the entire hallway. I ask her to pass me the spray bottle and then begin the important process of applying a mist to the path of pot. The herb on top of the newspaper looks like it's resting on a conveyer belt that has stalled. I carefully walk down the edges of the newspaper and continue to mist, making sure to spray evenly. Rocky looks at me as if I'm insane, which I may be. "Okay, what's going on now?" she asks.

"Joel is going to be here in 20 minutes. I am going to temporarily turn 3 pounds of pot into 3 1/4 pounds of pot."

"You're a magician too?"

"Yes, boys and girls, right before your eyes, watch the magic weed." I continue to spray water. "The trick is to make it moist but not wet. When we put the pot back into the half-pound baggies there can't be any water drops or condensation on the plastic. We need a light mist that's just enough to add weight, but not really detectable."

"That's some skill," Rocky comments.

"I think of it as an art." I carefully begin filling each bag, and when it reaches what should be around half a pound, I measure again on my scale. I continue to tweak the contents of the bag, sometimes adding pot from the newspaper and sometimes subtracting, but when I close that ziplock, the bag weighs half a pound.

"By my calculations," Rocky says, "there should be a quarter pound of pot left over on this newspaper. Is that right?"

"Uh-huh." I smile.

"What happens when it dries up and these guys figure out they were shorted?"

"Joel will buy 3 pounds that will be weighed right in front of his eyes. By sundown, these bags will be broken down into many forms, and between all the sample hits, transfers and lack of business acumen by the stoner community, I don't anticipate any issues. I haven't had a problem yet. And I've been buying for free for a while now."

"Buying for free?" Rocky asks.

"Buying for free. It was an important lesson I learned. The 15 pounds I received today will yield 16 pounds. There's one extra pound for my own retail distribution. But even more than the money, there's buying for free and that's beyond business; it's an attitude. I need to get knee-deep in it."

"Okay," Rocky says and pauses, "I have a couple of questions."

"I was hoping you would ask. Shoot." I might sound like I'm joking, but talking to Rocky about this is very liberating.

"What do you consider retail distribution and what does buying for free mean?"

"Well, take Joel. He buys wholesale so he can sell it retail, just like in the real world. While I'm making a nice chunk, I have to give him a chance to make money. He'll break this up into ounces and dime bags, and possibly he'll sell a quarter pound somewhere. He's selling it to the dorms and frats. I have other guys here in the Lakes who hit the lawyers and lobbyists." I tell her that I try not to send someone out onto someone else's turf. I like to have some idea where it's going because if it ends up in an elementary school playground then it would be a real shitfest.

"I see," Rocky says. "You sell in bulk to Joel, but give him a chance to make money."

"You got it. Joel is buying this for $1,200 but by the time he's done retailing it he will bring in $2000. So he's got $800 profit and all the weed he can smoke."

"If Joel is buying it for $1,200 a pound, are you able to make money?"

"Yep. I'm buying it for $700." I answer. I'm glad she's interested. I think this is going well but we are going to get into some murky water soon.

"So you have 15 pounds and you earn $500 a pound... that's $7,500, right?"

I remind her of the pound of pot I "bought for free." By wetting this down I'll end up with an extra pound, I tell her, which I can retail for $2,000, just like Joel.

At least, that's the way it's supposed to work. "We have a little fun with our extra bag. If we wanted, we could sell it without even leaving the apartment complex. Loot and Carey take some and act like Big Men on Campus and turn people on. They've gotten to be buddies with the Gorilla basketball team mainly because of this excess supply. Loot and Carey believe the players respect them because they, too, are good ballplayers and fun to be around. I suspect, though, that if the dope supply dried up, Loot and Carey would be a lot less fun to hang out with."

Finally we finish filling the last half-pound bag. We have three pounds of pot. There is a fair amount of weed still left on the newspaper that I carefully put into a separate bag to be weighed later, but I suspect I'll have my typical quarter pound extra. There's not a crumb left on the newspaper. It's good to be a pro.

We have about 10 minutes before Joel arrives for his three pounds. So I guess these 10 minutes are as good a time as any to roll the dice. We start crumbling up the newspaper from the hallway, dispose of the pile and open the window so the smell can escape. "Hey, Rocky, you have a minute to talk about something?"

"More serious than 15 pounds of pot? Sure, I'm all ears," she says.

"Look, I've really enjoyed spending all this time but...."

She interrupts to ask, "Are you breaking up with me?"

"No. Hell no," I say. "Look, these things I'm involved in, I told you that it's something I'm doing now, but I have no desire to continue with it after school. Right?"

"Yes," she says, "to get you through school and help out at home."

"I appreciate, you know, staying with me and giving me a chance," I say gratefully. "I know you wouldn't want to be involved in this stuff long-term, so I appreciate you giving me some leeway here."

"Well, it's been my pleasure," she says with a smile.

"Rocky, I don't want to freak you out, but there's something I have to tell you because it's important." She looks at me seriously, her brown eyes large and intense.

It's always been difficult to speak to anyone about my father's and sister's deaths and the effect they've had on my mother and me. Speaking to anyone about this always causes that awkward silence and uncomfortable comments meant to console. People ask what happened to your father, but the truth is, people do not have a lot of experience hearing about someone being murdered. I haven't heard a good response yet. Rocky's silent attention is such a relief that I hate to unload the rest on her. But I do. I tell her about my job at Kosher World and how I discovered Jimmy Balducci's buying for free and his involvement in so many killings, most importantly, my dad's.

"What about the police?" she asks. "Have you told them?"

"Rocky, my father was the police. He was the district attorney, and there were people inside who sold him out." I tell her about George Skolinsky cooperating with the police and then getting his head cut off. "Believe me, working with the police and wearing a wire is not the way to go. So right about now, you may be wondering why I am telling you this"

"Kevin, why are you telling me this now?" she asks seriously.

"When I told you these money-making activities are temporary, I left out the fact that I'm really not using these transactions to pay my college bill. The truth is, I would have been able to scrape by without all this, but I need real money to stop these guys. They're killing people. They're ruining families, and no one knows how that feels more than me. I have an idea how to stop them, but I need to build up a presence. Getting Balducci is the least I can do for my father."

I know that Rocky's mind must be racing. To distract herself, she grabs her auburn hair and fits a band around a newly created ponytail. I can sense that I'm losing her. "Rocky," I say, "I didn't count on having feelings for you. Not like this. I care about what you think and I don't want to see you hurt. The truth is, anyone involved with me could get hurt."

"That's why you're telling me this? You don't want me hurt?" She pauses to look at me, tilting her head. "Is this some sort of elaborate breakup line?"

"Rocky, that's not what I want to do. I know I just dropped a bomb on you. There are so many normal situations for you here. I don't want your time wasted and, more importantly, I don't want you physically hurt. I didn't want to get too serious too fast, but damn, I can't stop thinking about you."

"Any shot you let this Balducci stuff drop?"

"I can't. It's what I was put on this planet to do."
Rocky is staring at the floor and nodding in acknowledgement.
"Everything seems to have a purpose. I used to caddy on golf
courses, deliver pizzas, sell on the telephones and work in the
meat factory. I thought I was doing it to get enough money
to get through school so that I could launch some career. I
thought I was doing it so I could get into the social circuit
around here. But that's not the case. Everything I've done has
been put in front of me to get Balducci, to finish the job my
father started."

"All right, let's say you get Balducci, let's say this
works. What then?" she asks.

"Baby, I don't know. I can start living my life, I guess.
I sure as hell don't need this shit. There's no way this can be
done for any length of time without getting nailed at some
point. I might last another year, at best, before I run out of
luck.

"It wasn't long ago that swinging this kind of money
around was all I was dreaming about doing. It was just something I seemed to be missing. Everyone seems to have money,
everyone seems to be having fun. I thought that's what I cared
about, but now I know better."

The doorbell rings. Joel has arrived. "Coming," I yell.
Then I turn to Rocky. "I have to take care of business. I hope
we can talk later, but I understand if you don't want to have
anything to do with me. You know, good people can be put in
bad situations. I didn't ask for this; it happened to me and my
family. You have choices, and even though I'm crazy about
you, I want you to have those choices and not be ambushed by
my cavalier behavior."

As Joel comes in, Rocky slips out. The transaction
with Joel is a blur. I am trying to gauge Rocky's reaction to my
revelation, but I am trying to stay focused on Joel as well. It

sounds strange, but I met Joel through his best friend Bartner
– a policeman. Bartner lives in the building with his lobbyist
girlfriend but occasionally stops by here and I turn him on for
free. I figure it's good for business to keep him happy. He's a
tall, powerful guy with a long chain-link tattoo on his neck that
makes me think of the time I strangled Zog.

Joel and I go through the typical dance, beginning with
him taking a few sample bong hits to make sure the quality of
the merchandise is to his liking. He occasionally gives an ap-
proving nod or comment like, "Awesome weed, it's chronic."
We measure out his purchase and he says, "Dude, three elbows
on the screws, here's your cashish." With that he hands me
money and puts the six bags of marijuana in a large gym bag.
Joel holds up a fist, I close my hand into a fist and gently bang
his knuckles, and then he leaves.

The money I pocket for the quick work seems pretty
small compared to what I risked today. I'm not sure why
Rocky was hanging with me before I leveled with her. Shit, if
she's not calling the travel agent to New Boyfriendland now,
then somewhere cats are sleeping with dogs and it's snowing in
the rainforest.

I feel better that I told her everything, but I suspect
she'll dump me. It's crushing me, thinking that we are done.
Maybe I shouldn't have spilled my guts just yet. Maybe I
should have waited to let her know me better.

CHAPTER 16

As it turns out, Rocky doesn't bolt. The Balducci story doesn't make her run, but I ain't gonna say the jury has come in with a verdict, either. She is still with me and I am grateful. There is another level to reach in what is developing in, dare I say, our relationship. I want to be at that level, but I don't know if she does. As good as things are with Rocky, anytime we begin to get physical, it feels wrong. We're having a lot of laughs and I know she likes me. I feel she wants more and I know I do. But then, she pulls back. I can't put my finger on what pushes her away…that is, until this night. I call her at 11:45 p.m. on Sunday when the weekend's work is wrapped up to say goodnight.

At first it's our usual repartee, but things change when I ask, "How did you get the name Rocky? I can't be the first person to ask you that."

She laughs and says, "No, you're not. It doesn't surprise me that you ask. What surprises me is how long it took you. It usually gets asked sooner."

"Oh, hey, I'm not looking to…."

"No, it's not a big deal. I was born Raquel Olivia Campbell. Get it? R.O.C. It sounds like 'rock'."

"Aahhh, I get it, so the rock would become Rocky," I say.

"Well, there is a little more to the story," she concedes. "My father was a huge boxing fan. He can talk that stuff for hours. He was also a wanna-be actor. His biggest success was a tiny part as an extra in the first Rocky movie. It came out before VHS and DVD, and Dad saw the movie and himself 25 times in the theater. He laughed that he spent more on movie tickets than he was actually paid."

"How about the other Rocky movies? Did he see them a bunch too?" I ask.

"That's my point. Somewhere between Rocky and Rocky III, I was born. So it's no accident that my initials are R.O.C. It was a great way for my father to introduce his new daughter and gloat about being in the movie, even though a million other Rocky movies were made without my father."

"Hmmm, would you rather not be called Rocky? Do you like Raquel better?"

"No. I like Rocky. I think the name is interesting, but the story behind it isn't as cool as my father intended."

"Are you and your father close?" As someone who hasn't had a father since I was 10, I always get a kick out of father stories.

Rocky shrugs and shakes her head. "We haven't had a reason to talk."

"When was the last time you spoke?" I ask.

"Seven or eight years now. I guess you think that's weird."

"Hah! I'm not the guy to judge what's weird." The truth is I do think it's weird, because from my vantage point, any day your father's above ground should be a great day. "I guess relationships with parents can get tricky." I try to be polite, but she can tell I don't really get it.

I notice how late it is and intend on wrapping up the conversation so I can get some sleep. But that's not what happens. "Hey, Rocky, why aren't you speaking with your father anymore?" Holy shit, did I just ask that? There's something about fathers that makes me overwhelmingly curious. I can't help myself.

There's a pause on the other side of the phone. How do I take this question back?

"Kevin, if I tell you, it might change things. I don't

think you really want to talk about this, do you?"

It's a rhetorical question at this point. I mean, could you imagine if I said, "No, thanks anyway." The truth is, I'm captivated. So I say, "Yeah, Rocky, I'm really interested in you. Hell, I got a screwed-up situation too. Maybe I can help."

"I don't think so. I have it resolved."

"C'mon, you said you haven't spoken to your father in eight years." I might sound altruistic here, but to be honest, I have my selfish reasons as well. I'm no Sigmund fuckin' Freud, but I suspect I've found the reason she is pulling back from me. I hypothesize that her father was a player and Rocky walked in on him with the town nun. Therefore, she can't trust guys. "Rocky, we can let it drop here. I'm not trying to pry. I'll tell you this, though. I'm glad I told you about the situation with Balducci and my father. It was risky, but I'm glad I told you."

I hear her sigh on the other end of the phone. "Okay. Here goes. My father didn't work much, so he was around a lot. Most of the money we had was from my mother, who's a terrific dancer and owns a few dance studios. Dad and I hung out a lot and we always had a lot of fun. The weekends were busy for my mother, so my dad was the one taking me to carnivals and the playground.

"Dad's acting career wasn't going anywhere, so, to help support me and my brother, he took a job with an uncle of his who runs a plumbing supply business out here in Albany."

"Wow, that's a big change, from acting to plumbing. How did it work out?"

"Not too well. Uncle Allen says that my father never put any effort into the job and wanted a piece of the business as his birthright. Dad says Uncle Allen got him to move out to Albany but was never going to make him a partner."

"So who was right?" I ask.

"I don't know. I'm sure the truth lies somewhere in

between the two stories. We were fortunate because my mom developed her dance studios. Money-wise we were okay." Her voice falters, she pauses for a moment, and when she continues, her voice is softer. "This is where it gets fucked up." She pauses again and says, "You have to understand, my dad got by on his looks his whole life, but when he hit 50, his hair – what's left of it – started losing the battle of salt vs. pepper and he gained a lot of weight as well. But the worst thing for him was that the young girls he used to love flirting with weren't interested anymore. He looked average now and the rest of the world was running laps around him. He wanted to feel like a young stud again, and he turned to a young girl who couldn't say 'no.' Me. My father molested me. Okay, he raped me."

"Holy shit!" is about all I can muster. I'm thinking to myself, What a dog! "I can't believe you had to live through that."

"Living through it was awful, but living with him was unbearable. Anytime he had a few drinks, which was fairly often, he'd reach for me. I was only 13 then, and he had me believing that if I said anything, my mother would throw us both out."

"I can't even imagine how tough that must have been on you." I always thought there's nothing worse in this world than not having a father, and now I've changed my mind. "How did you get him to stop?"

"My mother suspected something going on. She knew I never wanted to be in the house and would find any excuse to get out. But this one Sunday afternoon she wouldn't let me out. She had a birthday party at the dance studio and took my brother to help. She put her foot down. I had to stay in and study. My father came into my room and started grabbing at me. I was pleading with him to stop. He was on top of me and getting angry that I was resisting. Out of nowhere my mother starts pounding him on the head with a log from our fireplace stack. So he was on the ground bleeding and my mother was dialing the police. She puts the police on hold and she says to Dad, 'Here are the keys to the car, get the fuck out of here. If you ever try to contact us again, you're going to jail.'"

"Fuck, why didn't she throw his ass in jail?"

"Kevin, she knew I couldn't go through a trial. The last thing I needed was to be stared at. The town was real small." Rocky pauses. I can hear her weeping, but she fights through the sobs and says, "What if that perv is out there doing it to someone else, and I didn't put him away? How do I live with that?"

I jump in, saying, "C'mon Rocky, you're being too tough on yourself. You can't have the whole world on your shoulders; you had to take care of yourself. You did what you had to do. It's not like this is marketing class where you lay out a strategy and follow a plan from a textbook. You went into crisis management and you weren't wrong. You were a kid who got thrown into a tough situation."

"I know," she says through a voice still broken by sobs.

"So that was the last time you saw him?" I ask.

"Never saw him or spoke to him again," she says. "So, are you still with me, Kevin, or did I totally freak you out?"

"Baby, I'm here. I'm here more than ever. My only regret is that we're on the phone and I'm not there to hug you." I never said anything truer. I didn't expect anything like this from Rocky.

We spoke about the gamut of emotions she has. She tries to date. Guys think she's a tease or a prude because she always stops short of getting intimate. She moves on to other men before it gets to the crossroads. She's had a lot of therapy and it's working, but despite the progress, she hasn't been able to stay in a relationship for an extended period. She would like this one to be different, though, if I'm willing.

I'm so into her that I swear I don't care if she ever gets

intimate with me. I never thought I would feel that way about anyone, but man, Rocky is special.

CHAPTER 17

Shit, that was a great conversation. That should probably qualify for Loot.

I'm remembering Loot laying it out for me. It was
when I wandered into the living room, where Loot and Carey
were getting high. We don't usually pry into our own supply,
but every now and then we need some relief, so we got stoned
and Loot took over. We were watching a mind-numbing TV
show where celebrities were getting pranked. Loot refused to
put a ball game on. "You pretty into her?" Loot asked and I
refused to answer.

When the TV show broke for a commercial, Loot tried
to pick up on the conversation about Rocky. "But you ain't really hitting that yet?"

Pretty blunt comment, even from Loot. "Watch the
show, Loot."

Carey jumped in as best he can, but with all the pot
smoked, he's approaching outer space. "Leave the man alone
Loot."

"I'm helping the man out," Loot said defensively.

"Loot," I snapped. "Just shut the fuck up and watch the
show."

"It's a fuckin' commercial!" Loot barked.

"Then watch the fuckin' commercial."

"That's what I'm talkin' about!" Loot screamed.
"When you want to get some real bad and you ain't hitting it,
then you get ornery."

I said, "Maybe I'm ornery because you're such a dick."

"Man, why you got to disrespect me so much? Shit,
if we're just playing around then you're laughing and joking

with me. You've gotten some with girls and not gotten some with girls, but you just deal. You haven't been this jumpy since C.W. Wellington; and that bitch got you all sorts of ornery. Now you listen to the Oracle of Love…"

"The Oracle of what?" I asked in amazement. I turned to Carey and I asked, "The Oracle of what?" Carey was laughing and shaking his head. You think you can never be surprised by one of Loots self-given nicknames.

With righteous indignation, Loot stood and said, "I am the Oracle of Love and as soon as you come to terms with the greatness of my powers the better your life will be."

"Loot, I don't want to hurt your feelings, but I'm handling…"

"Do not interrupt me!" Loot commanded as he put his fist in the air. "When the Oracle of Love receives his powers, there is no turning back. So whether you like it or not, you will hear from the Oracle of Love."

"Listen Loot…."

"Oracle," Loot corrected.

"Okay, Oracle, please make it fast." Like I had any chance to stop him.

Loot looked at me for drama's sake and in his deepest voice said, "This is the real thing and the key to opening the door will come from the reach of speech."

Carey and I looked at each other to see if either of us can make any of this out. "Man, you are so fuckin' trippin'. Now you're talking Chinese."

"Stop this disrespect!" He hollered. "This is not like other situations. This is not the waste of time like them other bimbo women that you been spending time with. This is not her high holiness C.W. Wellington, who is an aberration of reality."

"A what of reality?" Carey interrupted.

"Silence! You might try to make a mockery of my

greatness, but you need to heed my wisdom." Loot brought
his voice down from the bark of a preacher to the consternation
of a teacher. "You are frustrated and feel incomplete because
there are deeper feelings and physical attainment yet to be met
with this woman. You can not get there until you have the
great conversations. The reach of speech will open the door.
Do you understand me?"

"Yeah, Loot," I answered sarcastically, "I hear you,
conversations. It's outstanding insight, but don't you think
over the last bunch of weeks we had conversations?"

"There you go, you do not hear me. You might hear the
volume but not the sound and thusly you're missing my point."

"Thusly, what the fuck is thusly?" Carey laughed.

"Listen," Loot said, reverting to his preacher voice,
"the great conversation; a conversation where nothing is held
back and where trust is exchanged. That, my disciples, is what
unlocks the door. I know you've had sex before, but we're
talking more than sex here, my brother. We are talking about
unlocking the door, yours and hers. You thought you had that
with C.W. Wellington, but you did not. You think you miss
C.W. Wellington and you don't want to let it go. But let me tell
you this—what time erases, the heart replaces! And while you
are ornery now, I am here to tell you, wait, be patient and embrace the great conversation. The Oracle of Love has spoken."

"Thank you Oracle. You want another bong hit?" I
asked.

"Yes, yes I do. Oracling is a lot of work."

As ridiculous as Oracle Loot is, he happens to be right.
That last conversation where Rocky told me about her father
was a great conversation. I never felt closer to anyone. Yet
sometimes the closer I feel, the more frustrated I get and that's
not just because we are limiting ourselves on the physical front.
It ain't easy exchanging everything when you know everything

can ruin it all. I can tell her more and frankly, so can she. I do figure out what's gnawing at me. The question I need answered: Why me? After all she told me, I would think more than ever she would want to find some nice, normal lawyer, lobbyist or banker to settle down with instead of a small-time crook. I need to find it out and I need to talk to her more.

As part of my plan of self-disclosure, I decide to take Rocky to my office, the Albany branch of Luke's Action Sports, a few minutes from the apartment in a remote yet very open office park. Luke Birdman is the greatest sports handicapper ever, according to him, "The Einstein of the Line." Luke Birdman presented me with an opportunity to make real money and make it fast. Luke Birdman, whose real name is Barry Rothberg, unknowingly gave me the opportunity to fund a pretty damn impressive bookmaking and drug-dealing operation.

Our building has just two floors and a lot of glass windows that are always blocked with curtains and blinds. It's not that sports marketing is illegal; it's certainly not exactly ethical, but when you're running a boiler room operation, you don't need views, you don't need light and you don't need distractions.

In the short drive over to the HQ, I offer Rocky an explanation of what to expect. "Think of it like a stockbroker, except, instead of saying that IBM is going up 10 dollars, our guys are selling expert advice, telling investors that the Philadelphia Eagles will win by 10 points. For this technical advice, clients pay a chunky fee."

She thinks for a moment and then answers, "Sounds like you're a bookie, but we already knew that."

I tell her that, at the time I started doing this, I was not a bookie. I started the sports handicapping with the intention of legally funding a drug business.

"You do know how fucked-up that sounds, don't you?"

she asks.

"Of course, but I'm hoping you don't rat me out to my ethics prof."

She laughs and I continue. "I had drug customers lined up and I had suppliers lined up, so according to most business classes, I was on my way. The problem was that the pesky element of working capital was still missing. I didn't think the bank was going to lend me money for this business venture, and I ruled out the reality of an initial public offering as well. My other jobs got me enough money to stay in school but not enough to finance school and this business. Luke's Action Sports was my plan B."

"How much did you need?" Rocky asks.

"It might as well have been a million dollars. At that point my drug customers weren't paying half up front; why would they? They barely knew me. I needed to lay out all the money to get started. For me to make an impact, I had to get ahold of $40,000, and in a hurry, too."

"How'd you know you could make that kind of money at Luke's?"

"I had no idea. I was trying everything I could get my hands on, but I still couldn't get close to the kind of money I needed to put my plan for getting rid of Balducci into action. Then lo and behold, I spotted an ad in the paper."

"Which paper, the New York Times?" Rocky says with a smile.

"Nope," I answer, "the ad appeared in our very own student newspaper, the Gorilla Gazette. It was just a few words, but the right words: SPORTS, more money than you dreamed you can make. I call the number, and the guy says he needs a killer salesman.

"The truth was, I had sold over the phone and had made some decent money. The one thing I learned was that more than actually selling, you needed to be able to listen. First you listen; then you close. So this guy is barking at me, but he's also telling me what he needs. So when he fires off some weird questions, I'm ready. I tell him I am hungrier than anyone he will meet. I tell him that if I'm stuck in the ocean with my mother and father and can only save one person, I save myself.

"He says he'll give me $500 for the weekend. 'I know it's a lot,' he says, 'so before you start strokin' yourself, understand this: after Sunday you're on commission, so it's your time and your dime. If you think 500 bucks is a lot of money, you're in for a nice surprise, because if you can do this, then it's a tiny shrimp cocktail appetizer to a big motha-fuckin' steak dinner. How do you think I can pay a piss-ant like you 500 bucks on a yo?'"

Then I tell her the rest of the story. The guy gave me the address and the directions to a townhouse in Saratoga. Not too far from the famous race track, which I'm sure was not a coincidence. I was greeted by Milo Weeder, the C.F.O of Luke's Action Sports, a disbarred lawyer with a nasty coke addiction. He's a quirky guy, standing 5'3" and all of 105 pounds. He was hospitable enough as he enthusiastically showed me around the townhouse office.

The basement had a bunch of desks scattered throughout with salesmen howling about point spreads and opportunities into the phones. There was a living room on the first floor with a big-ass plasma TV and plain couches. "We watch the big games together," Milo informed me. The dining room and other bedrooms were occupied with a few private big producers as opposed to the zoo in the basement. The top floor was Milo's office, as well as his bedroom. As it turns out, this is Milo's home. The first thing that crossed my mind was that this crib must be a real hit with the ladies.

Milo took me to the bedroom to the right of the bathroom. Standing at his desk was Red Sullivan. Milo tried to introduce me, but Red shot him a look and pushed out the palm of his hand like a crossing guard demanding a stop. His headset nearly fell off as he leaned over the desk and screamed, "Luke! Luke!"

A nasal, high-pitched voice from the bedroom to the left of the bathroom answered, "Yeah, Red, what's up?"

"Luke, I got Bailey Zelmo on hold. I just sold him the 'lock-of-the-year' for five thousand. What game do I give him?"

"Give him the Eagles getting three vs. the Vikings," Luke said.

"Naw," Red answered. "He's got that game already. Gimme another lock-of-the year." While he's waiting for Luke to dole out another selection, he says to Milo, "That's why you never tell the gamblers which game until you know what he's playing. Why would he pay me if he got bucks on the game already?" At this point I realize that Red was the gruff voice I spoke to on the phone.

"Give him the Detroit Lions giving seven and a half points vs. the Seahawks," Luke screamed.

Red answered, "No way, man, I hate that game."

"Holy shit, Red, gimme a break." With that, Red smiled at Milo and me, finally recognizing that I exist. The nasal voice answered again with, "Give him the New Orleans Saints giving the Jets five." Clearly, Luke was throwing darts and reaching for anything with his picks.

With this piece of information, Red said into his headset, "Bailey, the play is the New Orleans Saints. They're giving five and I don't care if they were giving 50, we love this play. It's not part of the regular service and that's why I have to charge you extra, so please promise to keep this on the QT." There was a pause while Red listened to his client. "Yeah, big deal, the Jets are home. Don't let home dogs scare you today. Believe me, we're in the huddle on this one! Yeah, load up on it; we don't get this kind of info all the time." He listened

again. "Yeah baby, it's gonna be great. Hey, you need my
home address to send me a bottle of champagne after we win?"
Red laughed and says, "Take care, Bailey. I'll talk to you later."

Red wrote all the vital credit card information on a yel-
low order sheet, crumbled it up in a ball and tossed it at Milo.
"Okay, Milo, you ring that up." Red pointed to me and said,
"You the guy I spoke to on the phone?"

"Yes," I answered.

"Leave him with me, Milo. It's time to learn how to
collect fees for prognosticating. He might be in college, but
school's really in session now."

I look at Rocky as I pull into our parking lot and say,
"So that was the beginning, I'll show you what I learned when
we're inside the office." I pull the Saab into my usual spot and
say, "You are coming in for show-and-tell today, aren't you?"

"Wouldn't miss it for anything," she answers.

Inside the office on the first floor there are two long
tables. Each table holds 15 sales guys. The raw noise coming from these tables is dramatic, like the sound of 100 people
vibrating the foundation of the building, pumping the phone
lines with hope and greed. Papers and notebooks are scattered throughout the tables, but also adding to the clutter are
15 phones with crisscrossing wires. I explain to Rocky that
Gorilla college students are working these phones. Yup, I con-
vinced Red and Luke that if they liked what I was doing, they
would love multiplying it by 10 or more. Thus, the Albany
office of Luke's Action Sports was created, complete with its
sales manager, Kevin Davenport.

"These guys are all working for you?" Rocky asks.
She has to raise her voice over the chaotic banter that's filling
the room.

"Override," I say loud enough for her to hear over the
noise. "I get a piece of every sale in here. Override, it's some

concept."

"But who are these guys calling? There can't be this many gamblers to call."

"There are. It's hard to believe, but on the other end of every one of these phone calls are hard-core gamblers from all over the country. And they all have their own bookies."

"But how do these sales guys know who to call?"

"Good question," I say. "Luke gets his potential clients from a variety of places. First he takes out newspaper ads in any paper that will let him advertise. But his primary source for clientele is his TV show. He buys TV time for an infomercial that appears several times a week. In this show he is screaming about computer programs and inside knowledge. He always claims to be hitting about 80 percent of his picks."

"Is that good? Is 80 percent a good number?"

"Hell, yeah, if he came close to that it would be amazing. Picking sports games against the gamblers' spread is tough business. No one, and I mean no one, comes close to 80 percent. Good thing this business isn't regulated very well."

"If people are losing money," Rocky insists, "how does Luke keep getting customers?"

"You see these two tables? You see these 30 guys? They are calling the 'torched' list," I say.

"I can't wait to hear this," Rocky shouts over the din.

"The sports handicapping business has been around for awhile. It's not surprising that some people didn't fare so well by listening to the advice of these experts. It's fair to say these people got torched. Now, the guys who answer ads from the newspapers and Luke's TV shows are hot prospects." I point to the row of desks and cubicles along the wall. "Those hot prospects go to the elite salespeople." Then I point to the noisy table in front of us. "This table is selling to the torched list until they can prove they are real closers."

"Isn't the torched list a complete waste of time?"

"No," I answer. "To me, the torched list is incredible. Even though these clowns got burnt, they're so greedy and so dumb that they're still ripe. Which I guess isn't far-fetched, but the thing that cracks me up is that this torched list comes from all of Luke's competitors. There's a whole industry of sports prognosticators. All the different sports handicapping businesses know that they need leads, so after one company accumulates a list of guys it torched, it trades it with competitors, fully knowing that the new salespeople at the next sports marketing company will be bad-mouthing the previous prognosticator."

Rocky stares as the guys at the table continue pounding the gamblers into submission. "Every one of these guys they are calling has been torched by another service?" she asks.

"Without fail. You can't create gamblers from scratch. You can't just cold call a bunch of people. You need established gamblers with bookies. These salespeople are not asking if guys are interested in gambling. They call and say, 'Who are you playing today?' knowing that the person they are calling has been exhausted by Empire Sports, The Sports Doctors, or one of our other competitors."

I point out two guys standing next to the table, watching the activity. "See them? They're salesmen, too. If someone goes to the bathroom, a seat will open up for them."

"You're kidding."

"Nope. Hey, Rocky, you want to hear what it sounds like from the other end? You want to listen to a few calls from my office?"

"Oh, in your office," she says teasing me for trying to sound like a hitter. Rocky doesn't let me get away with much. "Yes, let's view the office." She smirks.

Unfortunately, the office isn't very impressive. The room has a desk, a few chairs and one of the master phone systems. I set up Rocky in the seat behind the desk where I usually sit. Then I pull up a chair next to her. The phone system has two rows of buttons that continue to flash brightly and then briefly go dark as the call ends. As sales manager, I like to see that light go bright again real quickly, signaling a new sales call. "Ready to hear this?" I ask.

"Ready, Mr. Sales Manager!" She shoots back.

I can't get mad at her for busting my balls. She has that smile on. "Okay, there's one that looks like it's starting. The idea here is to create excitement and overcome objections. When this guy picks up the phone, it's going to sound like he's being pitched on a sports service where he pays a fee, but what he's really being sold is excitement. That's what these guys are really looking for. Sports is just the messenger. They want to be players, they want to feel alive. So no matter how much this guy says 'no,' the salesman will try to overcome him by creating excitement." With that, I hit the speakerphone button, press the mute button and press on the newly bright light. "They can't hear us, so we can talk."

I tell Rocky that we're listening to Don, one of our better sales guys. "Jerry! How are you? It's Don Moses from Luke's Action Sports! How are ya, buddy?"

The other side answers, "Hey, leave me alone. You guys suck!"

The salesman is ready and says, "I suck? What are you talking about? I'm hitting 82 percent. How 'bout you?"

"You guys suck! Suck! I used the Sports Doctors and they crushed me!"

The tug-of-war is in full bloom now. Don is doing a good job finding out about Jerry's fiasco with the Sports Doctors. "Look, Jerry, I understand you got burnt, and I'm sorry it happened to you. Honestly, you used the wrong guys." Don explains that real prognosticators exist and that the scams will piggyback off the legit ones. The trick is to learn the difference between contenders and pretenders. "If you go to a bad restau-

rant you're never going to eat out again?" Don keeps bringing
up the Giants vs. Redskins game and the inside information
he is sitting on. Jerry is wearing down and is asking questions
about where the information is coming from.

"Jerry, we're in the information business," Don says.
"We spend hours making connections and gathering information. But our real value-added is inside information. We get
it from trainers, managers and coaches." Don pours it on. He
needs to touch Jerry in a way that ignites anticipation and pleasure in order to make him cough up a fee. "So here I am today
with a combination of information from the home team, the
visiting team, the guys that make the line at Union Plaza, Las
Vegas and on top of all that, we have a very prominent wiseguy who's interested in the game, so he's added an insurance
policy, if you know what I mean. This game is a human lock.
Are you going to tell me you don't want a game like this?"

Jerry's resistance is weakening; Don moves in for the
kill. "C'mon, Jerry, shoot me that Visa card! This play alone
will wipe out all the bad plays from the Sports Doctors and pay
for my service all in one play. This play here is the mother-
load!"

Don won't let him think it over or call back; it's go
time. "Jerry, it's something special and you got to be able to
go for the jugular. Have the guts to win. This is the one your
friends will be jealous of. You'll wipe out the bad plays and be
able to buy your girlfriend something special."

"I'm married."

"Hey, don't be greedy. I don't know if there'll be
enough left over for your wife and your girlfriend."

"That's pretty funny. At least you have me laughing."

"Don't worry Jerry, we're gonna have a lot of laughs
together. It's fun to win."

It's just semantics after that. Don obtains the credit
card number and gets Jerry to load up on the Redskins and

place his biggest bet of the year.

Rocky looks at me, her mouth slightly agape. "Wow!" she says.

"Pretty wild, but there's a good chance when we run the credit card through, it'll be maxed out. These degenerate gamblers often have the nerve to lie to the full-of-shit sales-man. Then it becomes a numbers game. Our boy Don will be back on the phone in less than a minute, setting someone up for the exact opposite play by giving the Giants instead of the Redskins. If he's any good, by the end of the day he should have 10 people playing the Giants and 10 people playing the Redskins. And if he's really good, he will spread out both sides of four more games as well. If he's a stud, he'll have a hundred guys all rooting for different sides of a game."

"But what's the purpose of that?" Rocky asks.

"Because right after the game he will have 50 people who love him. Tomorrow's call will offer, in the rarest twist of fate, an even better game. You always need another game to hook them long term. But to get the next one, they have to join the service for six months. No more of this one game stuff."

Rocky asks, "So if the Redskins win the game, Don calls Jerry back, and magically there's an even better game?"

"Wow, you're good." Then I add, "You ready to pick up a phone and start selling?"

"I'll pass, but thanks for the offer. What's surprising to me is that you really do this. It seems so out of character for you."

I explain, "You have to get in character. That's the whole trick. There's a lot of rationalization happening and nei-ther side are angels. A great salesman named Sean Gallop is an animal lover who hates hunters. When Sean sells, he uses the name Hunter Pierce, and in his mind everyone is some back-wardass hick who is bagging a deer or moose after his phone call, unless the mighty Sean Gallop can bring him down. He's actually saving animals in his mind. The bottom line is that these salesmen are not themselves. That's how they rationalize this existence."

Rocky looks at the phone lights flashing. "How do you rationalize? What do you pretend?"

"Me? I don't pretend. It's not a joke for me. The stakes are very high and I need a lot of money to nail Balducci. I'm bringing in an ungodly amount of drugs and that costs money. This business is hard to fund, but right upstairs from here I have my bookie operation, and that has huge profit and loss swings. So I guess my motivation remains to get Balducci no matter what. In this case, sell my ass off in this sports scam and keep my head above water and my body above ground. It's enough for me."

"That's motivation," she agrees.

"C'mon," I say, "you want to see the bookie operation?"

"How can a girl say no to an offer like that? You really know what to say to a lady."

A flight of stairs separates Luke's Action Sports from the bookie operation. Rocky and I walk up these stairs and I take her to the office marked at eye level by a black name plate and white letters reading, Hempstead Equipment. Rocky looks at the name on the door and before she asks, I say, "It was Loot's idea to pay tribute to our home town and all. Seems harmless enough."

"It's nice to see sentimental guys in this day and age," Rocky says.

I open the door with my key, which catches the guys inside by surprise. Carey is seated and running numbers on his spreadsheet. Loot is standing behind Carey, no doubt giving him instructions on what was probably something already done correctly. They're shaking, but when they see Rocky and me enter the room, they give us a big grin.

Loot walks over and gives Rocky a hug, which surprises her, as she has been gazing at all the display boards marked up with felt markers. Details like point spreads, underdogs, favorites, home teams, away teams, parlays, teasers and exactas are scrawled on boards that have more numbers than a Wall Street trading floor. When Rocky realizes that she is in Loot's grasp, she hugs him back. Loot embraces me next and says, "We got some sweet business going."

"Where's most of the action?"

"Pretty spread out, Kev."

Carey barely notices us as he continues typing on his spreadsheet. When it gets close to game time he really gets his game face on. "Carey, where's the overall risk standing right now?"

Carey checks the spreadsheets and asks, "Without the junk?"

"No junk." I see Rocky is confused by the last comment. "Junk means the gimmick bets that gamblers are offered, like a parlay. Parlaying is a way to link together a number of wagers on a chance to make even more money. So you might link three bets together and if you win, you win a lot. But if you lose any part of it, that's it. You lose the entire bet. Picking three winners is tough; it gives the gambler better payouts, but it's a huge advantage for the house. So we discount the risk of junk when we try to gauge how much we will potentially pay out if we lose."

Rocky looks up again at the writing on the display boards. I can see her calculating. "There are so many ways someone can bet on the same game. Do you guys lose a lot?"

I smile at Loot and Carey. "Yeah, we lose. It's good that we lose also. If our clients never won, they wouldn't be back. They wouldn't be telling their friends how much fun they're having."

"Yo, Kev," Carey barks. "$45,000 total wagered.

$25,000 is matched."

"Okay, so we have exposure to $20,000?"

"Yup," Carey answers.

"How much in junk bets?" I ask.

Carey answers, "Not quite $8,000."

Knowing my next comment will curl their skin, I say, "Good, let's lay some off."

Loot and Carey look at each other, startled and frustrated. Carey is laid back about most things, but it kills him when I lay the risk off. "C'mon, Kev, there's nothing special about tonight, we can handle it," he pleads.

I don't want to make a big deal in front of Rocky and I don't want to pull them over into a sidebar that excludes Rocky. "Guys," I laugh in an effort to soothe egos, "please just humor me. Don't ya want me to be able to sleep at night? Just give Petrocelli a call."

"Kevin, if we got to do it, if we have to lay some bets off, let me go to this other guy I met," Carey pleads. "He charges a five percent vig and Petro charges 10 percent. And Petro is such an asshole about collecting and paying. We can do better."

"Yeah, I know, I'm gonna think some more about that, but in the meantime, do me a favor and lay 15 dimes off with Petro."

"Fuck meeee!" Carey blurts out. He storms off in frustration with the look of a pissed-off three-year-old kid who was just instructed not to stick his father's screwdriver in an electric socket. Carey dramatically plops down and starts dialing the phone, no doubt to call Petro. Loot shoots me a look; he doesn't say anything, just rolls his eyes, like my decision is so wrong that it's not worth wasting words on me.

The phones are ringing and Rocky notices the other bookmakers, six in total, working the lines. We can hear them confirm the team, the point spread and the amount. The good ones remind the players about teasers and parlays, attempting to rope them in.

Carey hangs up a phone and screams, "The Whale just came in. He's in for five dimes today."

"The Whale is a well-respected New York senator, if that makes any sense," I explain to Rocky. "Let me guess, he's playing three dimes spread out to the tune of a nickel each on six games, all being the favorites. Then with the other $10,000, he's betting against the Gorillas. Is that right?"

Carey checks the wagers and says, "Yup, that's it. You know your customers."

Loot notices that Rocky is a bit lost and explains, "The Senator has a very strong gambling bug. We bookies love it when people consistently take the favorites, which is to the advantage of the house, but we also love emotional gamblers. No matter who the New York State Gorillas are playing, Senator Murphy, or as we affectionately call him, Senator Whale, will always take the Gorilla's opponent. The best theory on this pattern stems from when he himself was a student at New York State and caught his sorority-president fiancée in bed with two Gorilla football players. He always plays a bunch of favorites and bets against the Gorillas every game without fail."

"We call him the Whale because he bets so damn much," I add. "Ours is not to question why, ours is to collect his money."

Suddenly Carey breaks in. "Let's not lay this new bet that just came in from the Whale. Let's run with the number." He's got an uncharacteristically irritated look and I don't want to get into anything with him in front of Rocky.

"Okay, Carey, let's go with it. If you don't want to lay any of the Whale off to Petro, it's cool."

Loot perks up and says, "Way to be a man, Kevin."

I laugh and give Loot the finger. I face Rocky and say, "I could use some fresh air. You feel like taking a walk?" After saying that, I look at Loot to make him think he's the reason I need fresh air, and he affectionately gives me the finger.

The truth is the last thing I need is cold Albany air, but I do need some alone time with Rocky. Now that I showed her these operations, I needed to talk with her uninterrupted somewhere.

In front of our meager office building there is a quiet bus stop. We sit on the bus stop bench, surrounded by billboards plugging movies and featuring anti-drug messages. I don't read the ads but I am thankful they are there to block the wind. Rocky asks me, "So were Loot and Carey right? Does Petro charge you too much money to lay off bets?"

"Yeah, he charges way too much," I answer. "And we always catch him trying to get cute with the betting lines. Plus, he's hard to collect from. It's easier to pick up a 300-pound barbell than it is to pick up money he owes us. The funny thing is when we owe him money, he wants us to make like Star Trek and beam it right over to him. The guy is a total asshole."

"But, Kevin," Rocky asks, "if you have other options, why go to him?"

I explain that this is the point that Loot and Carey don't really understand. Sometimes they think I'm trying to run a business here. Like I care about making any more money. "This guy Petro is a snake, but I need him."

"How so?"

Now I'm in that tough spot. I want to tell Rocky everything and show her everything. I'm scared like hell she's going to leave me, but it's important for me to show her what I'm involved in. "I don't want to be doing shit behind your back," I say. "Then again, there's also a point where if I tell you something, it might be worse for you in the long term. I can put you in some unnecessary danger, or I could send you running for the hills. I think talking about Petro would do one or both of those. Will you let me off the hook and let me not talk about

Petro?"

"Sure." She hesitates, then says, "I can live with that. And by the way, I won't run for the hills. You're stuck with me."

Yeah, that's what Rocky is saying but what about when she knows more? Shit, how am I ever going to explain Petro to her? When I said I would do anything to get at Balducci— even hanging with Petro is going above and beyond. Well as dumb and as ruthless as he is, maybe Rocky will appreciate how creative he is. It's certainly what he prides himself on.

A few months back, Petro shot and killed Al Lasiter a 6'2" 280-pound gregarious guy with a huge personality to match. The problem was, his huge personality couldn't pay the tax money that Petro was charging him as Big Al's Steakhouse was failing.

Petro wanted me to accompany him to the funeral two days later. A rabbi presiding over the service was nasal and insincere. It was clear his eulogy was a canned speech, but what was most surprising to me was that instead of calling him Al Lassiter, the rabbi referred to the deceased as Hilda Goldberg. Petro usually presents himself as the ultimate stone-cold bastard, but witnessing my confusion was making him giggle like he was watching Bugs Bunny.

I asked, "Who the fuck is Hilda Goldberg?"

Before Rabbi Nasal could finish, Petro said, "C'mon, let's go."

Petro situated himself a few feet from the black hearse that was waiting for the coffin at the bottom of the steps. While waiting, Petro explained that Hilda Goldberg not only made the greatest kugel in the world, but never missed a Petro tax payment. In his infinite wisdom Petro explained, "You haven't lived until you ate good kugel and good pussy."

"Petro, aren't we here to see Al Lassiter's funeral?"

Petro explained, "The woman in that box wasn't 5' tall and she weighed 90 pounds tops, but she was one tough broad. She had a restaurant for 50 years. Shit, she ran it for 20 years on her own after her husband bought the farm. Tiny little woman like that, and she never missed a fucking tax payment to me. Not one. And the kugel she made was fucking unreal. But that fat-fuck Lassiter, he couldn't make his payments, could he? Lassiter should've learned from a great gal like old Hilda. Then maybe, someday everyone would've called him Old Man Lassiter."

The congregation fell into a respectful formation to allow the pallbearers to bring the casket to the hearse. While the men holding the casket looked healthy enough, there were problems. The eight men wobbled on the ice, nearly tipping the casket, and Petro kept laughing. Another man from the congregation jumped in to help this tricky procession down the steps. The additional pallbearer made Petro laugh even harder. Petro turned to his favorite goon, Rich Bennett, and almost choking with laughter said, "Geeee, you see that, you see that? They had to add another guy. Geeeeee."

Bennett was laughing. "Yeah, Petro, they still might not make it."

Petro not even trying to suppress his laugh said, "Yeah, kugel, you should put that on your list to do before you die. Eat some kugel."

"But what about Lassiter? Is his funeral next?"

The coffin swayed all the way from the left and then nearly as dramatically to the right but there were still many difficult steps before this group of pallbearers could orchestrate a smooth landing. Petro in between laughing said, "C'mon, Rich, tell me the truth, geeee. You put some bricks in there for effect? These guys carrying the coffin can't be that lame. C'mon, tell me the truth, Rich."

Rich answered, "I swear on my mother, no bricks Petro.

No fucking bricks, just Fat Al Lasiter."

Petro wiped tears from his eyes as the struggle down the stairs was winding down, "Oh, this is too good." Petro saw my confusion over Rich Bennett's comment and in between gasps for air said, "Double-decker coffin. Inside Hilda's coffin, under all the nice silk and bedding, we added some extra cushion for her. We put that fat-fuck Al Lasiter underneath her."

In amazement I looked at the group wobbling and struggling and asked, "Right now? He's in there right now?"

"Geeeeeeee, it's un-fucking real. These assholes think they are carrying a 90 pound old lady, but they got her 90 pounds plus Fat Al's pounds. All 280 fucking pounds of him."

All I can muster was, "Holy shit."

Petro stopped laughing enough to compose himself. He looked at me and said, "Fucking Al, would eat all his fucking profit and try to leave me holding my cock. Like I'm not entitled to my tax payment or something. Now he can spend the rest of eternity learning from that great gal Hilda Goldberg, who never missed a payment.

He explained with his ingenious system there's no need to chop people up or drop someone in a lake wrapped in chains. "Hell, we used to boil people to make them unidentifiable. It was all so messy. With this system, who is ever going to find guys like Fat Al? The best part is, we get to watch people busting their nut carrying the load for us. We don't even have to dig the fucking ditch." Petro sees my amazement and asked, "Whaddaya think of my system?"

I tried to stay calm. Petro was looking for some reaction and I needed to be in his good graces, so I said, "I can't help thinking that when rigor mortis sets in and everything gets stiff, that Fat Al Lassiter could be sporting wood and giving it to Hilda in the pail for eternity."

Petro drew that far-fetched mental image and broke out laughing again. He slapped me on my shoulder and screamed,

"Yeah, getting it in the ass for eternity from Fat Al Lassiter; Ha!" Then he asked, "So, am I brilliant or what?"

I'm thinking now, I'd be pretty brilliant if I can explain this to Rocky. Let her digest my business first, then I'll get into my relationships.

I put my arm around Rocky and kiss her neck. Her skin is cold from the frosty weather but still so soft, the contrast from my warm kiss and her cold neck adds to the sensuality. Rocky closes her eyes and moves her head back, offering more of her neck. "See what I mean?" she says. "Why would I run away from this?"

I look at her seriously so she knows I mean business. "This whole college is full of winners. There are guys lining up power jobs, guys really going places. All of those guys would step over and crush each other to be here with you. Why are you wasting your time with me? Why aren't you running for those hills?"

"It's kind of funny to me. I see you managing all these different things and you have a confidence and certainty like no one that I ever met, including those so-called winners you talk about. But then you say things to me like, why aren't I running away?"

"Maybe because the stuff I do can land people in jail and also promote physical harm," I remind her.

"Yeah, I'm not naïve about those risks. But even if those risks didn't exist, for some reason, you don't think you deserve to be happy. For some reason, you don't think you deserve to get the girl. I've been giving this whole thing a lot of thought lately. It's hard to get you out of my mind. I'll admit, now that I'm involved with you, I wish you weren't part of these businesses, but I knew going in that you were doing this. The drugs and bookie business don't scare me. My feelings for you…that's what's scary."

"Yeah, that's what I'm trying to figure out. Look, I went out with a lot of girls. Of course, they weren't like you, Rocky." I also can't help myself from thinking that they weren't C.W. Wellington, either. "And by the way," I continue, "you weren't doing too bad yourself in the dating department."

"Yes, but I never dated anyone for more than two weeks," she explains.

What's that even supposed to mean? Does she have some sort of time limit? Why only two weeks? What's up with that? "What? Why?"

"That's what I've been giving so much thought to," Rocky says, her cold breath rising about her head like a halo. "You talk about all these bankers and lawyers like they are the greatest catch. I was looking for the opposite, for the anti-catch. I was looking for the escape hatch."

"Obviously, you can explain that," I say with an uncomfortable smile.

"As half-baked as this may sound, a lot of girls around here judge a successful college experience by having a cool boyfriend. I didn't make that concept up; this philosophy exists and, right or wrong, I felt the peer pressure to a degree." I nod, but I don't really know what I'm nodding to. Rocky continues. "I know I should be a big girl and say, if I'm ready for a boyfriend great, if I'm not ready, then that's my own business. But in reality, I started dating guys I thought my friends would like.

"The one thing I made sure of," she goes on to say, "was all these guys had some faults I could make clear to my friends, so that I could dust them when the time came. I honestly don't think I was doing this on purpose, but in any case I'm not particularly proud of this behavior. It wasn't like it was two weeks every time, but when a certain expectation to get physically or emotionally closer came due, I would push the eject button, you know, open the escape hatch. All these guys had an escape hatch. I didn't realize I was doing this, but I know it now. The truth is I just couldn't get comfortable with guys. It comes pretty easy to a lot of people; it used to come easy to me. I used to be so proud of how close I was with my father. Who in this world are you supposed to be closer with?"

Rocky is beginning to choke on her words. I have my arm around her, with the intention of making her feel better but hell, I might be pushing her away further. "Rocky, what you went through was crazy. We don't have to talk about this any more."

"Yes," she says, "yes, we do. I want to show you everything. I want you to know what you're getting into also. Please, ask me stuff."

I hesitate and say, "So you wouldn't go out with me originally because I didn't fit in with your friends' profile of the right guy?"

"Just the opposite. My friends think you're way cute." She sees me blush a little. "Look, Kevin, you keep thinking when you were asking me out, I was saying no because of what you didn't have. It was just the reverse. I knew you were different; I always thought there was something special about you and it took me by surprise. It was hard for me to put my finger on it, but I felt something was there. Then, the more time I spent with you, the more it started getting clearer.

"Because of the illegal stuff, it would have been real easy for me to dust you in a couple of weeks. But while you were trying to be honest with me and scare me off, seeing your motivation made me want to stay. The thing I admire about you the most? You're not willing to be a victim. I am so damn frustrated being a victim! I've been totally and completely changed because of what happened to me. I don't act like I should and I don't feel like I should. I feel helpless and power-less. But not you. You're doing something about it. I don't care how dangerous your plan is. I admire you so much for not letting yourself be a victim."

"Rocky," I say at last, "not a lot of people can imagine how I feel about the situation I'm in, but you understand. I know you feel alone with your issues, but I don't want you to be alone. Let's just keep talking. I'll help you any way I can. There's no hurry for anything, and I'm glad I made it past the two-week mark with you." I laugh as I wipe away two tears that have trickled down her face. "I'm looking forward to a bunch of two weeks. Believe me, I didn't plan these strong feelings for you, either, but I'm glad to have them. Nice surprises don't happen often, but when they do, you really got to appreciate them. And, baby, I really appreciate every minute with you."

We both pause and start to embrace but an extremely old man with an empty fold-up grocery cart sits down next to us and smiles. He's bundled in an old Army jacket and brown scarf; patches of grey hair sprout from the sides of his AFL-CIO union cap. The old man says, "I think I missed the bus. Won't be another for 40 minutes."

I feel sorry for the old gent. "Listen," I reply, "I was going to leave my car and take the bus today, but it looks like I'm driving now. Where are you headed?"

"Down by Rector Street Market," he answers.

"Yeah, that's exactly where we're going. C'mon, we'll give you a lift."

"Oh, great, it's cold here." The old man perks up.

Rocky smiles at the old guy and then grins at me. We weren't going anywhere near Rector Street Market. Sometimes you need to make a few detours. I call Loot and let him know I won't be back today.

Funny, but the best moment I have had to date with Rocky is segued into a cramped ride in the Saab with a faded old man. Rocky is generous enough to yield the front seat to our new friend, so we are separated. But it ain't how it ended.

CHAPTER 18

After we dropped off the old guy, Rocky herself suggested we go to my apartment. How about that? And here
she is in my arms, in my room, in my place at The Lakes. She
is trying to be the same confident and playful girl, but she's
nervous. I sense the normal poise being overcome by a strange
fear; I can hear a difference in her voice. I don't want her to
do something she doesn't want to do. "Baby, there's no hurry
here, I know this is diff...." But before I finish, Rocky pulls
me in for a long, hard kiss.

She walks over to the light and dims it. We are standing and embracing each other and I want to feel every part of
her. I run my hands through her thick, wavy auburn hair and
I kiss her neck, inhaling and bringing in her subtle fragrance.
My hands move around her shoulders and then lower. Her
body is firm and athletic from dancing but her skin is so soft
and smooth.

Rocky is kissing my neck and unbuttoning my shirt. I
am doing the same to her shirt. When we can't unbutton each
other anymore, we take off our shirts and remove our jeans.
She smiles at me and while we are supposed to be shadows, her
smile is clearer and brighter than ever. How do you halt time
and make this never stop? Is there anywhere else in the world
anyone would rather be right now?

We lie down in bed and I run my hands up the curves
of her hips, caressing and feeling her smooth skin. She tells
me how nice it feels, but I still sense that Rocky is nervous
and I wish I could make her comfortable. It's taken a lot to let
someone over on this side of the wall, the wall that her father
created. I want this to be right for her. I want to give her the
feelings she has given me.

My hands are drawn to her body, and it feels as if my

fingers are dancing on onyx. Her skin is precious and rare and I'm amazed that something like this exists. I wish she could relax and give herself completely to this moment. She is trying, there is no doubt about that, but this isn't exactly like jumping into a lake.

My mouth moves down her body, kissing her navel. I can hear her breathing deepen as I continue. I kiss her inner thighs and her breathing gets deeper.

I want so badly for this to be great for her. This has to be great for her. Her breathing is getting deeper still. I stay down and continue; I feel her apprehension drift into the cold Albany night, I feel that quiver of nervousness replaced by shaking desire.

Just above the back of my neck, Rocky has taken a fistful of hair. Both her hands are filled with my hair and her grip is getting tighter. Her breathing is getting still deeper and transitioning into a light, low moan of pleasure. Her grip on my hair tightens, actually causing pain. But trooper that I am, I continue. Rocky pulls my face in deeper as her hips move up and down, offering a rhythm to follow. Her grip on my hair gets tighter, she pulls me in deeper, her moan is picking up volume and duration. Her legs are slowly opening and closing, as if she is looking for a comfortable position.

"If you stop doing this, I'll kill you!" she blurts out. I almost start laughing, but I need to concentrate. I'm thinking, I love that you're enjoying this, but please don't throw me off my game here.

Her legs stop moving, and her body is no longer rocking in a rhythm. Rocky's back is arched with her hands grabbing my hair with the tightest grip yet. I feel her body shake from top to bottom as she climaxes. Her body arches even further as her climax continues.

I begin to kiss her body, by her tight stomach, moving slowly around her navel again. She pulls me up and motions for me to roll over. There is no uneasiness anymore. There is passion and it feels right. I am on my back with Rocky straddling me and I enter her. She is grinding slowly and my hands slide up that silky skin and caress her breasts as she moves, more rapidly, her head is tilted backwards, her long hair swaying.

We fall asleep cuddled in a combination of satisfaction and, exhaustion. I look over Rocky's shoulder to see my clock radio reading 3:18 a.m. I glance down at Rocky's smooth back and marvel at the feminine but muscular valley that divides the left from right side. Like a baby reaching for a toy in a crib, I can't help myself. I need to touch her more. I don't want to wake her, but I have to run my fingers along the perfect valley streaming down her back. If I am soft enough I can satisfy my selfish need to feel her body and still let her sleep. I run my fingers up once, then twice and by the third time I hear a muffled giggle. She turns over and smiles her brilliant smile at me. I roll on top of her and I'm delighted that this night is not over.

CHAPTER 19

Sunday mornings are a special tradition here. I've always been the first to wake up because no matter how tired or how late I went to bed, by 7:30 a.m. my mind is racing and there's no turning back. Sundays are important days for us as the National Football League, and their little ecosystem provides the potential for a very nice income stream. All three of us are out of the apartment by 10:15 to get to the office and open the phones by 11.

This Sunday morning I look at the alarm clock and, true to form, it's 7:25 a.m. The only difference today is that Rocky Campbell is sleeping next to me. Before I get out of bed, I stare at her motionless body for a few minutes. It's been a long time since I've felt lucky. But this morning I feel flat-out lucky. She looks at me differently and talks to me differently than anyone I've ever met.

I make a huge breakfast, four ham-and-cheese omelets, bacon, bagels, and fresh-squeezed juice. I flip the last omelet and drop the pan in the sink. The bacon has been done for a while; I scoop the strips out of the pan and put them on a separate plate from the omelets. I turn to bring the plates to the table and am surprised by Rocky. She's wearing her jeans from last night and one of my Gorilla sweatshirts. I wonder how long she was observing my hectic culinary preparations.

"Hey! Good morning," I say. "I was going to let you sleep." I know I am probably smiling a little too wide, but I'm looking at her smile and damn, she has an extra huge smile

herself. She leans over to give me a kiss. I'd like to give her
a hug but it's tough with a plate of omelets in one hand and a
plate of bacon in the other.

"Sleep?" She says. "How can I sleep with this huge
breakfast out here?"

"Ahhh, the aroma of fresh bacon lured you out?" I set
the plates on the table.

She playfully says, "Yes, of course. It had nothing to
do with the three pans you dropped or 15 times you slammed
the cabinets."

"I only dropped the pan twice. I can see you don't appreciate sheer brilliance."

"No, you're wrong. I appreciate it." She walks over
and hugs me. Now that my hands are free I am able to recip-
rocate. This is nice; it's the Kodak moment you keep in your
mind. We could stand here for hours but will have to settle for
these few moments because, rather than a romantic sunrise to
cap this magic moment, we will have to settle for the sight of
Loot Hightower scratching himself outside his boxer shorts. A
bright green pick is sticking out of the mound of hair that has
been unleashed from the cornrows. Loot has a shit-eating grin.
Rocky's been hanging around a lot, but she has never spent the
night. "Yes, Loot," Rocky says, smiling at him, "last night I
kind of used your boy here."

Loot, who is never at a loss for words, says, "Damn,
that's what I'm talking about!" He high-fives Rocky. "C'mon
Rocky, don't you got a friend or a sister or something for me?"
he asks.

"I'll keep my eyes open, but I have to find something
special for you," she says.

Both Carey and Loot are big supporters of Rocky.
They've seen some of the other girls I've been going out with
and they weren't too taken with them. Rocky likes hanging
with the guys, and we all have a lot of laughs when we're to-

gether. It means a lot to me that my buddies approve of Rocky.

Carey wanders out, much less animated than Loot. It was clearly an effort for him to get out of bed at this ungodly hour of 8:30 a.m. He looks approvingly at the full spread on the table, nods to all of us and eloquently says, "Waz up?"

We sit down and enjoy our nice family breakfast. Loot hits the TV remote so we can watch MTV as we eat. I think Rocky is pretty impressed with my cooking. Hell, it's another reason for her to want to spend nights over here.

After a slow, enjoyable repast, it's almost time to clean up. I'm buttering a last bagel half when suddenly a show on TV grabs my attention. It's a story about something called "the annual Celebrity Best in Show Dog Extravaganza" at Madison Square Garden. Are those my buddies, Buster Wellington and his charming daughter C.W., mingling with a batch of A-list celebrities? The camera shows them awarding prizes to Robert DeNiro, Tim Robbins, Tori Spelling and a gaggle of other actors while the announcer gushes about how much money the event has raised for charity. The catch is, the dogs are all untrained and definitely not show material; the whole thing is a spoof of the famous Westminster Dog Show, which also runs at Madison Square Garden. I watch as Susan Sarandon's beagle takes a crap on the green carpet. Turns out that the Wellingtons have been running this event for seven years now; all the money raised goes to the Juvenile Diabetes organization. What they show next stops me mid-bite: It's a close-up of C.W. Wellington as she hands a best-in-show trophy to Ben Affleck, who's standing next to his bored German shepherd.

Our cozy and jovial breakfast table goes quiet as Loot looks at Carey and Carey glances at Loot and Carey and Loot both look sideways at Rocky. Rocky, noticing something is irregular, looks at me, but I'm just staring down at my plate,

refusing to show a reaction. You would think that, after the
night I had with Rocky, today would be the day I would be able
to break my streak of thinking of C.W. Wellington at least once
a day. But today is not the day.

Heaving sounds from alongside the couch in the living
room interrupt our awkward silence. At first I think it might be
part of the TV program, but of course, dry heaves are not usually part of an MTV celebrity dog show. The retching sounds
are coming from below a small coffee table by our living room
couch. There's not a lot of room there but somehow our friend
Ray, of Ray & Cindy distinction, managed to crawl into a ball
and camouflage himself under the coffee table. Seeing Ray
banged up is pretty standard, but this is different.

Loot lifts Ray and says, "Big night even by your standards, my man." He's joking with Ray but he's not getting a
response. Loot props Ray's limp torso on the couch and gently
slaps his cheek and says, "My man, are you with me?"

Loot smacks Ray's face again. Loot is trying to be
gentle but the smack is crisp and loud. To our relief, Ray opens
his eyes and looks at Rocky. He shines a flirting glance toward
her, and before we can rag on him, those flirting eyes roll back
in Ray's head. Only the whites of his eyes are visible as a
rapid-fire shudder overtakes his eyelids at subhuman speed.

"Hey man, this is fucked up!" Loot exclaims.

"Are we losing him?" Carey asks in amazement.

We all look at Rocky like she should know something,
but she just shrugs.

Ray's eyes continue to flicker and then his body starts
shaking.

"Hey, should we give him mouth-to-mouth or something?" Carey asks in confused frustration. No one knows
what to do, but when Ray gives three quick coughs, a soapy

foam oozes out and runs down his cheek. We all know mouth-to-mouth is out of the question.

Carey blurts out, "Guys, this is beyond our means here. We got to call in the professionals. How about I call an ambulance?"

"It's not that easy," I interrupt. "We got 20 pounds of pot in here, a half kilo of coke and a closet full of X. We can't have the place packed with strangers now."

Ray tilts his head and says through the foam, "I'm fine, guys," then closes his eyes. His head droops on his limp neck.

"Shit," Loot says, "let's bring him down to his ol' lady's apartment and let Cindy deal with this."

Rocky says, "That's not a bad idea."

"Guys, I'm going to call first. We need to make sure she's there," I say. The answering machine picks up in Cindy's apartment and voicemail stops me on her cell phone. Ray's limp body begins twitching again.

Carey demands, "We got to do something here. Let's bring him down and bang on that bitch's door. If we hammer that door long enough she'll wake up."

"Calm down, Carey," I insist. "If she's not in the apartment, she ain't gonna wake up."

"Where she gonna be?" Loot asks.

"I suspect she's gone on to another project. I suspect that's why Ray's been here so much lately. Recently she's been whining how Ray can't handle the real world. I may be wrong, but what if you bang the shit out of her door and wake up half the building while Cindy is cuddling with some up-tight lobbyist 10 floors away? If you play that out, we get plenty of attention back here where we can't afford any attention."

Rocky is flushed with frustration. "We got to do something," she says. "He's your friend and he's really sick."

"I know," I say. "I'm thinking that I should take him to the emergency room. I can get him there in the Saab just as fast as it would take to get an ambulance up here."

"You sure?" Rocky asks.

"No, I'm not sure about anything, but I'm doing the best I can. We've got to get a move on here. If I take care of Ray at the hospital, we need to keep business moving. We have a lot riding today. Loot, can you handle the bookie room?"

"Yeah, not a problem," Loot says.

"Okay, but listen to me, lay everything off to Petro. Don't fuck around. Not today. I have my reasons."

"Yeah, yeah." Loot shrugs in contempt for the money he believes I'm leaving on the table by dealing with Petro.

"Carey," I say, "we're scheduled to move eight pounds today. Can you leverage it with the spray bottles and move it if I walk you through today's customers?"

"Hell yeah, I'll be the rainman on those precious little buds."

"Take it easy, Carey. Don't be too obvious and don't get us caught. Leveraging dope is an art. If you get us more pot but leave water all over the bags, we're gonna get black-balled by everyone."

"Okay, Kev, I got it, it's an art. I'll take care of this. You take care of Ray."

I look at Rocky and say, "Do you want to take a ride with me to the emergency room?"

Rocky says, "How about I handle Luke's Action Sports?"

"Yeah, that might work." I look over to Loot and Carey and they give me a subtle nod of approval. "Okay, that's great. The mere fact that you're there would stop anything crazy from happening. Just hang in my office and peak out now and then."

I look over at Loot. "You'll be at the bookie operation. I don't care how busy you get today, pop down every now and then and check in on Rocky."

"I know, man," he says in disgust. "I was gonna do that anyway."

We get Ray propped in the front of the Saab and put his seatbelt on because we would hate to see him get hurt. Next stop, Albany General emergency room.

CHAPTER 20

    I text Cindy and leave seven messages on her voice-mail before I even reach the hospital. "Cindy, I'm not fucking around, call me back." It's been hours and I'm still dealing with Ray. I should have just dropped him here and bolted. Then again, who am I kidding? As fucked up as Ray is, he was always good to me. Hell, good to Carey and Loot, too. I can't just abandon him. Still, I wasn't equipped to handle questions about insurance and healthcare. I'm like, "Shit, the guy is sick and you help sick guys. Let's get going." It's just not that easy. So I'm here all these hours and I can't get cell service to get Cindy's ass up here. Maybe all the X-ray beams being blasted from the hospital's equipment are challenging my cell service. When did I ever give a fuck about the effect of X-rays on cell service? Waiting room bureaucracy can turn you into a philosopher. I don't know why I can hardly use the phone, but I can't use it and that sucks. Sundays of all days, this is happening. I have Luke's Action Sports and the last few hours before game time to offer the miracle tip to the promised land. Not to mention the Sunday drug crowd. Yeah, those hard partiers were burnin' it up in the fast lane on Friday and Saturday. As much as they try, there's never enough to last the entire weekend. It's Sunday morning and God forbid they go a day without something to get them through. Their miscalculations are an important transition for our weekly services.

    I have the gambling lines moving and degenerate gamblers looking to arbitrage. January of all times is huge. Pro football is in playoff mode, pro basketball is in full swing and college basketball has finally started playing intra-league; those rivalries attract the most emotional gamblers. Bookmak-

ers love emotional gamblers. Luke's, bookies and dope, we do
business all week, but there's nothing like Sunday mornings.

I can't get a straight answer from any doctors or nurses.
Shit, they told me how serious this is, so why aren't they acting
that way? When I first brought Ray in here, he was foaming
and twitching and doing everything one would do to be taken
seriously in an emergency room, but no answers. A guy came
in here wailing like every bone in his body was just crushed.
It turns out he fell off a ladder. Ladder Guy left an hour and
a half later with a cast on his arm. Maybe Ray needs to be a
squeaky wheel, but Ray can't bitch and moan very well with all
that foam he's coughing up. I'm not looking for all the answers, but shit, they're not even dealing with this. Meanwhile,
I want my friend back and I want to go run my business. It's
not a ton to ask. Still, no matter how many different ways I
word the questions, Nurse Katims is giving me the same standard answers.

"Sir, you have stated you are not an immediate relative
of the patient, correct?"

"Yes, that's right but...."

"Sir, I appreciate your concern. Please sit down and
we'll contact you when there is some information to share."

I can't take this. I'm going outside to call and check in
with Loot, Carey and Rocky. With my luck, just when I leave,
the doctor will come out to speak with me.

The moment I'm outside the door, my cell rings. "Kevin, where the fuck you been?" Loot sounds dramatic even by
Loot standards.

"I know, doesn't it suck? I can't get any reception in
the hospital and they're slow as balls here. How's everything
over there?" I ask.

"Shit, you better get your ass over here, now! We got
some problems, dude!"

"What's up?" I ask.

"No way, man, we can't talk on the phone. You need to get here, and I'm not fucking around."

"I'll call you right back," I say. As I disconnect the phone I notice a bunch of missed calls and voicemails registered to my cell phone. They hit up in one fell swoop, but they must have been kept at bay all morning with all the X-ray beams and thick hospital walls.

I frantically dial Rocky's cell phone and before the second ring she picks up and blasts, "Hey, we've been trying to get hold of you!"

"I know. I just hung up with Loot. He says he can't talk on the phone and that I should get back. Do you agree?"

"Without a doubt, you need to be here," she says firmly.

"Yeah, but I haven't heard anything about Ray. I can't just leave him here."

"Kevin," Rocky says sternly, "I'm sensitive to your friend Ray, but my advice is that unless you have some medical experience that can help the doctors, you better get back over here. It's bad."

"Okay, I'll tell the hardcore nurse where to reach me and I'll be there in 10 minutes."

In the reception area of the emergency room, I recognize Ray's parents. I never met them but I recognize them from the pictures that Cindy would always push in front of us. That is, until she came to the realization that her straight-as-an-arrow, church-going, cutthroat, soon-to-be father in-law would never let a waste-product like Ray anywhere near the family business. That realization got Cindy cutting her losses and moving on to the next empire.

Ray's mother is a basket case. She's weeping into her hands. Ray's father is on the cell phone but is frustrated by the service. He's doing better than I was with his cell reception, but only marginally. He is speaking too loud and has already called the person back three times due to an abrupt disruption in service. At least his conversations are giving me a chance to piece together some information I haven't been able to obtain yet. His voice is loud and deliberate with no thoughts of privacy; his mission is to convey his information.

Ray's dad says, "No, it's not the substances, although that couldn't help matters, I'm sure." There is a pause as Ray Senior listens to the other party, but then Senior says, "No, Stan, it's alcohol poisoning." Okay, so from listening to Ray Senior, I know he's got alcohol poisoning, whatever that is. The fucking moron practically drowned himself in vodka. At least now I know what he's got and I can go back and clean up the mess that Loot and Carey created. That is until I hear Ray Senior bark into the phone, "No, I can't move him, not yet. He's in a coma."

Holy shit, Ray is in a coma. How can you get yourself into a coma from drinking? "Damn," I hear myself say out loud.

Rays Senior continues. "I don't know what to do. I want our doctors to look at him, but they are telling me not to move him out of here yet." There is another pause as Ray Senior listens to the other end. Then he says, "They're not being optimistic or pessimistic, but they told me this coma is as serious as if he got himself into a car accident. Hell, he might never be the same. Stan, I'm scared. What do you know about alcohol poisoning? Stan? Stan? Are you there, Stan? Shit!"

I decide it's time to leave. The 10-minute ride back to work gets more frustrating with each mile. What is going on here? You drink, you throw up and you feel like shit the next day, but you don't die from it. Right?

I get to Loot's Action Sports, grab Rocky and pull her upstairs to Hempstead Equipment. The bookie room will be the best place to talk.

Loot sees me, but he doesn't look relieved. Loot, who is black, looks as white as chalk. As a matter of fact, Carey doesn't look much better. "Spit it out," I say.

Loot, Carey and Rocky all exchange meaningful glances but no words. For the first time ever, Loot is speechless. In an effort to bail him out, Rocky says, "It started at Luke's Action Sports." I tell her to go on. "Two salesmen got into an argument. Apparently one guy was calling the other's leads."

"This happens all the time," I say, figuring it can't be too bad. "It's usually about a woman, though. There's too much damn testosterone in that room when it's cranking." Everyone here thinks they had such a bad morning, but fuckin' Ray is in a coma. That's a bad morning.

Rocky cocks her head and looks at me, "Fights break out all the time? So you let me volunteer knowing that could happen?"

"Yeah," I say, "that might have been bad judgment."

Rocky takes a deep breath and says, "I didn't see how the argument started, but when I got there, one guy was stabbing the other with pencils. By the time I got there, one pencil was stuck in his neck and another was sticking out of his shoulder. There was blood, there was fighting, there were pencils flying...it was awful!"

"What were the other salesmen doing while this was going on?"

Rocky looks at me deadpan and says, "They were cheering and betting on the outcome."

Loot, Carey and I simultaneously catch each other's eye and wryly nod to each other, noting, that kind of makes sense.

Loot chimes in with, "Compared to fights in the past, this was pretty bad."

"Thank you," Rocky says. "Knowing I was in over my head, I called Loot."

I look at Loot and say, "So, you couldn't take care of this fight?"

The three of them are visibly frustrated, and Rocky

says, "Kevin, the problem isn't over this fight. That's just where it all started."

They do seem pretty rattled. "All right then, please continue." I am trying to sound all poised and everything, but they're taking so damn long to get to the point.

Carey breaks in and says, "I had a problem with the law today. A cop came to the door and said he was going to bust us."

"Please define 'problem'."

Carey hesitates and looks at Rocky and Loot, but then looks back at me and says, "They were going to bust us. They said so."

"Who said so?" I ask.

"The cop said so," he answered. "The one that kept coming to the door."

"Go ahead," I encourage him.

"The cop bangs on the door at 10 in the morning, again at 10:30, and by 11 he was pounding and screaming to open up or he'll kick the door in."

I ask, "Does the cop have a tattoo on his neck?"

Carey looks at me with amazement and said, "Yeah, how did you know?" I laugh a little to calm Carey down, but I should play this up and scare him. "What's the deal? You know this dude?" Carey demands.

I better let them in on this. "Hell yeah, you do also. He's been over a bunch of times. He's gotten stoned with us a bunch of times."

"Kevin, I don't know any cops," Carey insists.

"Yeah, you do." I inform them. "Bartner's been in the apartment a bunch of times, lounging on our couch, watching ball games and getting wasted."

"He has?"

I smirk and answer, "Yeah, but he's usually in a tank top and jeans. Didn't you guys know he was a cop? When he was banging on the door, he must have just come back from work."

Carey is still confused. "Why is your buddy threatening to bust the door down?"

"He was busting balls. With all the confusion over Ray, I forgot to mention that I told Bartner to come over this morning. He's taking a vacation to Florida and I told him I would give him some dope for his trip. He was leaving this afternoon, so that's why he came back a few times." I laugh and say, "It's all good. We're not getting busted."

"He was joking when he was pounding on the door?" Carey says incredulously.

I laugh and start imitating Bartner, "Open up or I'll kick this shit down." I laugh some more and say, "Yeah, Bartner's got no bite." But Rocky, Carey and Loot still aren't smiling. Hell, they don't even seem relieved.

Carey says, "Kevin, you should have told us."

"What's up, guys? No one's going to jail, so what's the problem?" Why aren't they laughing and ragging on each other?

"The dope is gone," Carey blurts out.

"What?"

"Kevin, you should have told us about Bartner," Carey insists.

"How much is gone?"

"Kevin, you should have told us."

"Okay, Carey, you could have called me also." It was clearly a mistake offering that suggestion because simultaneously all three of them scream in an off-key chorus how they called a bazillion times but the messages weren't reaching me. "Carey, what happened to the dope? Did you eat 20 pounds of pot, a half kilo of cocaine and a thousand Ecstasy pills? You don't look like you gained any weight."

The moment of truth comes when Carey says, "I

flushed it, man. I'm sorry, Kevin, but I flushed it all."

"About $50,000 in street value? It's all gone?" I calmly ask.

"Yeah, man, it's all gone. I didn't think I had a choice."

It's a banner day today. My friend is in a coma and I just lost 50 fuckin' grand. I sit down at the chair in my barren office. I put my hands over my face and try to regain my composure. You know, try to make some sense of this. I am fuming but I am trying to rationalize how it's just some money and that's not what I'm really after. This setback will sting, but my plan to get Balducci is in motion. This won't kill that. While I am coming to grips with this situation, I hear Carey, Loot and Rocky talking quietly, almost whispering. I look up and see them conferring nervously. There is more.

CHAPTER 21

"I had a big problem in the bookie room," Loot admits.

My left hand is covering my eyes while my thumb is massaging my left temple. I don't know how to act as I begin to feel the weight of this garbage truck that is dumping its contents on me. I am doing everything to show grace under pressure because I have a hunch this is developing into a defining moment. I calmly smile and say, "Sure, lay it on me and we'll figure out how to fix it."

"This one won't be that easy, Kevin."

"Quit fucking around and tell me what happened." So much for grace under pressure.

Loot hesitates and finally says, "Senator Murphy was in this morning."

I need to find out what the fuck is going on. "So what? The Whale is in every weekend. He plays six favorites and bets against the Gorillas."

Loot can barely make eye contact with me. "Right before I left to help Rocky with the pencil-stabbing dudes situation, the Whale called in. And he called in big. He bet his six favorites, and took the Gorilla's basketball team getting eight-and-a-half vs. Cleveland University."

"You mean he took Cleveland and gave eight-and-a-half," I correct him.

"That's my point. He took the Gorillas," Loot insists.

"That's strange. What made him change? Why today?" I look at my friends but they are silent. "How much did he play?"

Loot meekly says, "10 dimes."

I feel my eyes widen. "You mean after years of protest

wagering, the Whale bets 100 grand in favor of the Gorillas? He hits his betting limit with us on that game? Get the fuck outta here!"

"It's true," Loot says. "He wanted more, but I told him he was at his limit. He used his color and number: Blue-425, plus I recognized his voice. When it was over, I did our mandatory checkout process and went over all the plays, spreads and amounts. The Whale bet on the Gorillas."

"Okay, then what happened? Did you lay it off with Petro? You didn't have us go naked on that big amount, of course. Tell me exactly what happened next."

"I went down to help Rocky."

"Before you layed off that big bet?"

"Kevin, it was bedlam in there! The girl called up screaming!"

I look over and Rocky is nodding to confirm what Loot just said. "Okay," I say, "then what happened?"

Loot says, "I broke up the fight and sent the kid that got stabbed home. I figured if I got stabbed with pencils all over the place I wouldn't be a very productive salesman. So I kept the guy here that did the stabbing." Everyone nods in confirmation and I have to agree that's good business.

I look at Loot and say, "So that's when you laid off the bet?"

"I was going to lay it off then because it was getting late. By now it's 1:30 and the Gorillas play at seven and it's a pretty big number to lay off. I thought I might need a couple of guys. I thought if Petro didn't want all the action, I could maybe use some of the guys I told you about."

"Loot, did you lay the bet off?"

"I couldn't."

"Please explain this," I plead.

"Okay. I had every intention to come back and lay off the bet. But Carey was calling about the cops banging down the door. He's freaking because he's going to get arrested with a mountain of drugs. The dude's about to kill himself and I am trying to calm him down. We can't get hold of you, and we're going off the deep end over here. Finally we agree to flush the dope."

Go on."

"We get it done, and that's when it happened. I am so bummed that I then proceed to fuck up. I was like in a trance. I call Petro to lay off the bets and I'm going through the motions. I go to lay off the entire Whale bet; we don't need to let any of this ride today. Who has time to manage the book today? So, I'm laying it off."

"I agree, so where is the problem?" I ask incredulously.

"Like I said, I'm really distracted, so I call Petro and lay off the eight favorites and then, like an asshole, by force of habit, instead of betting against the Gorillas to offset the Whale's typical bet, I lean the way we usually do and bet with Petro for the Gorillas. So with the Whale's action, add another $100,000 on the Gorillas with Petro."

"You bet the Gorillas for 100k?"

"Yes, I'm sorry," Loot states.

His story takes a while to percolate through my brain. "So," I say, "instead of offsetting the bet, instead of making that bet zero, you double it up. We actually have $200,000 exposure if the Gorillas cover the spread?"

"That's right," Loot confirms. Then he bites his lip and says, "But it's actually about $250,000 because a lot of other dudes bet on the Gorillas today. Even Stinkfinger hit his limit with a dime bet on the Gorillas."

"The gynecologist? C'mon!" I shake my head in disbelief. "Did Petro give you a hard time about the action?"

"No, as a matter of fact, he was thrilled. They confirmed, but they were trying to rush through the checkout process. At first I thought it was because he must be real busy, but now I think they were pushing it through as fast as they could."

"So when did you realize you that we were exposed to $250,000?"

Loot says it was about an hour ago, just before he reached me at the hospital. "I was organizing shit around here and planning on how we were going to tell you about flushing all those drugs, and then I heard some guys talking about the Gorilla game and something clicked. I looked at my notes and saw how I confirmed everything with Petro. At first I thought my notes were wrong, then I started remembering my conversation and I thought it was possible that my notes were right and I fucked up. I called Petro's office and they confirmed that we have Cleveland University getting eight-and-a-half from the New York State Gorillas for ten dimes. So at this moment we have $100,000 on with the Whale and $100,000 on with Petro, not to mention 50 grand with our regular customers."

"Did you try to lay off the big number?" I plead, "Tell me you reversed it. Tell me you got worse terms, but you got it done."

"Kevin, I tried," Loot says apologetically.

"What do you mean you tried?"

"There are guys dying to get some of our lay-off action. They've been bothering us for a long time. And I've been bothering you because I hate dealing with Petro. I called these guys up, telling them that this is their big chance."

"So what did they say?" I ask, trying to hide my desperation.

"No line," Loot answers. "They took it down. Everyone took it down because the game stinks."

"Loot, this is important. Tell me exactly what the guy said. Do you remember?"

"Yeah," Loots says. "'That line went down faster than a priest at a Boy Scout jamboree.' That was exactly what he said."

I feel a little faint; I have to sit down. It's fucking amazing. Everything I worked so hard for and then some is about to come apart. How can I finish the job my father started? How can I stop us from getting killed? I look at Carey, Loot and Rocky, and there is no hiding my panic. "The game is fixed. Cleveland University is laying down," I say wearily. "Everyone in the universe got wind of this, so why didn't we?"

Carey attempts to answer. "Kevin, we were dealing with guys foaming on our carpet, police banging on our door and dudes getting stabbed with pencils. It was the perfect storm and we didn't pick up on the fix. But we can deal with this. Even if we lose, we've been making pretty good money. We got to be able to cover that or at least come close enough to work through it."

I give a gallows laugh because Carey has no idea how wrong he is. "Not only can't we come close to covering that action, but can you think of any two worse people to be on the hook with? Any other schmuck we owe money to, what could they do? Squat, that's what. But now we have a senator we owe big bucks to. Do you think that's a good idea? Do you think he can make life hell?" More blank stares from my posse; no one has ever seen me in full rant mode. I laugh and go on. "I just remembered something. Senator Murphy can't make my life hell because I owe 100 grand to a mobster like Petro. I won't have a life. It's really just a matter of how he decides to kill me. And by the way, it was always you two guys doing the laying off, so if you aren't scared shitless right now, I would question your common sense."

That certainly got their attention. I don't think anyone thought about the mob being included in the worst-case scenario analysis. In the bookie business, if you are flat-out busted, most of the universe has no recourse. They ain't calling the police, that's for sure. A senator, that's a different story; he's got ways to make your life miserable. A mob guy, shit, this is what they jack off to.

Loot is the first person to speak. "What the fuck is your drugged-out ass talking about? How sure are you he's Mafia?"

I shake my head and say, "Oh, about 150 percent sure."

"You know he's a mob guy and you made us deal with him? We hate the fucking guy and could get better rates and treatment from almost anyone else in the country. What the fuck gives?"

I look over at Rocky and she is looking intently at me. Carey is looking toward the dirty floor and Loot's neck veins are bulging. "Remember on the bench, the bench at the bus stop?" I ask Rocky. "I told you everything I could about my business, except anything to do with Petro. I explained that if I tell you certain things it could put you in danger. Now maybe you can understand why I was so sensitive."

Rocky looks over and shakes her head. "I knew you were going after Balducci in Queens, but I don't understand what a mob bookie in Albany has to do with any of that."

Loot, who is still fuming, says, "The girl is making a good point. Why didn't you tell us about being involved with the mob?"

"Because the less you knew, the less at risk you would be."

Loot screams back, "Well, I don't know shit and I don't feel too safe right now. Keeping us in the dark was a pretty stupid fucking idea!"

"Hey!" I scream back, "Petro never would have been a problem for you. So shut the fuck up. You made him a problem when you bet an extra 100 grand on the fucking New York State Gorillas."

"Fuck you, Kevin!" Loot screams. "If you weren't

playing fucking nursemaid to your spoiled shit friend, then maybe you could have done better!"

"Fuck you. Ray is in a fucking coma. What was I supposed to do, just let him die?"

Carey finally speaks. "Damn, your boy is in a coma?"

"Yeah," I say, "it's pretty serious shit."

The concept doesn't reach Carey all the way. He is quietly speaking, almost mumbling in a numb tone, "Man, I thought I was going to get arrested today. Now, I got some mob guy going to kill me."

Loot is about to boil over. "See what you are doing to him?" he yells. "Carey can't handle this shit! How can you do this to us?"

"Guys," Rocky interrupts. "Guys, we've got to stop pointing fingers. We got to figure this out. Please, let's figure this out!"

"She's right." I say. I'm glad she spoke up. We need some cool heads around here, and mine is about to explode. I don't know how I can pull this off. "Look, I'm not going to kid you, we're in a tough situation. But we got to try to fight through it."

"Yeah." Loot struggles to calm down. "Let's figure something out. But first tell us what you know. This time, tell us everything. Tell us what we're up against. The next decision we make is going to be big. I want to do it intelligently."

"Fair enough," I say. "I'll tell you everything. We are going to owe big money to the Senator and Petro, but our real problem is Petro. He's a bad guy and the worst to owe a shit-load of money to."

"Wait, wait," Loot says. "Exactly how bad a guy is he?"

CHAPTER 22

How bad a guy is Petro? As much as I'm trying to do this full-disclosure thing with Rocky, Carey and Loot, I just can't manage to talk about everything. For instance, I can't admit to them that I killed Zog. The group knows I mean business, but there's something about killing someone in cold blood that has me thinking I'll lose a little something with them. I should tell them, because I shouldn't hide anything, but I can't tell them.

How bad a guy is Petro? Loot is asking me a straight question, but if I tell them what I know, they'll panic. They won't be able to function. It's fucked. I can't rationalize like this; their asses are on the line now and they have a right to know. I don't have to tell them about Zog the Cellophane King, but I have to tell them what I know about Petro.

Petro became my target because I discovered that Petro and Balducci are colleagues and that Petro wants something from Balducci. I let Petro know I was tight with Balducci. Petro had ways to check up on me; he knew I was working at Kosher World, he knew about the Industrial Road fights and the fact that I'm buddies with Balducci's son, Richie. I used the gambling business to hook Petro and throughout, I dropped in plenty of comments about Balducci.

Petro has a way of showing his teeth like no one else in this world. He is flat-out mean. At first I wasn't sure if Petro was putting on a show for me. He knew I spoke to Balducci, so I was thinking Petro wanted to make a point that he is some ruthless, sick fuck and that I could somehow convey his brutal merits to Balducci. The more I hung with Petro, the more I realized that it was no act. Petro was always a bad guy, but being stuck in Albany made him a bad guy with a huge chip on

his shoulder. Petro wanted more than Albany, and I made him
believe I could help.

Like a cop who has to fill a monthly speeding ticket
quota, Petro needs to fill a killing quota, his own self-imposed
killing quota. By the end of a month, this guy is practically
twitching if he doesn't waste someone.

So I tell Rocky, Loot and Carey about Mack Gregory,
who disappeared from this planet about a month and a half ago.
There are no leads to Mack's whereabouts, according to the
police.

I know differently. I know exactly what happened. I
know Mack's 30-year-old, knockout wife Carina made breakfast for Mack and their six-year-old twin girls one ice-cold
morning because I was standing outside their house, feeling my
balls shrink to raisins. I was there with Petro and a bunch of
his goons. Petro was barking out orders and the smoke from
his breath mixing with the cold air made him look like a dragon. A big, fucking, badly-dressed dragon.

Mack and Carina sent their twin girls to school. A few
moments later, when the twins were out of sight, one of the
goons broke through the front door and four of Petro's men
barged through the back door by the kitchen. With the pathway
to the house clear and open, Petro waltzed in; he motioned me
to follow. In the kitchen, partially eaten waffles still lay on
their chipped plates. The empty drinking glasses still had a
milky residue.

Carina knew her husband Mack gambled too much;
so did everyone. That's why the police can't really decipher
which of Mack's bad gambling debts caused his disappearance.
I don't think it was Petro's intention to do anything to Carina
when we first barged into the house. I think when he saw how
pretty she was, with her smooth skin and jet-black hair, it overwhelmed him. It was too tough to contain himself. Carina's
tight-as-paint black tank top was failing to enclose her large,

shapely, attractive breasts. That poorly designed shirt is probably what put Petro over the edge. All bets were off. And so were Petro's pants.

The other guys worked on Mack first. They pistol whipped him in the head. Another one of Petro's guys broke through the door and nailed Mack in the legs with a baseball bat, all while his wife Carina was being held down on the kitchen table. Mack never had a chance to protect himself. I always heard rumors of breaking knees, but these guys kept swinging the bat and hitting three, four then five times in the center of Mack's shin. Again and again. Those guys shattered his legs to a point where they could never function again. The sound of the aluminum bat cracking against his bones will stay with me for as long as I live, for whatever short time that may be. The sound of Mack's cries and his wife's cries will stay with me after I'm dead.

When they were done crippling Mack, the thugs held him down and forced Mack to watch Petro mount his wife on the kitchen table, right next to the waffles that his little girls didn't finish. Watching a 6'4", 320-pound slob like Petro raping his wife was probably more painful to Mack than it was to be crippled.

Petro finished, and then matter of factly picked up his gun and shot Carina in the throat. I don't think he originally intended to kill her, or Mack for that matter. I'm confident Petro's intention was to break Mack's legs beyond repair for being a deadbeat. The guy owed money, and no one owes Petro money. He came into the house to set an example. Then things just took a different direction. After he shot Carina, Petro nodded to his goons to finish off Mack.

One goon, Billy Shaps, tossed the baseball bat at me and said, "Go ahead, make yourself useful and finish this."

I tossed the bat back and said, "Yeah, like I'm your fucking laundry boy."

Shaps shot back, "You don't have the stomach for this?"

"No, Shaps, I don't have the stomach to clean up after you." Billy Shaps didn't like me because he viewed himself as Petro's right hand man and thought of me as a threat. I wanted to fuck this guy up, but Sev taught me better than that, like the time in the meat factory when I went after Bino because of my ego. This guy Shaps was a piece of shit, but I wasn't about to ruin everything I'd worked for because he was antagonizing me.

Shaps looked at me while he squeezed the bat. He stared me up and down; turning to the whimpering Mack, Shaps smashed him in the skull four more times.

Petro wanted me along to see my reaction to a leg breaking. Maybe he hoped I would tell Balducci what a real player he was. I guess seeing my reaction to a sick murder that left twin girls as orphans was a bonus. Externally, I tried to stay cool but internally I was going bat-shit. What Petro did to these girls was what Balducci did to me.

Now Carey, Loot and Rocky know how bad a guy Petro is. I guess I should explain how he became my target. Ha, he became my target. What a fucking joke. In a few hours, he'll be after me. In the meantime, I need to let these guys know what I found out about Petro and how it relates to Balducci.

"I guess the best place to start is right in Jimmy Balducci's house," I explain. "I would go back to Long Island every now and then and catch up with my old high school pal, Richie Balducci. We would go out clubbing and I would listen to the most boring stories about how great Wall Street is and how smart he is. I shit you not. Richie believes they all think he is a rising killer, but I had the opportunity to hear the other side. When I met up with him at the bar by his office, a couple of the traders were ragging on Richie behind his back when he went to the bathroom. These guys didn't know I was there with Richie and they were relentless. But this was as bad as it got for him; the traders knew that Richie's father has some major connections and that's what got him into Bank of America for the summer. They'd been instructed to take it easy on the mental abuse."

Loot is frustrated and interrupts, "So why deal with Richie Balducci? You ain't friendly with him anymore and if the bitch bothers you when you're hanging out, why deal?"

"Believe me," I say, "I'm not disagreeing with you. He's turned into a Wall Street maggot. It's a bunch of months later and I still hear all about his Bank of America summer internship. It's all he wants to talk about. But to answer your question, hanging out with Richie allowed me total access to his dear old dad. It worked like this: We would go to the clubs, I would get the dork fucked up and then we would go back to his parents' house and crash. Whenever Richie was coming back to town to visit his folks, I made an effort to find an excuse to get back to Long Island."

Rocky asks, "Did it work?"

"Hell, yeah," I answer. "The house was like hitting the lottery. Balducci has a ton going on and he can't keep track of it at Kosher World. His house was like my own information highway. At around two in the morning I would go on an expedition and snoop around in his home office. That's how I came up with this brilliant, though obviously flawed, master plan for bringing down Balducci."

"Yeah, you and what army?" Carey asks sardonically.

I point to Carey and say, "That's my point; you don't bring these guys down without an army. As a matter of fact, you need two armies."

Loot is shaking his head wildly. "Man, what are you talking about?"

"I had it totally under control until today, when it derailed. Army number one is Petro."

All those times sleeping at Balducci's house and doing
my research, I found out the Balducci family exiled the Petrocelli family. Balducci thought of himself as this new frontier
of organized crime. It was so much grander than all the bone
crushers of the past. He once told me that it's not a *gumba*
thing anymore; it's like the United Nations. Balducci came
to the realization that the mob business wasn't what it used to
be. You had thinner margins and low job satisfaction, mainly
because the cops were getting sentences to stick. Undercover
cops were infiltrating mob operations. The witness protection
program was working and successfully getting guys to squeal.
This was a huge problem for Balducci, so he went global. He
was going after foreign government contracts and getting control of construction and factories in crazy countries like Uganda
and Myanmar. Anywhere there was a corrupt government, he
was able to duplicate a model to control all the work, just like
he had done over here. He set himself up to buy for free in different languages.

"What does that have to do with Petro?" Loot asks.

"That's a good question," I answer. I tell them that it
really started with Petro's father. Old man Petro was resisting
this great expansion. He was happy with his turf in Queens and
thought that this new mandate was too risky. It would bring
attention, and old man Petro thought attention was an invita-
tion to get caught. But mostly, these new initiatives would be a
cash drain, and old man Petro wasn't willing to kick in. It was
causing a roadblock. As global as Balducci thought he could
be, nothing could get done without going through Queens. Old
man Petro was a respected leader in good standing and he flat-
out disagreed. As long as he was resisting, other leaders would
resist. Old man Petro was a major thorn in Balducci's big
expansion plans.

Rocky looks at me and asks, "Is that why Petro is in

Albany now?"

"Yeah," I answer, "there was an internal war about 15 years ago. Balducci got control in the old-school Mafia manner and wiped out guys who were resisting the big expansion. Old man Petro was a bigger tree to chop down. Petro lost, but for political reasons, still couldn't be killed, so a truce was worked out and a territory was carved out for old man Petro. Albany."

Loot asks, "So you had this idea to get Balducci and you lucked into finding Petro?"

"Just the opposite," I say. "I've been hanging out with Richie Balducci all this time. I've been making special trips down to Long Island to get access to his house, and I would choke on his Bank of America stories. For months I have been pouring over information and trying to get ideas. I had thousands of ideas and then ultimately dead ends. But finally I found it. Here I am going to New York State University and someone who hates Balducci almost as much as I do is right here in Albany as well. So now the issue is, how do I get this guy to team up with me? That's my real motivation for the drugs and bookie operation."

"I'm confused," Rocky moans. "Who was exiled from Queens? Was it old man Petro or the Petro we deal with?"

I catch myself and say, "Sorry, my fault. Old man Petro was exiled in the late 80s. But he was an older guy and he grudgingly accepted his fate. He keeled over about five years after his exile. He's breaking thumbs in that better place right now. The younger Petro was in his 30s and had been strutting around New York as the heir to the Petro Dynasty. This exile crushed him. Petro was going to be running Queens, the center of the universe, but instead he's in Siberia. He turned into a joke. He thinks he should be The Dude and just doesn't have any of the muscle to back it up. In the younger Petro's mind, which is our Petro, he believes he's a man in a boy's body and this is causing frustration. This frustration created one of the most outright meanest motherfuckers I have ever seen."

Loot asks, "You know all this for a fact?"

"There's no doubt," I say. "I've been rummaging through Balducci's mail, documents and e-mails for months now. As much as correspondents try to stay under the radar, a lot of info is still passed the old-school way, just with different acronyms so the writer and the reader aren't actually talking about prostitution or extortion. You should see all the ideas and suggestions that Petro sends Balducci, trying to get back in. He's desperate, and that was my hook."

Loot tilts his head and asks, "I see a Petro vs. Balducci situation here. Exactly how do you win?"

"I win by blowing Balducci out of the water. That's always been how I win. I got Petro on board. It wasn't easy and it was pretty expensive but I got him on board."

"Expensive!" Loot interjects.

I am trying to hold my head up and lay out my idea, but based on our recent turn of events with the NY State Gorilla game tonight, it's hard to be bold and proud, so I belt it out quick and straight. "I gave Petro most of our money. We can't cover the fixed Gorilla bet when we lose because I gave Petro most of our money." There is stunned silence.

Loot is the first to awaken. "Kev, there was over $100,000 in our rainy day fund."

"More like $133,000," I say, "but I gave Petro $125,000 about a month back. "

"Oh," Loot says, "at least you still have $8,000."

"Okay, Loot, I know this is going in different directions. This is where it starts coming together. I started out by laying off bets with Petro. That was my in. At first I only worked through some of his staff, but when the size of the wagers got dramatically bigger, Petro, as expected, wanted to talk to me in person."

I sigh and continue. "It didn't take me long to win him

over. We were giving him good-sized bets, and I never haggled over paying his ridiculous rates. At the same time, I kept feeding him info about Balducci. What a coincidence that we had Balducci in common and Petro desperately wanted to get in better with Balducci. By the way, I may have slightly exaggerated my relationship with Jimmy Balducci."

"I see," Carey says.

"Here's the thing. Petro actually started kissing my ass."

Loot says, "Huh? Petro was charging us the worst rates in the universe."

"Look, guys, when Petro first met me, I needed to dazzle him. I had to sell him hope. I was introducing another market but I also slowly offered access to Balducci and a doorway back to the big time.

"This college town was always thought of as a bullshit nickel-and-dime proposition. It's messy getting involved with students from a public relations standpoint, and the income stream proved very unreliable. But I showed him a whole different level of organization and profit. I knew most of Petro's money is earned from bookmaking, offering protection from his own leg-breakers to local business owners and of course, prostitution. After all, there're plenty of politicians in Albany to earn from.

"I told Petro about the drugs, sports handicapping and bookmaking that he was ignoring and how it was overflowing to the lobbyists and whatnot. I told him how I wanted to show him respect and that I needed his help. There was so much more potential and I was only scratching the surface. I needed financing and protection to get heroin going, and H was making a huge comeback. My bookmaking was a complementary business to his bookmaking, and I needed protection from people starting to grab at my territory."

"Heroin. That's such bullshit! We never once talked

about heroin," Loot interjects. "And no one's trying to grab our territory; if anything, more guys want to merge with us. Kevin, what's with this shit?"

I answer, "I told him how we already cleared a million dollars and I'm frustrated because there is so much more to do...."

Carey interrupts. "What? Why would he believe a fucking nothing like you cleared a million bucks? How fucking stupid could he be?"

"How fucking stupid?" I answer, "I gave him ten percent of our fictitious $1,250,000 profit. In old-school fashion, I let him wet his beak. I gave it to Petro out of respect for past business done in his territory and made plans to do some great things together in the future."

"Fuck me!" Loot says. "You gave him all the money we had. You gave him $125,000. You fucking gave it to Petro!"

"How else would he believe I cleared a million bucks? Money talks, baby, money talks. Now I have Petro amped up to make millions of dollars and more importantly, to topple Balducci."

Rocky asks, "Petro is going to topple Balducci?"

"Yep, Petro is going to take down Balducci."

Rocky persists, "But if Petro wants in so badly, how are you going to get him to work with you? It doesn't make sense. If he works with you, he can never get back in with Balducci."

"Yeah," I answer, "I had to play on that slippery slope that Petro was climbing. Obviously, he hated Balducci; he just wasn't willing to admit that to himself yet. Balducci humiliated his old man and demoted them to the minor leagues. On the other hand, Petro needed Balducci to get back into the big dance; there was no way around that. I had a theory..."

"Oh great," Loot interrupts.

I shoot Loot a look. "It's not that crazy." Pointing to

Loot and Carey, I say, "It was fucking working until today when you flushed our drug money down the drain in a panic." I move my finger and vent further. "And you bet the wrong side of the fixed Gorilla game. So fuckin' hear me out."

"Okay," Loot says calmly. "No need to point fucking fingers."

I blow some air from my cheeks and say, "When I was spying in Balducci's house, Petro was always offering up ideas to Balducci, trying to get a bigger role. For business' sake and his own ambitions, Petro tried to play the past off like it was all ancient history. It wasn't anything personal with the exile, just business. As it turned out, Balducci did get to go global, so it's hard for the old guard or Petro's family to fight the results. Therefore, I have to believe Petro's unrealistic, rationalizing mind is thinking that if Petro ever came up with a valid business opportunity, Balducci would welcome him back.

"Balducci and Petro have reasons to talk from time to time because, get this, Petro has to kick money up to Balducci. That's the rules. Petro has to pay a tax on his Albany earnings. I know for a fact it's gnawing at his guts sending hard-earned income Balducci's way. The money Petro kicks up wouldn't affect Balducci's clothes shopping habits. Petro is paying for something that already belonged to him and was stolen by Balducci. It's like asking the guy who stole your watch to tell you what time it is.

"So, back to the theory. Petro wants back in and it's all he can taste. When he found out I was hooked up with Balducci, he was always asking me questions. 'Hey, Kevin, you ever hear Balducci mention my name?' Or he would say, 'You going to Long Island this weekend? Say hello to Balducci for me.' Then when I got back, the first voicemail waiting from me was from my new pal, Petro."

"So what did you tell Balducci?" Rocky asks.

"Nothing, not a thing. All I had to do was manipulate

the information to Petro."

Loot interrupts, saying, "The guy is a mob boss. Isn't he smart enough to see through your manipulations?"

"Fair question, but let's get one thing clear. Petro is a mob boss because he is once removed from a mob boss that got sent packing. Petro himself knows he jumped off the line early when they were assigning smarts. Petro makes up for this deficiency by being the meanest asshole in the land."

"We get the mean part," Carey says; he might as well be in a different room. Loot is trying to figure out which question to ask next and is dangerously close to an internal electrical malfunction.

Rocky sighs calmly and says, "How did you answer Petro when he asked you about Balducci? How did you manipulate the information?"

I start thinking to myself how good Rocky looks. C.W. Wellington could get a modeling deal if she wanted, but as weird as it sounds, C.W. is too pretty, untouchably pretty. Rocky, on the other hand, with her auburn hair and sultry eyes, is so attractive that she makes me want to grab her every minute of the day. I could be dead by the end of the week, and yet the mere sight and I need to embrace her. Man, I like Rocky, but damn, I thought about C.W. Wellington again today. I get back to the task at hand and say, "I might have added some fuel to the fire."

"What do you mean?" Rocky asks.

"When I was spying on Balducci, I saw stuff about Petro. Petro would occasionally offer up a less-than-brilliant business idea. Then Balducci would forward these ideas to some of his guys, laughing his balls off at Petro. Balducci thinks he's in the year 2100 and Petro is still pitching ideas on how to pick a caveman's pocket. Petro is a big fucking joke to Balducci. So you know what I do?" I pause for a moment because I really need them to understand what I am going to say. "I take the stuff mocking Petro and I show it to him."

Rocky says, "When Balducci finds out, he's going to kill you twice."

"Yup," I say, "that's when I jumped into the deep end of the pool. So I really needed this to hit home. One day, when Petro was asking me questions about Balducci, I acted like I just had to crack. I made like I didn't want to see Balducci make such a fool out of Petro any longer. So I showed him all the stuff I had where Balducci was ragging on Petro. I made him understand that he had no shot at getting back into Balducci's inner circle. I showed him everything I had found and I even made stuff up."

"Fuck me, why did you have to make stuff up? Weren't you doing enough?" Loot asks.

"Nope," I answer, "it's one thing for Petro to get angry at Balducci; it's another thing to have Petro turn on Balducci. So I explained to Petro that Balducci was planning to kill him."

"What?" Rocky shouts. "Is that true?"

"Fuck no. Balducci couldn't care less about Petro. But when I show Petro all this stuff and tell him he's a target, it's ballistic time."

"You got to be kidding me," Carey chirps.

"It worked. Think about all the emotions I put this guy through. He wants Balducci to accept him and bring him back into the fold. Then I show him that he's nothing but a joke to Balducci, which should turn on a switch. But then I got him believing Balducci is going to kill him. So now he's scared shitless. He's a fucking caged animal and I got him teed up."

"Teed up for what? Holy shit, did you ever think you were in over your head?" Loot demands.

"Look, even if I came up with the perfect plan to get Balducci, it would still have risks. The fuckin' guy ruined my life. I'm not saying it has to stay ruined, but as long as that cock and his 'buy for free' organization is breathing, I can't think about having a life. Did I think I was in over my head? No, it's not my head right now. Don't you realize that Balducci put the hit on my father? He ruined my life, and he's still doing it to other people. It's not my head right now; it's my father's head. I don't know if you can understand what I mean, but it's not my life until I get him. I had to jump in sometime. If not now, then when?"

Rocky asks, "Okay, so what next?"

"I sold Petro on the fact that I am just short of being the messiah. I have a business going here that is already allegedly netting me over a million dollars. I have connections back in New York where Petro's family was bounced. I have inside information out the wazoo and I have a great idea to expand my business and take back all of New York, including what's Balducci's. I know where Balducci's weaknesses are and I can exploit them. I told Petro I was approaching him because I needed manpower and experience. It was a big job and I needed a partner. No one's ever been able to get Balducci because no one has ever been able to penetrate like I have."

"Wow," Rocky says, "if he doesn't push back at Balducci, he thinks he's a sitting duck. Why wouldn't he want to hook up with you?"

"That's what I was thinking. Petro hears the clock ticking and he's looking over his shoulder. If he thought he was a target, then he needed to defend himself, but I also had him amped up for this business idea. After all, I handed him $125,000 like it was lunch money."

Loot says, "So he saves his own ass, takes the egg off his face that Balducci put there and when the dust clears, Petro gets a bigger business. I see where you are going. But even if he didn't believe in your business, the thought that Balducci was going to waste him would have Petro scrambling for ideas anyway. It's pretty crazy, but I see it."

"Yeah," I add, "But when the Gorillas win tonight, he'll be able to see through it. I am going to owe him $100,000, and I won't be able to pay him."

Rocky asks, "But you already gave him $125,000. Can't he call it even?"

"No chance," I answer with a laugh. "That money is yesterday's news. Not only are you as good as your last 10 minutes with these guys, but there is so much more at stake than the dough. I know how Petro responds to anyone who owes him money. After the bill of goods I just sold him, if I sweat paying this money, as dumb as Petro can be, he will smell a rat. Trust me, the charade will be over when I owe him money. Even if I keep Petro at bay with some story, he'll find out about the other chunk of money we won't be able to pay."

"The Senator," Carey blurts out, "Kevin's right. It's a small world when it comes down to it. All the bookies know who's a deadbeat. Word gets around. Petro will know we didn't pay Senator Whale."

"Right now, I have Petro so pumped to go after Balducci, I swear I can hear his brain cells sizzle. In his mind, he is climbing on the throne. Do you have any idea how he will react when we can't cover the Gorilla bet? At first Petro thought he was in Balducci's crosshairs for a good old-fashioned whacking. Then I offer him a solution to not only save his ass, but also grab everything back that was taken. It's an emotional whipsaw, and it will be ugly."

CHAPTER 23

As scared as I am, it's crunch time, and everyone is
rallying. After combing the universe, Carey finds out why
this particular game is dirty. It's a weak fix and under normal
circumstances, we would have spotted this crap from 10,000
miles away. Everyone got wind of this fix, and that's why it's
off the board now. Carey is furiously trying to mitigate our
exposure by attempting to lay off even small amounts, but so
far it's only pennies to two-bit bookies who aren't in any loop.
We can't even dent our overall exposure.

Cleveland University has only two guys who matter:
Jake Mitchell and Snake Frye. It's usually the Jake and Snake
show, except tonight, they plan on laying down. Cleveland
University is a perennial doormat, but Jake and Snake have
made Cleveland a force this year. They're local products from
Marshall High School and continue to frustrate all the big
programs that dissed them during the recruiting process. They
can play college ball, but they know the NBA is not an option.
Some enterprising student at New York State put two and two
together and arranged the fix. This student knows these players come from poor families with plenty of brothers and sisters
to support. Jake and Snake are decent enough guys, but this
student offered them a payday they are not likely to see again
in their lives.

The problem is, the fucking student couldn't keep his
mouth shut and now the universe knows, including the wiseguys. This is a circus. The fucked up thing is that I'm the
asshole on the other side of this bet and it feels lonely. But it's
time to fight back.

Carey and Loot have been friends with and drug deal-
ers to a lot of the Gorilla players, so we knew we had a decent

chance to get into the locker rooms. Hell, they even lit up the equipment manager and half the guys who worked for the team on several occasions. I'm sure Loot and Carey never imagined that their free flow of drugs could actually save their lives.

Loot and Carey head for the subterminal of the Gorilla locker room while I begin working on Jake and Snake. I've done a lot of fucked-up things in this quest to get Balducci, but I'm really rolling around in the gutter now. If I weren't so desperate or if I had more time, I'd figure out a better way, but I can't. I obviously can't get to Cleveland by game time at 7:30, but through some of my drug-dealing connections I am fortunate enough to have a hard-up client who is dying for a lifelong discount on our intake. Larry "The Sultan" Joshi agreed to beat up Jake's little brother. I don't mean to drag in innocent participants, but this situation is desperate. I rationalize that one person getting bloody is worth keeping Rocky, Carey, Loot and me from being dead.

The Sultan hustles over to the Cleveland area. He finds and beats up Jake's kid brother. The kid is only 16 and no match for the Sultan. While pounding the kid brother, the Sultan is able to procure Jake's cell phone number. He gives it to me. It's getting close to game time.

"Hey, Jake," I say into the phone.

"Who's this?" the player asks.

"Trust me, that's not important," I say. "I don't want to take up too much of your time because I know you have a big game tonight and frankly, I'm a big fan of yours. You're playing a ranked team tonight. If you beat the Gorillas, that's part of your legacy. Don't throw it away. Don't lay down tonight."

There is a long pause but then Jake says, "Who is this?"

"Jake," I say calmly, "stop worrying about who I am and worry more about your legacy and how you can ruin it by shaving points tonight."

After another silence Jake says, "I don't know what

you're talking about."

"Sure. Don't get me wrong, I appreciate the way
you're talking to me. Honestly, sometimes ballplayers can be a
pretty rude group. I hear you're a pretty good guy and that you
are shaving points to help your family but frankly, it will turn
out to be the exact opposite." There is more silence, so I continue. "Look, Jake, a funny thing happened here and a bunch
of wiseguys all over the country got wind a little too late about
tonight's antics. You see, this rather short-tempered group of
gentlemen had already given the points and bet on you and
your team. They believe in your legacy."

"I got to hang up now," Jake states.

"Jake," I say, "I need you to call your little brother
Tucker and check in on him. It's important. I know you want
to help out your family, and getting a few extra bucks from
shaving points can go a long way, but sometimes things aren't
what they appear to be. If Cleveland University doesn't cover
the point spread and you have a bad game, well, there may
be some side effects you didn't count on. When you talk to
Tucker, please understand, this is a warning. Ramifications
can be far and deep. Your decisions are not just yours. I know
you care deeply about your whole family and I think that's
wonderful, but you have a big family. I'm going to let you go
now, because I know you have some difficult thinking ahead,
but I'm sure you'll come to the conclusion that a New York
State Gorilla student who paid you to shave points doesn't pack
a ton of muscle. You do the right thing here and I'll get you
some dough, but the important thing is not getting the big guys
pissed. You will be less torn after you talk with Tucker. Please
pass this information on to Snake and tell him what big fans we
are and how excited I am to meet Snake's family." I turn off
the phone and think to myself, That went pretty well. At least I
did everything I could.

　　　The game is about to start and I have never been more

nervous in my life. I have over $200,000 and my precious ass on the line. Not to mention the precious asses of my friends. This is going to be a long night. I hope Loot and Carey did some damage.

I grab a few beers and sit down in our living room in front of the TV. I hand Rocky a beer and begin to pour us both a shot of 151 rum. Rocky gives me a strange look and I say, "These are supposed to be lucky."

Before I light the shot, Loot and Carey come through the door. Carey drops down on the couch, still in his winter coat and says, "Better pour me one of them."

I look at Carey and say, "You're asking for one of these?"

"Dude, I've had a hard night. Pour that fucker and light it on fire."

I crack open two beers and slide them across the coffee table. I try to pour Loot and Carey both a shot of 151 and they notice my hand shaking. In these situations you want to look like Clint Eastwood, but it ain't happening.

Carey grabs my wrist, which actually helps me pour the rum. I manage to fill two shot glasses, but my shaky hand leaves at least a shot of overflow on the coffee table. I got myself into this mess because I didn't care if I got killed doing it. But now that I am at a crossroads, frankly, I'm scared. I don't want to die. Loot continues to try to calm me. "Kevin, there's some hope here. We might've done some damage."

I turn my attention to the TV and the game that is just starting. Gorilla Arena is buzzing as usual. Gorillas win the jump ball and score on a quick alley-oop to Homer Wingate and the place erupts. Jake brings the ball upcourt for Cleveland and fires a pass to Snake, but the ball goes right through Snake's hands.

Loot's voice cracks as he asks, "Do we need to do another flaming shot?"

"Maybe we should do shots of cyanide pills," I suggest.

Gorilla sharpshooter Darren Veal sinks one from long distance. The ref extends both hands in the air, signifying a three-pointer.

"Fuck me," Carey groans.

The score is five to nothing and nobody's even broken a sweat. Before I can complain, fucking Jake dribbles the ball off his legs and gives possession back to the Gorillas. Bam Graham slashes down the middle and converts for a seven-nothing lead. Jake gets a look at a 15-foot shot from the side. He lets it go, but it bounces off the inside rim and is grabbed by Veal. Veal passes it to Wingate, who dunks it one-handed. That's all Cleveland University coach Bill Madden can stand. The coach calls timeout in an attempt to stop the runaway train. We're just a few minutes into the game, but the score is already nine-zero. There's a break for a commercial.

Carey moans. "Those guys are still shaving points. You didn't get to them, Kev."

"Guys," I answer, "I honestly don't know. Even if they are trying, they still have to play well. Shit, they're playing on the road and against a ranked team, and it's hard enough to deliver under these situations. Now Jake and Snake have to worry about who they are going to piss off if they win or if they lose."

"Yeah," Carey says, "but the Gorillas look strong. Too strong."

"What exactly did you guys do when you got inside?" I ask.

"I don't want to tell you yet," Carey states.

"What the fuck does that mean?"

"I don't want to hear any fucking abuse about how stupid I am until it's absolutely necessary."

I look at Loot, hoping he will be more reasonable. "So, what did you do?"

Loot turns to Carey and says, "Oh, now all of a sudden it's important to talk about everything."

"Fuck!" I scream. But I catch myself and say in a normal voice, "Fine. You tell me when you are good and ready." I pour myself another 151 shot and mumble, "Like any of it makes a difference."

The first half of the game takes an eternity. Each bucket New York State scores is like a shark bite. The 151 rum is dulling my senses and occasionally my mind drifts. I remember how much fun I used to have playing hoops in Hempstead Park with Loot and Carey. The great trash talk, the powerful summer sun and the first gulp of beer when we finished playing. But then Petro barges into my thoughts and I can smell his dragon breath as he is nailing my balls to a hotplate. The only thing worse than this image is the sight of Darren Veal sinking a beautiful jump shot that snaps the net and the nylon pops back up 90 degrees. That shot ends the first half with the Gorillas leading by 18 points. Fuck, we are dead.

The second half opens with another nice drive from Bam Graham of the Gorillas. That makes the score 54-34, an even 20 points. A hopeless feeling overwhelms me. My eyes start to swell with tears. I look over to Loot and Carey and say, "This is killing me because Jake and Snake are playing okay now. They both have 12 points, which is easily within their averages, especially when you consider they are playing against the tough Gorilla defense."

"That's why we tried to take care of the whole problem," Carey says cryptically.

The Gorillas score on a rainbow jumper from Wingate and the lead widens to 22. Whatever they did doesn't seem to be working. Teasingly, Jake hits a three-point shot to bring us within 19.

Wingate throws a pass five feet over Veal's head. Snake capitalizes on the error by driving through the lane and dunking

like he was playing against an elementary school team. Down
by 17.

Loot looks at Carey and says, "That was kind of easy,
don't you think?"

"Indeed it was," Carey answers.

"C'mon, guys," I insist, "what's going on? Did you pay
some of the guys off?"

"Naw, the Gorillas have too much depth. You can't just
reach a few guys."

Snake steals the ball from Wingate and bashes another
monster dunk. All of a sudden we are down by 15 and the Gorillas call a time out. I cock my head, look at Loot and Carey
and say, "What the fuck did you do?"

Carey looks over at Loot, who nods. It looks like Loot
just gave him permission to tell me. But before Carey begins,
he points to the TV. "Holy shit!"

Loot starts laughing. "It's too good to be true." They
are laughing at the Gorilla huddle shown on the screen. The
coach is drawing up a plan, but Veal is clearly aggravated. He
is trying to concentrate on the strategy, but Wingate keeps putting his arm around Veal's shoulders. Veal has shrugged off
Wingate's arm three times already. "Carey, this shit is working."

"What the fuck is going on?" I demand.

Carey smiles and says, "We got to the water buckets
before they were filled up. They store them in the equipment
room. We didn't need to get into the locker room. No one saw.
We didn't have any dope left in the apartment thanks to the
flushing incident, but we got plenty of friends and we got all
the Ecstasy we could. We put a ton of crunched-up X pills in
the water buckets. You've been watching the game for scoring,
but we've been watching the equipment manager hand out cups
of water."

Loot stands on the couch. "Ecstasy, the club drug of

choice. You know how it gives you that close feeling? You know how you need to touch someone? Look at fuckin' Wingate touching Veal. These guys are going to be hallucinating. How are they going to make a pass, or a basket for that matter?"

"You doped the whole team?" I ask in amazement.

Loot, still standing on the couch, says, "I sure as fuck hope so."

"You know, X is also a stimulant," I point out. "Did you ever think these guys might play better?" As luck would have it, Bam Graham scores for the Gorillas to end the N.Y. State scoring drought. The Gorillas are still holding on to a 10-point lead, and we are midway through the second half.

"Well," Loot says with a smile, "we had a backup plan. We didn't have enough X to make an impact in all those water buckets, so we made a different cocktail in some of the other buckets."

"What did you use?" Rocky asks.

"It's a little hard to talk about it with a lady," Carey says. At this moment, Snake banks a 15-footer from the side and Cleveland is down 8 points. We are flirting with our magical eight-and-a-half point spread.

"Carey, don't you think we might be a little bit past the social niceties right now?" Rocky asks.

"In the coolers we didn't lace with X, we put in Bust-Ass," Carey says.

I interject, "What's that?"

Carey looks at Rocky and then, embarrassed, looks back at me. "It's a laxative used by heroin addicts," he says. "If one uses H, one gets constipated. That's a known fact, at least according to my friends."

"Nice friends," I say.

"Oh, like they're worse than your buddy Petro?"

"Good point," I say.

"It not like I have a ton of experience with this stuff," Rocky interjects, "but doesn't it take a laxative several hours to take effect?"

"Rock," Loot explains, "this ain't over-the-counter stuff. Bust-Ass is a synthetic street drug that works in under an hour. I imagine with ballplayers running around and speeding up their system, it should move even faster."

Sure enough, the Gorilla team is substituting players in rapid fire. Normally, players won't head to the locker room unless there's an injury that needs an X-ray. Yet Gorilla players are sprinting from the bench to the locker room. One is coming back and two are heading out, nearly knocking each other over.

"Hey, Loot, why not call into the locker room now and talk to one of your buddies?" I ask. "Let's see what they know."

"Good idea." Loot and Carey can reach an equipment manager or trainer even during a game. It was always helpful getting some inside scoop on Gorilla injuries. Obviously, being in the heart of Albany, our bookie business takes in a lot of Gorilla bets, and we take second-half bets as well. Knowing any inside information was pretty valuable.

Loot is on the phone and he is stunned. He is screaming in the phone, "Get the fuck out of here! Fuck you! You're pulling my leg!" He listens some more and says, "Okay, okay, I understand...sure, man, get back to what you got to do." Loot snaps the cell phone shut and smiles toward the sky.

"Well," Rocky insists, "you are going to share the news, aren't you?"

Loot lets loose a mighty sigh and with an ear-to-ear grin says, "My man in the locker room had to get Bam Graham into the shower 'cause Bam took a dump in a big garbage can and got crap all over hisself. Talk about shit-faced!"

"Wow!" Carey says. "Bam must have drunk from both

buckets."

"Hey Kevin," Carey says, "You want to pour a few more of those 151 shots?"

"Indeed I do." I pour the shots, light them up and proceed to watch the last eight minutes of the game, the most enjoyable 8 minutes of basketball I have ever experienced. Every bucket Cleveland University scores is loosening up my body. I can almost feel the throbbing veins in my temples relax and retreat back into my skull. The Gorillas are throwing ridiculous passes, the ball is uncatchable and they sometimes run into each other. All I can think is, *What a beautiful thing*. Jake and Snake have both scored career highs. Cleveland upsets the Gorillas by 15 points.

Rocky says, "You know, we could have given someone a heart attack out there."

Carey says, "I've seen those guys take in a ton of substances before, a lot worse than this. Partying is one thing; playing is another. I guess we're lucky."

The mention of a heart attack jolts my mind and I think of Ray. I make a quick call to the hospital and find out that he survived, that he's going to be okay. I tell the others, and everyone sighs in relief, in unison.

"Thank God. After a day of pile-on, we were due for some good luck."

"And there's more," Loot says. "Because of all those unusual bathroom runs, they'll probably blame the poor performance on a stomach virus or something."

"And not on two pushers spiking the punch," Carey adds.

We sit in silence, basking in Ray's recovery and our newly found personal safety. "We were so worried about losing that we never thought about winning," Loot says. "Since we were naked on that bet, is it my imagination or did we win 200 grand tonight?"

I laugh and say, "Yes. Yes, we did, so why don't you call Petro up and make arrangements to collect?"

The thought of collecting from Petro doesn't appeal to Loot. He looks at Carey but before Loot can even begin the question, Carey blurts out, "No fucking way am I collecting from Petro." They both look at me.

"Well, guys," I say, "we still won a hundred grand from the Senator."

"That's right!" Loot exclaims. "Not a bad night's work."

Carey looks at me and says, "Okay, motherfucker, come clean." I look at him, puzzled. "I remember when you explained about Petro," Carey continues. "You told me you were going after Balducci and I said 'You and what army?' You remember that?" I nod. "Well," Carey goes on, "you said, 'As a matter of fact I need two armies, and the first one is Petro.' That's right, isn't it?"

"Yep."

Carey is determined. "Who is the other army you referred to? Let's go, there's more here. What's your plan to get Balducci? When is this all going down? C'mon, asshole, it's time to come clean."

"Asshole?" I ask. "You're calling me an asshole? Aren't you being a tad harsh?"

Still determined, Carey says, "Just because this turned out okay doesn't mean you were right. We came pretty close to being a memory tonight. And you are an asshole."

"Look, things got hairy tonight, but how could I imagine shit would have gone so off course?"

"That's not the point! We're your brothers and you blindsided us. It's one thing if we knew what was up, but you fuckin' hid shit from us. That's the wrongest thing of all this shit. What's supposed to become of us when you're done with your search-and-destroy mission?"

I take a deep breath, sigh and say, "Yeah, I understand where you're coming from, but I didn't see it that way."

"Well," Loot jumps in, "which way did you see it? Did you think we were pussies and that if we knew what was what, we would run the other way?"

"No, man, it was just the opposite. I know you guys have balls, but this Balducci stuff is over the top. No offense, but I didn't want you guys involved because I didn't want to get you hurt. I needed your help getting these businesses going so I could get Balducci and his corporation, but I wanted to keep you guys at a safe distance. After all that happened today, I'm sure that was the right way to go. I couldn't live with myself if you guys got hurt. I fucked up because I never anticipated it could go down like it did tonight. Does that make sense to you at all?"

"Yeah, I see where you're coming from," Carey drawls, "but what's supposed to happen to us after this is over?"

"Dude, you were working in a dry cleaner," I say to Carey. "And Loot, you were a busboy in Hempstead. My plan was to give you some choices. It's the least I can do after turning us all into scumbag crooks. The bookie and drug business will be history. We all agreed that doing this for any length of time is pushing our luck. I needed some money and I needed something to dangle as bait; and that's what these businesses provided. I became one of these scumbags, and that could be the biggest insult to my father compared to anything else. Believe me, I'm not proud and I'm not kidding myself. I know I'm no better than any of these lowlifes right now, but I don't have a choice. Balducci doesn't go by any code of honor or follow any rules. He and his assholes have to be stopped, and working with the police got other people killed. Maybe I'm rationalizing, but I don't think so. I'm determined to do this job and put it behind me. But I will put it behind me. I might not end up being much, but I won't become this.

"I never had intentions of keeping the money. It's all fucking blood money. I expect to have a decent chunk of dough when the dust settles, and I will try to put it to good use. My mom was a big victim of Balducci, and I will set her up better. If my plan works, you guys will be instrumental in bringing Balducci down. That's certainly worth a lot. I'm giving you guys the rest. Maybe you'll open a restaurant or something like that, but I hope you do something good with it. I'm not taking a dime. You ask what's going to become of you? It's hard to say exactly, but you'll have some money and you'll have some choices. My gut tells me you guys will do the right thing."

More than anything else, I'm glad they're going to be okay. Despite what Loot and Carey say about how much fun they are having, these guys aren't meant for the drug and bookie business, and I should move them away from it. In retrospect, while I needed their help, I shouldn't have involved them. It was too risky.

Loot looks me up and down and says, "Yeah, I guess you're right. We'll talk some more about this. But for now, it's only 10 p.m. and I just realized that my life isn't over after all. How 'bout we go out and par-TEE?"

"Amen to that, Brother Loot," Carey adds.

I look at Rocky and she glances back. She coyly smiles and then shakes her head. I recognize that coy look, and the only place I want to be is alone with her. I look at Loot and Carey and say, "Pass."

Loot glances at me and then looks at Rocky and smiles. He nods in approval.

Loot and Carey grab their coats and get ready to leave. I look at Rocky, my eyes fixed on her face. I want to see everything and always remember it. I want to remember all the smooth and wonderful features. Remarkably, she is gazing at me the same way. While other people see a bookie or drug dealer, she manages to see something different.

As Carey and Loot are leaving, Loot says, "Don't think I got off track. You said you needed two armies to take down Balducci. If the first Army is Petro and the second army is not us, then where is this second army?"

"I'll tell you tomorrow." It's all going down soon anyway. That second army? It's commanded by Sev Reynard, the baddest man in the land. Who else would anyone want to go to war with? I thought this whole Gorilla mess with Petro could screw up my plans to get Balducci, but not any more. The train has left the station, and I'm going to get that cocksucker.

CHAPTER 24

I always knew that for this plan to work, I would need Sev on board. Although Sev put his Special Services life behind him and willed himself to blend in at Kosher World, I made the ridiculous assumption I could wake up the giant and get him to help me stop Balducci. In my more rational moments, I wondered what the fuck I was thinking. Fortunately, I didn't have many of those moments.

Two months before the Gorillas game, Sev and I met on neutral ground. He said I could find him at a blues bar on Francis Lewis Boulevard called Crossroads. When I entered the club, I noticed immediately that I stood out from the rest of the crowd. Not because I was one of the few whites, but because I was so much younger than most of the others. Sev was seated at a small isolated table meant for customers to savor an intimate moment and enjoy the music. The room was dark, but Sev's thunderstorm eyes could be recognized in a cave. He was part of the majority, but he didn't blend in; I think he was the only guy in the place not smiling, laughing or talking.

Bo Beard and his six-piece band were wailing with emotion. The band had a sax, trombone and trumpet player, and they were electrifying the room. Normally, this would have been a unique and awesome experience for me, but I couldn't focus on it. My concentration was on Sev.

Sev's eyes caught mine and he nodded. As I moved closer to his tiny table, I kept second-guessing my idea. What if he wouldn't get involved? What if he thought my plan would endanger the workers at Kosher World? He could blow the whistle on me and ruin everything. As I drew near, Sev stood up and we simultaneously shook hands and hugged. His hands were big and coarse and his hug was powerful. We sat down at the small table and I noticed a bottle that was already a quarter empty. Sev's strong eyes were glassy; clearly, he'd been hitting the bottle hard.

Sev smirked at me and said, "Let's go, mothafucka. What was so important you needed to talk to me off-line?"

Sev is not a guy to play games; he knows what he wants. But I couldn't just blurt out my reason for coming. "Wow, this place is rockin'. You come here a lot?"

"Let's go, asshole. What's on your mind? You got something to say, so why don't you?"

Wow! I'd thought I saw a smile before, but he wasn't fucking around. I was concerned so I asked, "Sev, you okay?" It's easy to get defensive when someone barks at you, but I meant the question because I was worried. He really had an edge. Sev hadn't gone after me like that since he sent me into the Tongue Room way back when.

Sev saw my concern and lightened up. "Yeah, I'm okay." He paused and said, "No, I'm not okay. I'm actually far from fuckin' okay. But that's not your problem."

"C'mon, Sev," I urged him. "What's the matter?"

Sev took a shot and chased it with a swig of beer. He looked at me and said, "You remember me telling you about Hector Pinto the other day on the phone?"

"Sure. How can I forget? You said he found a better job back in his home country, but Balducci's not letting anyone quit. Sev, did Balducci chop up Hector Pinto like he did George?"

"No, because when they chopped up George, Kosher World had to close for the day and that was bad business," Sev said. "Instead, Balducci had Hector skinned. He literally had his skin ripped off of his body like a carcass of beef at Kosher World. Then Balducci had some of his goons wheel Hector over on a long handcart and leave him to be discovered by people leaving the Locomotive Breath. Imagine the mob scene that caused."

"Holy fucking shit."

"Holy fucking shit is right," Sev echoed me with a sigh. "Everyone is walking around like zombies at Kosher World. This is no way to live. This guy Balducci is a worse tyrant than any dictator we tried to bring down when I was in Special Services. I hate that asshole. If there was anything I could do to bring that son of a bitch off his horse, I would do it."

I poured a shot of Jim Beam into Sev's shot glass. It looked like a good time to float a far-fetched idea in front of him.

Surprising Sev is not easy. Yet surprise him I did when I told him how I want Balducci more than he did. Bear in mind, up to that point Sev thought Balducci was someone I grew up around. Sev thought it was a matter of time before I became part of the corporation. That is until I asked him, "Remember telling me how Balducci sent Bino and Zog out to kill the DA before he could do major damage?"

"Yeah, when we were in the warehouse."

"Sev, that was my family. My father and my sister. I was 50 yards away and I saw Bino's big fucking red hair streaming from the open window. Every fucking day since you told me that story, I've been thinking how to get Balducci, and I know how I can do it."

It was a lot of information for someone to absorb, but Sev had seen and heard everything, so he wasn't completely shocked. He asked a few questions and soon we were on the same page. "Okay, let's hear this plan."

"Balducci's got something really big that's going down, and we can fuck it up big time. I'm not talking about just bringing Balducci down. I don't want to leave a vacuum where any asshole can jump in and take over. We need to take down the whole fucking corporation, and I'm telling you we can."

Sev asked, "We, like in you and me, are going to take down the corporation?"

"It starts with us, but we're going to need some help. Sev, you're the only one who can pull this off."

Sev looked at me for a full minute, then said, "Don't worry about my end. Do you know the consequences of what you're talking about? I know you want the results, but are you prepared for the consequences?"

"Hell, yeah. Sev, this is all I've been thinking about."

"I'm not asking what you're thinking," he said. "Are you prepared for the consequences? Me, I've been in Kosher World 25 years now. I was your age when I didn't think I had anything to lose. The thing is, you think you have nothing to lose, but there's always something to lose. Are you sure you are ready for the consequences?"

"Yeah, Sev, I'm telling you I was put on this planet to bust up the corporation and I'll do anything to do it."

"Good," Sev said with a stern nod. "I'm interested. Now tell me what you got."

I thought I would have to sell Sev on the idea; well, that part was easy. "We all know Balducci is more than a typical mob guy; he's way beyond that now. He's gone international and he's taking over things like factories and construction in places like Uganda, Croatia and even Vietnam."

"C'mon," Sev said. "How can he?"

"I've been spying from inside his own fuckin' house and I've seen some things that will blow you away. He's not doing it on his own, though, and that's where we have an opportunity."

"Who's he doing it with?"

I told him I wasn't sure. I'd come close to finding out a few times, but the trail went cold. There was some huge money backing Balducci, some big and powerful groups. "But here's our in. While Balducci is making a ton of money, this

group is taking a big chunk of the results and the group main-
tains control. Balducci feels he's moving mountains and giving
it away."

"Yeah, so?"

"Balducci don't like sharing his toys in the sandbox.
He's got something really big on tap, and this time it's just him
and one partner."

"Who's the partner?"

"I don't know yet, but it's someone who can open
doors."

"Don't you think finding that person is important?"

"Yes, but you didn't expect a perfect situation, did
you?"

Sev leans back in his chair a little and rubs his chin.
"Where's this sandbox?"

"A little place called Iran."

Sev grimaces. "That's a big mothafuckin' sandbox."

"He's betting it all on Iran," I said. "His partner seems
to have plenty of money, but more important, he's connected.
Balducci, on the other hand, is really reaching. This can put
him in a different stratosphere and he tastes it. It's not about
money anymore. He's leveraging every penny he has to go at
this."

"What exactly is this? What is he trying to do?"

"Him and his partner bought their way into factories
and road construction in Iran. They're dealing directly with the
Iranian government. Since 1979 when the Ayatollah took the
American hostages, there are all these sanctions on the United
States doing business with Iran. Balducci is going to fund and
start these entities and bring black-market American products
to Iran. Including weapons."

Sev's eyes opened a little wider than usual. "For real?"

I loved being able to surprise him. "Hey, let me ask
you this. Has Balducci been skimming more or less from Ko-

sher World lately?"

"Much more now than ever before," Sev answered, his eyes still wide. "It used to be like 15 percent he would take and sell directly. Lately it's been 50 percent."

"You see?" I crowed. "He needs the money now. He's taking half of all the merchandise. That's crazy risky, even for him."

"What else you got?" Sev asked.

"Balducci has been accumulating retail stores throughout New York. Then he fills them with products he skimmed from factories. It's not just from Industrial Road, but from factories all over the state. The ultimate profit margin, Balducci would buy for free, but then sell at full retail. Now he's dealing with whole shopping malls. The man personally has millions of dollars, enough for any man to retire with. But here's the thing: Balducci has pledged everything he's got to this new Iran idea. I mean everything. He's pledged the stores, the real estate and the malls. Balducci's balls are on the line. He's tied up tighter now than ever, and the beauty of that is, he is vulnerable."

"How so?" Sev asked.

"He can't borrow from banks and he needs money. This skimming business is strictly for the leg-breakers. Here's the major point: Balducci is relying on cash flow to keep him going right now. He's up to his eyes in debt, and the money he takes in is what keeps him going. But every time he thinks he is covered, back over in Iran there is another corrupt government official to bribe and another coincidental delay in work that makes this project further and further from completion. He's in too deep to bail and he needs more to support his position."

"I don't get it," Sev grumbled. "If he has tons of money, why do this shit at all?"

"Sev, this has nothing to do with money. Back in Remington Academy, Balducci was always rubbing elbows with all the white-bread dudes there. He wants to be white-bread. You can't turn back time and force your ancestors onto the Mayflower, but Balducci believes that if he reaches a certain level of power, even the white-bread world has to accept him."

Sev slumped over his whiskey bottle and concentrated on stirring the ice in his glass. "So how do we stop him?"

"Balducci doesn't have a margin of error now. He's got it all riding. We have to strike soon and we have to take back Industrial Road. Not only is Industrial Road Balducci's primary income now, but it's also the heart of his credibility. We stop him here, we can stop it all."

This idea began to penetrate Sev's body. He leaned back in his chair again, closed his eyes and raised his chin. Then Sev's eyes opened and he grinned. I saw the whites of Sev's eyes pushing away the haze of whiskey. This past year, Sev, the natural leader of men with the heart of a winner, took a back seat. Sev was a spectator as his friends were being browbeaten and demoralized. George and Hector were whacked and put on display in the most horrid attempts to intimidate and control. It was killing Sev, but now I had put some hope back into Sev's body. He didn't know shit about my plan yet, but the mere possibility of fighting back had resurrected Sev.

We talked for hours. We drank, we listened to blues music and we planned our attack. Sev had a whole different perspective on things and brought up ideas that I wouldn't dream of. Sev wanted to talk to his old boy Curtis, the guy dressed like a cop who pulled me out of the last Industrial Road bout. Sev thought Curtis would jump on the idea. "He's supposed to be stopping guys like Balducci anyway. If he breaks this open, it could be a big deal for Curtis."

"But he didn't do any of this."

Sev laughed. "Son, when he gets done back-dating the records, this plan will have been in motion for six years. Believe me, government guys know how to take credit for shit. Is that something you care about?"

"I don't." I really didn't give a rat's ass who took credit, especially since I knew that having Curtis on board would increase the chances of my plan's success.

Before 10 a.m. Sev had spoken with Curtis and got him involved. "Just like that, he's in?" I asked Sev over the phone.

Sev snorted, annoyed by the question. "Did you doubt what I said?"

"No, but I'm surprised he's willing to get involved, no strings attached."

"There may be a string."

"Well, what does Curtis want from us?"

"He didn't say."

"Okay then, what *did* he say?"

Sev told me that Curtis could dump a lot of resources on our plan and thought we could get the job done. "But he needs something from us."

"What? What does he need from us?"

"Christ! I told you, he wouldn't say. He said he needs something from us when we take Balducci down, but he wants us to concentrate on the task at hand for now."

"Sev, isn't that weird?"

"You think that's weird? Shit, do you see who we are involved with?"

"Yeah, good point," I agreed. "We can't avoid committing to Curtis?"

"It's a deal breaker. If you don't want to deal with Curtis, then fuck it. He'll stay out of the way and watch from the sidelines."

I paused and thought about that idea. "You trust him?"

"Yeah, I trust him."

"That's good enough for me." Besides, what were the

odds I'd be alive when this was over anyway? "Okay, I'm ready to go."

"Good. I'll tell Curtis."

I didn't know what Curtis wanted from me or what corrupt idea he had for the remains of the Balducci dynasty, but I figured I'd jump off that bridge when I got there. First, I'd fuck up Balducci, and then I'd worry about Curtis. I was almost hoping I'd eat a bullet during the process so I wouldn't have to worry about the consequences.

CHAPTER 25

That conversation took place two months ago, and now NY State University is beginning to emerge from hibernation. It's warmer, and the student body has shed overcoats and ski parkas for windbreakers and Gorilla sweatshirts. Albany is no longer gray from the winter, and daffodils and crocuses are splashing color around the campus. It's a fun time at school as the spring semester winds down. There are outdoor events with music and flowing kegs. Sure, there are some annoying final exams to take, but we normally manage to fit them in the schedule as well.

Unfortunately, I won't be drinking from those kegs, listening to that music or for that matter, taking those final exams. It's hard to believe that, after all I've been able to juggle, I won't be able to get my degree. I'm standing in the kitchen of my apartment with Rocky when I tell her this. I say that it's a temporary detour and that I'll be back in the fall to finish my last semester. It's not like I'm lying, because it's not completely out of the question, but realistically, if I'm still on this planet, I won't be the same person. It will be hard to jump back into the frat scene after killing Balducci. I think we both know that but aren't saying it. She's worried, and while we were all putting on a nice act before, now the guard is down.

Rocky faces me, slides her hands around my waist and rests her thumbs on the back two belt loops on my jeans. She tugs down and draws me closer. "You know," she says, "you can wait a few more weeks. Why not just finish your exams?"

"Baby, I haven't been to class in weeks," I answer.

"I'll write your teachers a note."

"Oh, I can just see that note: 'Please excuse Kevin because he has to kill Mr. Balducci.'"

Rocky releases my belt loops and says, "Seriously, just finish school first. I know your father would have wanted that."

Normally, I would consider that a low blow, but I know she's concerned and I know she's reaching for straws. "C'mon, Rocky, you know I have to do this."

"But why now?"

"Baby, the timing is out of my hands. There are lots of people involved now."

"I can't just sit here and wait for you. I want to go, too. I can help."

"No way, Rocky. We've been through this before. If I thought you were in danger, it would fuck up my thinking. You're the best thing that's ever happened to me. You're the reason I'm coming back. But you know I have to do this. We both knew this day would come eventually." I'm staring at Rocky and trying not to be weird, but I want to remember every feature of her face. Damn, she's the best.

All the chips are on the table, and the clandestine crap is done. Fewer than 150 workers show up at Kosher World today, the third day of our job action. The first two days were quiet, but the place is heading toward panic. Throughout the last few months Sev tapped all the guys he can trust and told them what was going down. Considering how ruthless Balducci can be, it's asking a lot. He couldn't let everyone in on this because some guys, like Bino, would inevitably run and tell Balducci. This is the ultimate union job action and we need to use stealth for full impact. Sev estimates the level of participation in his job action would be 100 percent, and damn if he isn't right. When Sev tells you to work, you work. I guess when Sev tells you, 'Stay away and get out of town,' you evaporate. I can't think of a single person we tapped who showed up against Sev's instruction.

These days, when union guys unleash a job action, they are fighting for more pay or better benefits. Back in the day when unions were forming, the workers were fighting for basic quality of life and dignity. That's what we got here and that's why this will work. It has to. Hector Pinto just wanted to go back home and make a better life for himself and look what happened. I hate Balducci for what he did to my family, but these Kosher World workers and everyone else on Industrial Road are looking to take back a freedom that Balducci refuses to relinquish.

Still, after today, we are vulnerable. There is no way the source of this disruption, meaning Sev and I, is going to stay secret. Thousands of people involved, and some have much less fortitude than others, especially given the way Balducci's people ask questions. Balducci will know Sev and I are trying to take him down.

Right now, Industrial Road is at a standstill. One hundred and fifty people can barely turn the lights on. How can you make the pastrami and hot dogs if you can't unload the beef from the trucks?

Holy shit, look at all the fucking trucks backed up by the loading docks! These 50 trucks full of beef will be completely worthless. It's real pile-on time for Balducci. Fifty truckloads of beef in front of Kosher World, a hundred tankers of dairy product lined up outside Moon Beam Cheese, and other products all over Industrial Road factories looking to get processed. The place is rendered useless just when Balducci is trying to parlay everything he has into Iran. The Iranian public officials waiting for bribe money will have a long wait. Fuckin' Balducci is wound up so tight this is sure to give him an aneurism.

Sev and I are holed up at the Astoria Diner nearby. Sev is getting updates from the few people he planted. Sev told

them to show up at Kosher World and some of the other factories and act as if they didn't know anything. So far, the reports
are encouraging. Not only is Balducci losing revenue but his
communications skills are taking a holiday as well. He is barking orders and screaming in tirades so laden with spit he could
fill the Hudson River. What's adding to Balducci's well-earned
paranoia is that even his most loyal captains aren't around. Sev
had earlier earmarked those scumbags so Curtis and his special
service guys could creatively detain them. I'm sure Balducci
has no idea who has abandoned him. For sport, we let Bino get
through, and that dim-bulb fuck is all the seasoned counseling
Balducci can muster.

Businesses throughout the area are looking for product
to no avail. Kosher delis in Brooklyn are looking for pastrami,
hot dogs and tongue, department stores in Ohio are depleted of
cowboy boot inventory and dairy cases wait for Moon Beam
Cheeses from Industrial Road. Phones are ringing unanswered,
TV crews are sending coverage and politicians are saying they
will intervene in this mysterious labor crisis. I ask Sev how
long we have until Balducci knows he and I are involved.

"He knows by now. He probably cut someone's fingers
off by now to find out. But make no mistake; he knows by
now."

The thought of some innocent guy getting his fingers
cut off because of our plan bothers me and makes me feel a
little queasy. I keep reminding myself that this has to be done.
I rationalize to myself that whoever got his fingers cut off may
have gotten something else cut off eventually if we didn't fight
back now.

My cell phone rings and the caller ID reads Balducci.
Jimmy. I show the phone to Sev and he doesn't react. By the
fourth ring he says, "Might as well answer it."

"Hello," I say. I hold the phone up in the air so Sev can
hear as well.

Balducci screams, "You little prick! Are you going to play fucking games with me? With me! You going to fuck with Jimmy Balducci, you little shit? I saved your ass when Zog was suffocating you. I looked after you all those years at Remington Academy. I made my home open to you. My home! C'mon, say it to me. Let me hear it with my own ears that you are doing this to me, you fuckin' Judas."

Sev wants me to hang up. He looks at me and makes a slashing motion across his throat. I shrug my shoulders, but Sev frantically slashes his throat with his finger. So while Balducci continues to spew venom, I snap my cell phone closed. While I have waited so long to put this in motion, hearing Balducci go at me like that rattles me. There is a knot tightening in my stomach. There's no backing down now.

CHAPTER 26

Still shaking from Balducci's rants, I get hold of Carey
and tell him to drop everything and grab Loot and Rocky, then
get my mother and take everyone someplace safe. I couldn't
get hold of Rocky at first but she finally texted me that she was
leaving. That was a relief.

I need to get this party moving. "Sev, we're four days
deep into this job action. Let's bring in Petro now."

Sev is quietly eating his afternoon pancakes at our
H.Q., the Astoria Diner. "Kids today, always in such a hurry."

This guy is eating pancakes and I can hardly breathe.
The knot in my stomach has grown to a full-blown roadblock.
"Why wait when it's working so well?"

"Kevin, you're too fuckin' jumpy. We have a siege
going here. Things look good now, but this is where variables
start to rear their ugly faces."

"What do you mean?"

"I mean, keep some cards up your sleeve. If we're
doing this right, Balducci is going to panic. He will unload
everything he has. And I want to know what he has before I
deploy my resources. Right now, the ball is in his court. Let's
see the variables."

"Sev, this is killing me sitting here."

"So get the fuck out. Your jumpy ass isn't doing anyone here any good."

"Thanks a lot," I mutter.

"I'm not saying anything to insult you. I'm pointing
something out. You ain't being productive here. Go out for a
while."

"Go where?"

"I don't give a shit, but we got at least two more days of this labor action and I'm worried you're going to boil over. I don't want you to influence me to do something too soon, so go take a nature hike and come back tomorrow."

My cell phone starts vibrating and while I'm relieved the caller ID doesn't say Balducci, nothing could have prepared me for what it does read: C.W. I'm getting a call from C.W. Wellington. Holy shit! I was so wrapped up in my crap today, this could have been the first day I didn't think of her, but here she is, calling me.

I flip open the cell phone and as naturally as possible under the circumstances I say, "Hello."

The unmistakable and incredibly well-bred voice says, "Hello, stranger."

I feign confusion and answer, "Who's this?" Like I would ever not recognize that voice.

"It's someone who is intimately connected to a washing machine in Nevis."

I take a deep breath and try to maintain my composure. "It's been a long time, C.W."

"Too long, Kevin. I miss you. Sorry for calling you out of the blue, but I've been thinking about you more and more lately."

I glance at Sev and he gives me a concerned look. I cover the phone and explain that I'm talking to an old girl-friend. He rolls his eyes and sticks a massive forkful of maple-drenched pancakes into his mouth. I stop covering the mouth-piece and say, "So, er, how are you?" Can you believe how fuckin' smooth I am?

C.W. answers, "Things have been going well, but I was hoping we could speak soon. Are you ever in New York?"

"I'm here now," I answer.

"Don't you have finals?"

"Yeah, but I needed to come home for awhile," I answer.

"Oh, me too. I can't study at school, there are so many distractions. I'm locking myself up at home." After a brief, awkward pause, C.W. continues. "Let's take a break together. Could you meet me at Piping Rock?"

"I'm not sure that's a great idea."

"Oh Kevin, it's 80 degrees and sunny. Let's have a Southside on the beach and catch up for a little while. Please? what harm would it do?"

I'm thinking to myself, What harm? Does she have any idea how much her shit hurts? Maybe I can meet her for a few drinks, "Let me check on something." I cover up the phone and look at Sev who is 90 percent done vacuuming the pancakes into his mouth. "Do you think that I can…?"

"Kevin," Sev interrupts, "get the fuck out of here. Go chase a little tail for a while. It'll be good for you and I guarantee it will be good for me."

I tell C.W. that I'll meet her at the beach in an hour. The beach at Piping Rock Country Club. Holy shit, I can't believe I'm meeting C.W. there again.

"Good. See you then, Kevin."

I close the phone and give Sev one last chance to keep me here. He laughs and says, "Get the fuck out." Then he adds, "I'm going to ask Curtis to have a guy or two trail you, so don't get freaked out. You never know where Balducci's guys might be."

The beach at Piping Rock is rough with broken shells. The tide is rolling back, and a breeze coming off Long Island Sound cools the temperature to near perfect. I spot C.W. from 50 feet away. The warm weather has given her the opportunity to wear what I'm sure is a spanking-new sundress. I swear someone made that dress specifically with her in mind. It's so her. It's dark purple, not loud but tight and as sexy as hell.

Shit, and those legs! Christ, her legs are so long and lean. The dress stops well above her knees, and I can't believe that's an accident.

I lock into her green eyes. The 50 feet become 20 feet and then she's here. Shit, she's gotten better looking. I was hoping she got tagged with the freshman 15 but that's not the case. She's stunning. The breeze is whipping her hair around, and it looks as if it's moving with a purpose of its own. "Hello, stranger."

"I'm so happy you're here, Kevin." She leans over and gives me a kiss on the cheek. Now, I don't mean to over-analyze anything, but she kisses me on the cheek and not my lips. Then again, I swear she keeps her mouth on my cheek an extra-long time. I don't think I'm imagining that. How good she smells when she's close to me! The Long Island Sound smells like salt and seaweed, yet when C.W. is near me, I smell a special sweetness. Not perfume, mind you, or is it? It's not overbearing; I smell it just slightly over the scent of the beach. I don't know if they can sell this in a bottle or if someone has to be born with it, but that's what I smell.

C.W. shakes her head playfully. "Kevin, you want to walk along the beach for a little while?"

I nod. The beach is extra long because the tide is out. I take off my sneakers and she takes off her sandals. We begin walking on the area of the beach that's on the cusp of dry and wet.

"Kevin, do you ever think about me?"

Do I ever think about her? Every fuckin' day. "Yeah, sure, there are times I think about some of the stuff we used to do." There is an awkward pause, our first. I guess I'm sup-posed to say something. "How's your little sister?"

"Which one? Missy? She's fine. Just the other day she admitted she was spying on us that night in Nevis on top of the washing machine."

"No way!" I moan. I know I'm blushing. "I'm surprised she didn't tell your father. Buster would have beat me with a stick."

"She said it was tempting, but she kept it to herself. She knew Daddy would explode. Luckily she idolized me at the time."

We continue our walk along the beach and make small talk. It feels good remembering that brief time when I was happy. C.W. stops walking and asks bluntly, "Kevin, are you seeing anyone now?"

I pause, take a breath and say, "Yeah, I am."

"Of course you are. You're the most real person I know, and that's why I've been thinking about you lately. Some girl realized how great you are while I was too caught up in what wasn't important. There are so many jerks and pretenders around, just the opposite of you. You never played games."

I don't know how to respond to this but I try. "Wow, it looks like you're coming off a tough relationship. Did somebody hurt you?"

"No, it's nothing like that. I just seem to put myself in a position to be around people who want to out-impress the next person. No one's satisfied, no one's rooting for anyone else, no one's nice and no one's real. We insulate ourselves with private schools, private summer camp, and then we go to these liberal arts colleges and we meet the same damn kind of people. And I keep thinking of the one person I think is real."

"I don't know, C.W., you might be romanticizing my background. Believe me, growing up in Hempstead and working through college hasn't been easy. I've got a lot of baggage."

"Maybe, but at the end of the day, you value a person for who they are, not all this bullshit of what Wall Street firm he's working for or which celebrity he hung out with at which club. If you find a really great person who's not affected by that garbage, you should hold on. You should hold on to him and never let go." C.W. looks intently at my eyes. Those bold green eyes. She slips her hands around my neck, rests her forearms on my shoulders and says, "Please, Kevin, tell me it's not too late."

I shouldn't pause, but I do. Then I say the right thing: "It is too late." But I shouldn't have paused. When things were good with C.W. and me, they were awesome. It hurt when she moved on, but people do.

"Kevin, just remember what we had and think about what we could have." With that she moves into me and initiates a passionate kiss. My senses are ambushed, then overwhelmed. Her beautiful skin, her silky smell and the most sensuous mouth imaginable are all ganging up on me. Just when I am about to lose control I remember Rocky's amber hair and the sexy valley that runs up her back. But what if I just did this once, you know, to get C.W. out of my system? What's the harm in that? The harm in that is Rocky finally has gotten to trust someone and I'm going to fuck that up. Holy shit, what is wrong with me?

I pull away from C.W. and say sternly, "Look, I can't do this."

She moves closer, gently smiles and says, "Yes, you can. I think if you give this a shot you might enjoy it."

"It's not that. I'm not looking to enjoy it. I can't do this." I can't imagine anyone has ever said no to C.W. It seems impossible.

But C.W. is persistent. She moves closer and says, "We were born to be together. You know it and I know it."

"Yeah, I used to think so, but that's not true."

"I'm so sorry for everything that happened. Please, let's get past it."

"C.W., I got to go. I'm sorry, but this isn't right." I

turn and go. I try to break into a light jog and look cool, but I know I look like a dork running on the sand. I'm determined to not look back because if I do look, I might change my mind.

Finally I reach the Saab. I keep rehashing what just happened. I'm supposed to be kicking myself. I've been thinking of C.W. every day for years, and now I get my opportunity to get her back and I throw it away. Damn, it feels good. That big-ass monkey is off my back. I'm laughing to myself that I just dusted C.W. fuckin' Wellington. The last time that happened was probably...never.

CHAPTER 27

Sev moves our mobile HQ from the Astoria Diner to the Executive Diner in Elmont. One would think Sev could overdose on pancakes, but one would be wrong. You would think that maybe he'd want to rotate some waffles in the mix, but it's going to be pancakes.

We still haven't sent Petro in to take over Industrial Road; the wait is killing me. The only thing mitigating my anxiety is thinking about C.W. Yep, I guess for a little while I'll still think of her, but it's different now. That chapter is closed. I don't feel like I have to be running with any group, I don't need to chase any money crowd. I found the right place to be. I just need to get Balducci out of the way.

While this wait is challenging for me, it's really gnawing at Petro. He is chomping at the bit to storm Industrial Road. While at the diner with Sev, Petro calls me and says, "C'mon, Kevin, let me talk to Sev. It's time to go in."

"I can't do it, Petro. You know the rules. You go through me and only me."

"This is fucked up. Are you guys going around me?"

"Petro, what the fuck are you talking about? All I've ever done is deliver for you. I've earned hundreds of thousands of dollars for you, let you know Balducci was after you and came up with this idea for you; why would we leave you out now?"

"But why is it taking so long?"

"Sev knows what he's doing. The time has to be right."

"Well, what if I don't want to wait? What if I just move in?"

"You'll lose," I tell him calmly, as if I were talking to

one of Luke's customers. "If you were ever going to trust me on anything, understand this; you would lose. If we stay cool, we'll all win. There's so much upside here for you and everyone else. You've waited years for this opportunity. What's a couple more days? Let's stay cool, Petro, let's all win."

There's a slight pause and some rough breathing. Then Petro says, "Okay, Kevin, I hear you. I'll sit tight. Call me later when you know more."

Petro hangs up and I close my cell phone as well. Sev, who heard the whole conversation, stops slurping pancakes and says, "Nice job, way to diffuse him."

"Thanks, but I'm not so sure I can keep him at bay much longer. This guy is a wild card."

Sev says, "You want any pancakes?"

Two days and what seems like 400 stacks of pancakes later, we move from the Executive Diner in Elmont to the All-Star Diner in Rosedale. When I think the tension can't get any worse, I get a call on my cell phone. The caller ID says Rocky. She's not supposed to call, but still I can't help but appreciate that she does. I open the cell and say, "Hey, baby."

A deep male voice on the other end of the line says, "Fuck you, asshole."

Stunned, I stammer, "Who...who's this?"

"Never mind who this is. Get your ass up and excuse yourself from wherever you are if you want to see this bitch alive. Be very careful, college boy. Rocky never got your text to get out of Dodge. That was me who texted you on her phone. Now get up and move. If anyone hears this conversation, I'll chop her up like an onion."

That cocksucker Bino has Rocky. I excuse myself and because of Bino's threat, tell Sev that my ex-girlfriend is calling again.

He rolls his eyes and pours some syrup on the latest

stack. I walk outside the diner and say into the phone, "Bino you are so fucked up. You have no idea how bad this is going to turn out."

"Shut the fuck up before I start dick-whipping her. You did this, not me. You're the one ruining everything. What did ya think? That we're just going to sit here?"

"Bino, be smart. No one's looking for you. You can fly under the radar and get a good chunk of what's around after the dust settles."

"Fuck you, Davenport. How 'bout this for a deal? You get your ass over to Kosher World by 9 p.m. Alone. Right now, no one has touched this bitch, but if we even think you told someone about this meeting, I'll ram my dick up her ass so far she'll be coughing up my balls. How's that sound?"

"Bino, I'll come meet you. I won't tell anyone I'm coming, but if you do anything to her, I will smother you in pain before I kill you."

"Hey, asshole, did you forget who's holding the cards now?"

"Let me speak to her."

"Sure. You're hoping I just stole her cell phone and she's at home watching Oprah. Yeah, I got her cell phone and the rest of the package. I got all the buttons here I could ever dream of pushing."

Rocky's choked-up voice comes through. "Kevin?"

I try to maintain my cool; I don't want to spook her any more than necessary. "Baby, are you okay? Did they do anything to you?"

"No, not yet, but they keep threatening."

Bino grabs the phone back and says, "That's enough. You better get your ass over here tonight and don't fuck around."

"Where am I meeting you?"

"The Tongue Room. One more thing. Call the fucking

phone company and have all your calls forwarded to Rocky's
cell phone. I don't want anyone getting hold of you. If you're
not here by nine, she's my sex slave." Bino hangs up.

My head goes fuzzy. Panic overwhelms me. Anything
but this. Rocky is the only thing that matters. How can this be
happening? What do I do? I'll do the same to them. I'll grab
Balducci's kid Richie. I'll fuck him up. I'll grab Balducci's
wife. Yeah, I'll fuckin' grab both of them. Shit, shit, SHIT!
That's not going to work. There's no way Balducci didn't think
of that. Dealing with all that crap in Queens, I never thought
he would make a connection to Rocky way up in Albany.
Anyone that matters to Balduucci will be out of reach. I should
have been smarter. Damn, my head's so fuzzy. I've never felt
this kind of anxiety before.

I can't lose Rocky; she's everything to me. I wish I
could call this whole thing off now. I'll do anything to get
Rocky back.

I have to meet these guys alone. I can't tell Sev or
Curtis; they're not going to stop the Industrial Road takeover
because of Rocky. It's too far along. Balducci needs me so he
can figure out what he's dealing with. Then he'll kill me. As
long as I can get Rocky out, I can live with that trade. I never
thought I would ever feel this way. Stopping Balducci meant
everything until I was confronted with losing Rocky. I be-
lieved I would risk everything and accept all the consequences.
But I can't.

The Kosher World lights are low and my footsteps echo
as I walk. There was never an opportunity to hear an echo before. The place used to run 24/7, pumping out hot dogs, corned
beef and pastrami at warp speed. Now there are no machines
grinding, no orders being bellowed and no loud, lame excuses
being offered. It feels more like a museum than the hectic factory I had once known.

Every step I take toward the Tongue Room is scarier than the last. I feel like at any time, or at any moment, I'll take a bat to the skull or a meat pick to the heart. Balducci has thugs at the entrances, but nothing inside so far. I can only speculate that he wants as few witnesses as possible. I have no regrets about coming here alone. Sev's head is different now; he and Curtis are all military. They are in a different country, fighting a corrupt government. If Rocky is killed, they will view her death as nothing more than unfortunate collateral damage.

I pass the pastrami room and, although I'm trying to be cool and calm, my sneakers screech against the black-and-white tile floor. The lights are on in the Tongue Room. I walk slowly, waiting for something to happen, but they seem to be letting me get closer. Two dudes wearing black pants and black shirts flank the Tongue Room door. My breathing feels weird. I need to stay cool if I've got any shot here.

The two guys stiffen. I recognize one of them as Butch Bombart, the first guy I beat in the Industrial Road bouts. Great, I'm sure he'll be a load of laughs. They motion for me to stop. Butch frisks me. Nothing in my pockets or sides, but unfortunately he notices the knife I had desperately tucked into my sock.

Inside the room, Bombart shows the knife to Balducci. Balducci is stone-faced. He shakes his head in disappointment. He steps to the side and reveals Rocky. She isn't tied up, but Bino has a gun to her head. Rocky's eyes are bloodshot, as red as her auburn hair. She's been crying non-stop, that much is clear, and it's breaking my heart.

I have a gut-wrenching flash of insight: Rocky's not the bait; I am. Rocky is merely the bait to get the bait. I was thinking Balducci was going to pump me for information and then kill me. Now I've changed my mind. For some reason, he must think Sev values me. He thinks Sev will call off the

Industrial Road takeover to get my hide back. Of course, there is no fucking way Sev will trade me to stop this mission; that was understood from the beginning. When this twisted fuck figures out there's no trade, he's going to torture the shit out of Rocky and me.

I'm thinking of George's head in the locker and Hector being skinned alive and I know I can't let that happen here. If I get him to kill us fast, I might be able to save Rocky from horrible pain. The result is the same, but I may have some control over the method. If I go hard at Balducci, they'll have no choice but to kill me.

I'm up against Butch Bombart, another goon I never saw before, Bino and Balducci. I'm sure they all have guns, but only Bino is showing his. Here's the thing: I'm probably a few seconds away from getting my ribs broken or legs smashed. They're going to render me useless. When that happens, they control the whole agenda. They want me alive, that much is clear. I've been a sitting duck the whole time I was on the Kosher World premises, so they want me alive…but ineffective.

If I get to Balducci, maybe get to his throat, they may shoot me. I have to be on Balducci hard and fast. I fought Butch Bombart, worked with Bino and can't imagine this other goon is getting much action at the Mensa meetings. If I'm on top of Balducci, then Bino will have to move his gun off Rocky. If I can get at him efficiently enough, maybe, just maybe, Rocky can make a run for it. I can scare them enough to kill me, but it's a crapshoot with Rocky.

The endgame looks bad; I hate to admit it, but that's an honest overview. I'm accepting that I'm dead and I'm getting Rocky killed as well. Balducci doesn't leave loose ends. As shitty as it sounds, if I do nothing, we're both goners the slow, hard way; if I act, maybe she dies fast, but maybe she has a shot to get out of here in whatever chaos I can cause.

I calmly say, "Jimmy, before you do anything crazy, I think I have a solution here." I continue to spew some bullshit as tranquilly as possible. It's so absurd that even I can't fathom what I am saying. Then I sprint full speed toward Balducci and, son of a bitch, I make it to him. I knock him over and have him by the throat. I've got a grip on his neck that would asphyxiate an elephant. Balducci, being management, isn't much of a fighter. I roll him over on the ground, trying to make myself a moving target and tougher to shoot at, all the time, squeezing his throat. What a sight this must be. Maybe I can kill him before they shoot me.

Bino is screaming, "Shoot the prick! Don't let him hurt Jimmy."

Bombart shouts, "You got a gun, motherfucker. You shoot him. What if I miss and hit Jimmy?"

Balducci is turning purple and these assholes are involved in some Roe vs. Wade debate. Finally they realize they better not shoot, and they try to break us up, but I keep rolling Balducci. They start punching me but hit him a few times by mistake also. I swear I can kill him if they give me a few more minutes.

Bombart jumps on Balducci and me. It's a smart move, and now I'm no longer a moving target. Bino whips at my head with his gun handle and the other goon works on my hands and loosens my grip on Balducci's throat. I pop up and scream to Rocky, "Run, make a run for it!" The other three guys are attending to their boss.

Rocky is confused. She doesn't know I made this distraction for her. She probably wants to help me, but all I want is for her to get the fuck out of here. I begin to run toward her. Balducci motions to the other guys to stop me. Bino figures it out first and screams, "Davenport, you have two seconds to freeze." Which, of course, I'm not going to do.

Canisters of smoke roll into the Tongue Room and I

hear footsteps running all about me. I turn to Rocky and holler again, "Run, baby, run." Smoke is covering our feet and the fog is rising. I can still see the doorway of the Tongue Room. Before I can make my exit, I hear it first. Shit, it's so loud echoing against all the stainless steel tables that occupy the Tongue Room. Crack-crack. The sound ringing and echoing causes almost as much pain as the impact of the bullet into my flesh.

I feel pain radiating up my left side. Damn; I've been hit. "Rocky, you have to run. I'll catch up with you later. Please baby, run."

"I can't," she pleads.

"You have to," I insist. I nudge her toward the door.

The floor of the room is filling with smoke from the canisters; what must be Curtis' Special Service guys start coming in. Bino waves his gun menacingly and Sev empties one right in the middle of his skull. Brain and blood spray all over Bino's face. He drops hard to his knees and freezes there for a moment. Finally the crimson face tilts toward the floor and drops. His scrambled brains and bloody face disappear into the rising smoke, and I hear the loud thud of that pale fuck's lifeless body hitting the floor. The world has just lost a wonderful human being.

I reach down and feel my side above my left hip. The pain is too much. I look at my hand; it's covered with blood. My head hurts from the crack-crack still bouncing around in my skull.

I'm practically coughing my throat out from the smoke. The room is now filling with special service guys. I can hear the footsteps and I can see the figures in their gas masks and military equipment. I'm coughing too much to concentrate and my head is getting light. I need to get out of here.

Somehow I stagger out of Kosher World and out onto the street. I'm hoping I can catch my breath now that I've escaped the smoke. But it's hard; my side hurts and I can't lose the echoing in my head, crack-crack.

If I stay here, I could bleed to death. I need to get help. The streets are dark, much darker than usual. I'm disoriented, and I need to find a street that I know.

What if I can't make it? Will I bleed to death? Where the hell is Rocky? Did Sev and Curtis take out the streetlights? Is that why it's so fucking dark? I don't hear any voices. Where the fuck am I? I turn around to see the factory, but I must have wandered further than I thought. Man, am I fucked up or what?

I see some lights. I should be able to reach them and get some help, but it's a struggle for me to stay focused. If I black out I'm going to be in trouble. I want to stop and lie down for a while and get some strength back, but I know better. If I pass out over here, there's a good shot it'll be morning until someone notices me. That could be all she wrote. I'll just stay tough and keep moving forward.

Did I pass out? I started this whole shit-show at 9 p.m. but it feels like it's three in the morning. I've been on these streets before but they never seemed so dark and empty. I've got to keep focused on those colored lights in the distance. They get closer. I hear music. When I see the lights clearly, I recognize them. They are the neon signs for the various beers served at the Locomotive Breath.

The music is loud now, practically pulsating through the street. Over it I hear the sounds of wild cheering. I check my bloody side. I don't want to cause any commotion coming in all messy, but I think I might need a doctor.

As I swing open the door, I see a crowd of people around a makeshift stage. Harv Hatch is here, with his scraggly beard and beer belly, one arm around Little Steven Van Zandt, and the other arm around his idol, Bruce Springsteen.

The whole fuckin' E Street Band is here, singing "Tenth Avenue Freezeout."

I feel a tug at my shoulder as someone grabs me and turns me around. The yank causes my side to burn with pain. I close my eyes, grit my teeth and try to regain my composure. When I open my eyes, I see the unmistakable cornrows of Loot Hightower and Carey's bright grin. Carey screams over the music, "Can you believe this?"

What the fuck is going on?" I demand.

Loot interjects, "What's going on? Only the greatest party in history! We're celebrating your victory."

I grimace from the pain of the wound. "Huh? Someone explain what's going on. Is that really Bruce Springsteen up there?"

Loot screams over the music, "Yeah, that's Springsteen."

Whoa, in this dive? "Guys, I got to find Rocky. You know where she is?"

"Yeah," Carey says, "she's here, and she's been looking for you. Look, there she is." He points to the bar. I think I catch a glimpse of her, but then she's gone. The music's getting louder and the drums are pounding like thunder. Pain darts through my whole body and ricochets around inside my skull. The drumbeats remind me of the gunshot, crack-crack. I show Carey my wound and he gives me something called a Euphoria Martini and explains it's more than a drink. It's bright blue in a triangular blue glass. When I down it, the pain instantly dissolves.

There are tons of people around now, laughing and having a great time. I feel frustrated because I can't find her. "Let's find Rocky and then find a doctor to look at my side."

"Are you sure you want to go?" Loot asks seriously. "This is unreal and you're doing okay now."

"I guess I can stay for a while," I answer. "But let's

find Rocky."

"Sure, sure, let's go, she's probably in the back."

As we start walking, I see plenty of people I don't know but plenty that I do know. There are people here from Spring Valley Lakes, and damn if that guy over there wasn't on my Little League team back in the day when everything was good in Manhasset. People are waving at me, shaking my hand and hugging me.

We enter the back room. It's quieter here, but I wouldn't call it quiet. I can still hear the drums pounding. As I walk deeper into the back room, I am trying to spot Rocky's auburn hair amidst all the heads swaying to the music. I think I see her in the distance but I'm not sure; people are dancing around, blocking my line of sight. This back room is darker than the rest of the place, and it keeps getting darker as we walk on.

As we get close to the bar, I see two guys laughing and having a rowdy conversation. When they see me, they courteously move over in mid-story and yield some real estate so I can get up to the bar. I nod my thanks to one guy and immediately his face surprises me. He looks just like Hector Pinto. The problem is, Hector Pinto was skinned alive a few months ago. He notices my surprised look and says, "If I didn't cut my finger off, way back when I was supposed to fight, you may never have been in an Industrial Road bout. Think about it. If it weren't for me, you might never have taken a stand against Balducci. It's clear, I was the beginning of the whole thing."

I don't know what to say to this Hector look-alike. He's waiting for an answer and repeats, "It's clear."

I still don't know how to respond. I look at Carey and Loot but they just shrug.

The large guy next to him says, "You?" He shakes his head, but his head seems unsteady. "Shit, I was the first one to stand up to Balducci, that's clear. I got caught talking to the police, but I had the balls to try to do something. That's where it started. That's the only thing that's clear!"

Suddenly I recognize the guy's hairy fuckin' ears. "Holy crap, George, what are you doing here?"

"Drinking a shit-load of Euphoria Martinis, that's clear!" George and Hector high-five each other and start laughing. Loot and Carey both join in and soon everyone is laughing, except me.

George turns to Loot and says, "What's up with your buddy? Is he okay?"

Loot asks me what's wrong. I look at Carey and Loot and I'm so shocked that I can hardly get the words out. "Guys…these two dudes…died a while ago."

Loot and Carey begin laughing, and the George and Hector look-alikes join in. "Right!" George shouts. "We're dead! Oh yeah, that's clear!"

Loot, Carey, Hector and George are soon laughing out of control. What the fuck is so funny? What the shit is happening? Clear? This is anything but clear. All around us, people are laughing. I'd like to join in but my side is hurting again. My head is throbbing, and I can hear that crack-crack echoing in my skull. All the familiar faces are laughing, all laughing at me. Everyone except Rocky and my father. They are at the bar as well. Their faces are expressionless, their gaze fixed on my face. I look back and forth between them. I am locked into Rocky's eyes. Then I am locked into my father's eyes. I see tears streaming down Rocky's face. Aw, Rocky, don't cry….

I hear one word in the background: "Clear!" Again I hear it: "Clear."

I recognize the smell of rubbing alcohol. I feel my eyes flutter open and close. There's too much light and too much pain to keep them open for long. In between flutters I see someone holding white paddles. I see his eyes, but the surgical mask is covering the rest of his face. I hear him screaming to the others, "I got something. C'mon, people, get the 12-lead EKG. Give me some numbers."

I can't keep my eyes open.

CHAPTER 28

Sev and Curtis. I can't keep my eyes open. Sev and Curtis. Again, I can't keep my eyes open. I hear them talking. I hear the words but it's too damn much work to open my eyes. The first words I can make out are, "It'll be any minute now."

I feel my eyelids flutter and I see the doctor. I see Sev and Curtis. The doctor asks, "Can you hear me?" I nod. "Can you talk?"

"Yeah." My answer unintentionally comes out like a whisper.

"Kevin, I'm Doctor Reddy. You are in a hospital. You are recovering from a gunshot wound. Do you understand everything I am telling you?"

"Yes." I try to say it louder than a whisper. A nurse offers me a straw so that I can sip some ice water. It stings going down my dry throat. After several minutes of staring at the ceiling, I notice the faces in the room. Sev and Curtis. I look at Sev and say, "Man, I can use an aspirin."

"Take it easy for a few minutes. Then we'll talk," Sev answers.

As the haze lifts, the pain in my side rises. Sev tells me that I have been in the hospital for about two weeks.

"Get the fuck out of here!"

"You've been in bad shape, Kevin," he says. "Shit, you were flat-lining, man."

"For real?"

"Yeah, it was touch and go for a while. Once we had you back, the doctor thought you'd have the best shot to recover in a drug-induced coma. But I'm telling you, we thought we lost you. For a while, you were on the other side."

Curtis interrupts and says, "We got you up at a special hospital in West Point. Otherwise, I don't think you would have made it. Shit, I still can't believe you made it."

Sev says, "They say your life passes before you when you die." Then he asks, "What do you remember?"

I think and I concentrate. What the fuck do I remember? "I remember being in the Tongue Room. I remember charging at Balducci and I remember all the smoke canisters." I try to remember more but I'm having trouble thinking.

Curtis asks, "Is that all you remember?"

"I don't know. Everything is in pieces. Sev, didn't you waste Bino? Put a bullet right in the center of his skull?"

Sev matter-of-factly says, "Yeah, well it was a little off center." Then Sev turns to Curtis and says, "But I'm out of practice."

"Okay," Curtis says, "what else do you remember?"

"Christ, I don't know. Wait…I remember Bino nailing one into my side."

"Okay, we're making progress." Sev says. "What else do you remember?"

"I don't remember much else. Oh yeah, I remember being at the Locomotive Breath. Everyone was there. So was Bruce Springsteen."

"Kevin, listen up," Sev murmurs. "The Locomotive Breath has been closed for weeks. No one in his right mind is going to hang out there during this job action. It's too dangerous. Now let's go back to the Tongue Room. Tell me about getting shot."

"I remember hearing it first." I almost hear the crack-crack of the shot again.

"And I remember telling Rocky to run. I was hurt and I wanted her to bolt."

Curtis and Sev cringe. "Kevin, you need to think more clearly," Sev says.

"I rushed at Balducci, thinking it was the only chance to cause a distraction. It worked. After I got shot, I told Rocky to run. She didn't want to, she wanted to stay, but I got her to leave."

"Okay," Sev says. "Tell me about that."

Crack-crack. I think back to the exact moment I was shot: *I feel pain radiate up my left side, damn; I've been hit. "Rocky, you have to run. I'll catch up with you later. Please baby, run."*

"I can't," she pleads.

"You have to," I insist. *I nudge her toward the door.*

Sev looks at me intensely and says, "Kevin, dig deeper. Think more clearly."

I think and I think some more. Then I understand what Sev wants. The reality rises up. The agony overwhelms me. Crack-crack. There was no echo. Damn it, that wasn't an echo. There were two shots.

Then I remember something else. After I nudged Rocky, I looked at her face. Her expression was blank, just like in the Locomotive Breath. I thought it was confusion but it was more. I remember tears streaming down her face. I tried to nudge her to the door to get her to safety. She took five steps and could take no more. She dropped down to the smoky floor. I never saw her make it to the door.

Maybe she's not dead. Maybe she's in another room at this hospital. Sev and Curtis can see I remember what happened. "Is Rocky okay?" I ask.

Sev answers, "Listen, we relocated your friends Loot and Carey. Your mother, too; we moved her to Arizona. We did what we could, Kevin."

"Sev, what about Rocky? Is she hurt? How bad?"

Sev is poised and prepared. "Kevin, I'm sorry, we lost her. Rocky never made it out of Kosher World that night. Her funeral was last week. Curtis's guys moved her body out of

Kosher World, and we made her look like the victim of a random robbery."

I gasp. It's hard to breathe all of a sudden. How did I let this happen? How did it get here? How the fuck did I let Rocky die? Her of all people. She had nothing to do with this. I try to say all this out loud, but I hear myself whimpering like a little baby. I try to cover my face with my shaking hand but I know it's not covering anything. Tears are streaming down my face as the whimpering turns to full-force blubbering and I can't control it. I'm confused and I'm angry, but most of all I am so guilty. I am the worst person in the world for letting this happen to the best person in the world.

It's awkward. Sev and Curtis may have been prepared for this conversation; after all, I have been unconscious for two weeks. But were they prepared for my complete breakdown?

Sev and Curtis let me blubber and whimper. I don't think they have a clue what to do. I don't think they cover this in Special Service School. Sev and I have gotten close, but he's not exactly the type of guy to hold my hand and give me a hug. So I lie in bed with my hands over my face and cry. Sev and Curtis don't want to be rude and leave me like this, but clearly, they are squirming. I try to explain how bad I feel, but I'm sure they can't even make out the words I'm saying. It's all so frustrating. I try to ask them to leave me alone, but I'm not coherent. Finally, I simply wave my hand for them to leave.

A nurse says, "Mr. Davenport, I need to give you this injection. It will relax you a little bit."

I blubber louder because I don't want anything to help me. I don't deserve anything to help me. Frankly, I don't even have the strength to fight this nurse, and I'm sure if I did, Sev would help her anyway. She injects my arm and I am numb. My eyes close and I hope they never open again.

CHAPTER 29

I've fucked things up before, but this is off the charts. I can't believe what an asshole I am. I feel helpless, frustrated, disgraced, guilty and incompetent.

Sev visits me every day. He comes in and sits by the bed. He looks at me and I won't return the look. So he sits and reads the paper. He talks to the nurses when they come in to medicate me or change my bandages. When he's done reading and chatting, he excuses himself and says goodbye. This is kind of a cool thing. He's showing that he gives a shit. He's here for me, but he's not forcing anything. I suspect he's waiting for me to be ready to talk. Like I give a shit about anything now.

After days of this charade, I break my silence. "What's the situation now at Industrial Road?"

Sev folds the paper down on his lap and says, "Your boy Petro marched in there and set up shop. Business is going again and people are working."

I feel like crying again. But I won't. I won't break down like that again.

Sev notices my frustration and calmly says, "Isn't that what you wanted?"

"Well considering how much I lost, is everyone much better off with Petro instead of Balducci?"

Sev smirks. "Yeah, don't worry about that. Petro is just our cover for a while. We'll get him out soon, New Year's at the latest. Whether we go in and arrest him or kill him is really up to him."

"Where's Balducci?" I ask.

"At his fishing house in New Paltz," Sev answers.

"What's he doing there?"

"He's probably trying to figure out what to build with all the bricks that he's been shitting."

"I don't understand." I ask him why they didn't take out Balducci when they had the chance the night I was shot. What was the point in saving me if they let Balducci run off?

"Kid, I hate to break this to you, but we weren't saving you from Balducci. It was the other way around."

"I'm confused."

"We got wind that you were on your way to meet Balducci because he took Rocky. The bottom line is, we needed some more information before we could take him out. Mostly info about the guy Balducci was working with in his Iran project. I know it sucks, having Balducci in our crosshairs and not being able to finish him, but there are rules even for Special Service guys. Balducci has got some clout, but his partner has even more. When guys with those kinds of political connections get taken out, well, there better be plenty of proof documented." Sev pauses, sighs and says, "Lawyers get involved. So not only do you need documentation, you need every 'i' dotted and 't' crossed. By strict legal standards, we weren't there yet. So if you were going on a kamikaze mission and Balducci accidentally died before it was his time, it would have caused irreparable problems."

"Sev, are you telling me we were this far along and everything wasn't set up right? What were they waiting for? Why didn't we wait longer?"

"We didn't wait because the time wasn't right. As for getting all the documentation first, it could never happen. Curtis's department probably has more rope to run with than any government agency. But there ain't no government agency without its share of bureaucrats looking to cover their asses. To please them, you got to make things happen and convince them that you're going to win. So we're out there with our dick in the wind for a while. But you got to jump in at some point. Me and Curtis were almost done getting everything official when Balducci grabbed Rocky. Balducci was reaching for straws, acting more desperate than we ever thought. He almost got killed, and he almost fucked up this whole mission."

I ask if everything were legal, and Sev nods. Then I ask him what we were waiting for.

"You. Yeah, you. Me and Curtis have been talking, and Balducci is our gift to you. It's not like we need to, of course. We got everything we need from Balducci. We got wire conversations, pictures and cooperating witnesses filling up the house like it was the Playboy Mansion. Balducci is toast; it's just a matter of how the toast gets served. If you want to be the chef, he's yours. If you want to lie in this bed and feel sorry for yourself, we'll just arrest him. It's your call."

I pause as Sev's words sink in. "Are you telling me you know exactly where Balducci is right now?"

"Kid, I can tell you the brand of toilet paper he has in hand at this minute."

"And Curtis is okay with this?" Curtis never let anything take a backseat to a task at hand. "What gives?"

"Well, me and Curtis know how bad you want Balducci. Shit, now probably more than ever. If Curtis needed him any more, yeah sure, he wouldn't wait, but he appreciates what you brought him. This is turning out pretty good for Curtis. Before this he was chasing leads on a case going nowhere, and now you drop this in his lap. The whole Industrial Road manipulation was spreading to factories across the country, which in turn was affecting retail outlets. Think about this from the viewpoint of the bureaucrats upstairs. You have a corrupt situation that involved everyone from blue-collar workers to the ticking time bomb in Iran. With all the shit going down in the Mideast now, the brass is happy to stop this crap without sending troops overseas. When people get wind of who was involved in this little caper, everyone is going to want to be friends with Curtis."

"Wouldn't it be better if Curtis took Balducci in himself?"

"Hey, Curtis don't want headlines. He's looking for political clout on the inside. People on the outside can't know his face. For a while he needed information on who Balducci was working with, but as far as Balducci goes, Curtis could give a shit. That brings us back to you; you want Balducci?"

"I can do what I want with him?"

"Yup."

"If I do nothing, will you arrest him?"

"Yup, I already said so."

"Does he get life in jail?"

Sev starts to answer the question but then hesitates. He thinks for a minute and then answers, "The system can't be predicted. Did O.J. Simpson get life?"

I want Balducci. I want him bad. I got no other reason to get out of this bed, but on top of that, I can't let this thing go to trial and risk letting Balducci walk on some technicality. Fuck him and fuck me. I'm going fishing.

The fishing house is an elegant log cabin. It almost looks like a hunting lodge. The wooded landscape is impeccably groomed. It's like some Abercrombie & Fitch outfit that's supposed to look rugged and athletic, yet they put the clothes on some prissy looking model. I'm sure when Balducci comes to this fishing house he feels all macho.

I'm sitting in the back of a black Escalade; Curtis and Sev are in front. Curtis has a small television screen on his lap and he motions me to lean forward so I can view the screen. The screen splits into three windows, each showing a different location around the fishing house, each with a separate guard. Curtis says, "It's like a fucking zombie movie here. These guys don't know they're dead." He looks at his watch. "It's time."

We quietly watch the screens. Two of Balducci's guards are dropped with a silent pistol shot to the skull, and the third has his throat slashed while his mouth is covered. I ask Curtis, "Why cut one and shoot the other two?"

Curtis answers, "Personal preference of my guys. I don't like to micromanage."

Makes sense, I guess. I stare at the surveillance screen in Curtis' lap. The Special Service guys have disappeared and the guards are lying where they fell.

Curtis says, "C'mon, we're on a schedule tonight. We got to make a big arrest after this. We kept everything on ice till you got ready, but we can't fuck around anymore."

I guess that's my cue. I get out of the Escalade. "Okay, Curtis, I'm ready."

Sev rolls down his window. He asks if I've got the gun he gave me, and I say yes.

"You want me to come in there with you?"

"No, thanks. I got this one under control. Is Balducci still getting my calls forwarded to Rocky's phone?"

Both Sev and Curtis shrug; they're not sure. I ask to borrow Sev's phone, and he tosses it to me through his window. I catch the phone and thank him. Then I say, "Mom and Dad, if I'm late, you don't have to wait up for me."

Curtis says, "You got half an hour and then we come in and take care of business. I'm on the clock tonight." When I hesitate, Curtis adds, "C'mon, kid, you can get this done in a half hour."

I expect I can. I walk toward Balducci's cabin, stepping over one of his dead guards. I start to pass him, but I realize there's enough light from the house to take a picture with Sev's cell phone. I can't resist snapping a shot.

I wait by the window and look at my watch. Any

minute now. I look toward the Escalade concealed by bushes. While I'm waiting, I open Sev's cell phone and change the wallpaper to the picture I just took of the dead guy lying on the lawn. Finally, the house goes dark. The power has been cut off; that's my cue. I force open a locked window and crawl through. Balducci sticks his head out of another window, hollering, "Hey, Fleisher! What the fuck is going on?"

Obviously, Jimmy is going to have to wait a long time to get an answer from Fleisher. I pull out Sev's cell phone and dial my own cell number. I can hear it ring in the distance. It rings several times but Balducci isn't answering. My phone calls are still being forwarded to Rocky's cell phone. He still has Rocky's cell phone. I hang up when I hear the beginning of my own voicemail. The house is pitch black, and the ringing must be driving Balducci nuts. I call again, and this time I call Rocky's number. I'm assuming he is holding the phone, trying to get all the information he can if someone is calling me. I hear it ring from the phone I'm calling on, and I can hear Rocky's ringtone coming from only a few rooms away. The unmistakable voicemail picks up. *"Hi, this is Rocky, sorry I can't get your call, but if you leave a message, I'll call you right back."*

Holy shit, I wasn't expecting that. I dial the number again and I hear it ring in the distance. I miss her voice so much; I even missed her funeral. Her voicemail is all I have now. I dial it again just to hear her voice. I hear it ring again. Balducci surprises me; he picks up the phone. There is no greeting, only breathing from his side of the phone. If I can hear him breathing, his heart must be pumping through his skull. I let him breath for another minute. After all, how many breaths does he have left? Finally I say, "Jimmy, it's time." He doesn't answer. I still hear him breathing.

I want to get Jimmy talking so I can follow his voice, figure out exactly which room he's in. In a low voice I say, "I know you saw me get shot. You must have been wondering if I was alive or not."

"Fuck you, Davenport. I know you lost your girlfriend, but I lost a lot, too. Shit, I've lost everything I got."

"Not everything, Jimmy. Not yet." I use the light of the cell phone in my hand to navigate around the furniture, avoiding any unnecessary noises.

"Kevin, listen up. I helped you out. I got you a job when you needed money. You were always welcome in my house. I was going to take you into the business. I was offering you some opportunities. Things you always wanted. Why did you turn on me?"

Right on schedule Curtis's guys return the power in the house and the lights go on. There I am, staring into the frightened eyes of Jimmy Balducci. There is no gun in his hand, so I can put mine away. It can't be a coincidence that Jimmy is in this room; he was looking for his gun.

"You killed my father; that's why I turned on you." I shove Jimmy in the chest. "You took everything from me. Fuck you." I shove Jimmy in the face, nearly knocking his head into a lamp that's next to his desk. We are in the home office of the fishing house, a place where he undoubtedly bought for free and ordered hits that ruined hundreds of families. Probably he is trying to get to a drawer in the desk. "My sister's dead, my mom's a train-wreck." I shove his face again. "You gave me a job when I needed one? Fuck you. You're the reason I was so hard up for money. I had to take care of my family, you asshole." When I shove him in the face again, his head hits the wall hard. He slides down the wall and lands on his ass. I notice him looking toward the window. I pull out the cell phone and show him the picture of the dead bodyguard that I saved as wallpaper on Sev's cell phone. "Jimmy, your friend Fleisher and his pals are taking a nap, so they won't be able to help you right now."

A stunned and desperate Jimmy says, "Kevin, hold on a minute!"

"Don't pretend you didn't kill my father."

"Listen, it wasn't about your father. We were protecting what we built up. Your father was a freakin' pit pull." Trying to work me, Jimmy continues. "I see where you get it from. He was closing in on us. We had to stop him. You have to believe me, it wasn't anything personal."

I put my knee on Jimmy's chest. I have him pinned against the wall and the desk. Being in a drug-induced coma for two weeks took a lot of my strength away, but even at a fraction of what I'm supposed to be, Jimmy is no problem. "So what the fuck was I? Some sort of sport for you?"

Jimmy doesn't answer. He is trying to wrestle free but I have him lodged solidly. So I repeat, "Was it funny having me over to your house and having me work in your fucking meat factory?" My head is throbbing from pent-up frustration. Jimmy is cornered in every way imaginable. "It must have been a riot bragging to all your fucked-up psychotic friends how not only did you ruin my family but you have me jumping through hoops. I hope you had a lot of laughs, because now it's time to pay up."

"No, no! Shit, you have it wrong. Listen to me, you have it wrong."

"Speak. You have one minute."

"It wasn't sport. Shit, it wasn't anything like that. You came to Remington Academy; we didn't know shit about you except that you could help the school build a better basketball program. Who would have thought you were the DA's kid? A bunch of years had gone by since your father died. Trust me, we didn't know shit then about you. I'm telling you, Davenport, when we finally put two and two together, we almost crapped our pants."

I hesitate a minute. I'm trying to digest what he is saying, as if I care, but something does strike me as funny. "Jimmy, who is 'we'? You said we almost crapped our pants."

Jimmy hesitates. "You know, the guys I was working with."

I punch him in the face. His eyes briefly roll back into his skull. I say, "Cut the shit. Who is the 'we'?"

"Kevin, it's not too late. We can make this right. Let's talk business here. Don't make this so personal. I can get you more money than you ever dreamed of. Isn't that what you always wanted? You told me so. C'mon…let me go and we'll talk about this."

I take my knee off Jimmy's chest and stand up. I'm sure Balducci thinks I want to talk about the "business proposition" he just offered me. But I'm really looking for something to drive home a point. "Thanks for the offer, but even if I wanted to accept, which I don't, we both know you have no money. It's all gone, Jimmy."

On Balducci's desk, there is a brass letter opener in the shape of a dagger; that will do nicely. I grab Jimmy by the throat and throw him back down on the ground. I shove the letter opener into his right eye and drive it in. There's a sonic pop that booms through the house. It reminds me of the gunshots that ripped through Rocky and me. It reminds me of the pop the suffocating cellophane made when it finally burst. A combination of blood and eyeball fluid is flowing over Balducci's face and my shirt. I even taste some in my mouth. It must be all over my face.

Balducci shrieks like a dying cat. As much as I want to do this, the sight and sound of blinding Jimmy is making me queasy. "I'm not fucking around here. Who the fuck is 'we'?"

Understandably, Balducci is having a little trouble focusing. "Oh God, I can't see! Oh God, it hurts, oh it hurts."

"You want me to make this hurt more? Who the fuck is

'we'? Who else?"

"Wellington. Please stop! Buster Wellington. He's the one with all the political connections. We were partners. Oh God, this hurts."

"Keep going," I demand.

"I provided the muscle. He had the political connections. He stayed behind the scenes. How do you think my kid got into Remington Academy? I needed help and he helped me. Oh God, please don't do this!"

"Shut the fuck up!" I drive the letter opener into his throat. I was going to stab him in the heart, but you'd have to be a microbiologist to find it. The throat is working nicely though. He is gurgling and wheezing and he is suffering.

I slump down on the ground and sit next to Balducci. I want to see it all the way through. But give Jimmy credit; at the end of the day, he managed to steal something else from me. Him and his "I buy for free" bullshit; he's the ultimate thief. I lived for the satisfaction of taking Balducci down and finishing the job my father started. But then Jimmy told me about Buster Wellington. All that time at Remington Academy, I never saw Buster or Jimmy speak two words to each other. When I was dating C.W. Wellington, I never saw any connection. Shit, even when I was spying on Balducci inside his house, I never saw a connection. Was he bullshitting?

I'm about to ask him if he's lying when he begins to gurgle. Then he's gone. He still has a little air left, but he's not here. He's probably halfway down some giant sliding pond dropping him off at Lucifer's Playground for the Hopelessly Evil.

The gurgling stops. It took me 25 minutes. Five minutes to spare; Curtis will be happy.

CHAPTER 30

Sev and Curtis are standing and talking outside the black Escalade. The three Special Service guys that took out Balducci's guards flank them. When I appear from the other side of the bushes, they look me up and down to observe how soiled my shirt is.

Sev speaks first. "I sure hope the house is spotless."

"Not exactly," I say. "The house is pretty messy too."

Curtis frowns. "Damn, I don't think I've ever seen anything sloppier in my life."

I show them the letter opener and say, "I took this with me, you know, so I wouldn't leave any evidence."

Sev smiles and says, "Good idea, kid."

Curtis takes the letter opener from me and hands it to one of his guys. He says to the group, "You have three body-guards and Jimmy Balducci. Make the bodies disappear and take care of this house. I need a first-rate job here. By the time you're through, no one should be able to recognize even the foundation of this house."

Sev and Curtis get back in the Escalade. Sev looks at me and says, "Are you coming or what?"

I'm dazed. I nod and head toward the back door of the SUV. Curtis says, "He ain't coming in my car like that. You have any idea what that's going to smell like?"

Sev motions to a Special Service guy who is wearing a T-shirt under his regular button-down black shirt. The guy takes the shirt off and offers it to me. I take off my bloody T-shirt and, in a moronic move, offer the horrific shirt to the Special Service guy, like we are trading.

"Thanks," he says sarcastically.

"Oh, shit, sorry."

Curtis says, "C'mon, let's go."

No one speaks during the ride. I took down Balducci, but shit, Buster Wellington is just as bad, if not worse. Fuck. I want to talk to Sev about this but our car ride is over and we are parked in front of a helicopter.

Curtis says, "Let's go; New Paltz to Manhattan in 30 minutes."

The helicopter isn't what I'd pictured an Army helicopter to look like. The pilot is separated from the passengers by a partition. We are in an area with two plush leather rows facing each other and a coffee table in between. There is burl wood veneer throughout the interior.

"Nice ride," Sev says to me. "Curtis' department busted a big Brazilian drug cartel and they confiscated about ten of these. Curtis gets a chopper for his department to use as they see fit. That's how it works here; kind of a merit system." The helicopter takes off. I'm feeling frustrated. I want to talk to Sev and Curtis about Buster Wellington, but it's too noisy to talk. Curtis puts on a large headset with a big microphone and motions me to pick up a headset. Sev does the same. "You guys knew about Buster Wellington, didn't you?" I can hear my own voice in the headphones.

Sev answers. "Yeah, we knew." I can hear him perfectly now. Almost like we are on the phone, but we are looking right at each other.

"Why didn't you tell me? You must have known for a while."

Curtis says, "Is it my imagination, or am I correct in saying we gave you exactly what you asked for? Not only did we stop Balducci, we also waited till you were ready to terminate him. Think about tonight. It was like going to a fuckin' Mickey D's take-out for you. Don't make it like we did something wrong."

"Yeah, well fuck that. I want Wellington, too."

Curtis says, "Sorry, kid, that one you can't have."

My frustration boils to a fever. "You can't do that to me. He was Balducci's partner. He was just as responsible for killing my father and sister. He ruined my whole family. Look what they did to Rocky! I need this. Please, guys."

Curtis says, "Believe me, I know how you feel. I know how this stings, but we need Wellington. I threw a lot of resources at this; we can't come up empty-handed. If it makes you feel better, Buster's life is taking a dramatic turn for the worse tonight."

"That's why you needed me to finish Balducci in 30 minutes. You said you have a high-profile arrest to make."

"Yes. Buster Wellington is at a fundraiser at the Waldorf Astoria. The room is filled with senators, businessmen and socialites. When we take Buster in, it will be all over the news."

Sev laughs. "Kevin, you can't believe how much shit we have on this asshole. Remember when you were getting antsy because we weren't moving in yet?"

"Yeah, sure. Petro, too. We all were on the edge and you were eating pancakes."

"Yeah, pancakes help me think. Anyway, that's where the dominoes really fell. Balducci was a caged rat. He was desperate and he blew his cover with Wellington. There are direct phone calls, attempted meetings, and all the codes that they had throughout the years were revealed and deciphered. We located the money trails and linked them to both Balducci and Wellington. We have pictures and surveillance tapes. Balducci knew he was cornered, and he'd figured out that Petro didn't have the resources to organize this effort. He knew something was up and that being arrested wasn't out of the question. Shit, for Balducci, getting arrested was the best option. In the end, he was more scared of Buster Wellington than us. He knew

Buster wouldn't risk being exposed. He was right, too; Buster was planning to kill Jimmy."

"No shit?" I say.

"Yeah, Buster was more cutthroat than Balducci by a long shot."

Now I'm even more frustrated. I went after the wrong guy. "Curtis, are you the one who's going to arrest Wellington?"

"Hell, no. I can't blow my cover. We have district attorneys for that. If people know me, I'd never be able to get things done. Tonight, we'll be in a surveillance truck watching the whole thing."

I ask Curtis if he can give me five minutes alone with Wellington.

"Why? So you can strangle him?"

"I want to, that's true, but I understand everything you've been saying. You come away with a big-profile arrest and your department gets stronger. It's easier for you to go after other scumbags now. I wouldn't ruin that for you. But I'd still like to confront Buster Wellington. Can you arrange that for me?"

Sev looks at Curtis. Curtis pauses and says, "I'll think about it."

CHAPTER 31

I'm mad at myself. Did I let my feelings for C.W. Wellington blind me? Did I miss something while I was idolizing her? If I did a better job, if I kept my mind more open, could I have figured out Buster's involvement? For Christ's sake, I was at their house all the time. If I did the job better, maybe I wouldn't have gotten Rocky killed. I'm such an asshole.

The helicopter lands on a pad near Chelsea Piers. Another black Escalade is waiting for us and rushes us to the Lexington Avenue side of the Waldorf Astoria. TV trucks are parked out front to cover this big celebrity charity event. Sev and Curtis lead me to an NBC TV truck parked in front of the Bull and Bear restaurant, a block north of the Waldorf. Immediately, I can tell this isn't an ordinary TV truck. It holds an impressive array of TV screens that have every angle and every corner of the grand ballroom covered. One flat panel TV, bigger than all the others, is focused on a deserted table.

Curtis says, "That's the Wellington table. No one is there now, but the main course is about to be served."

Cameras are panning randomly through the crowd, highlighting the celebrity guests. There are major movie stars, models, athletes, senators and captains of business like Buster Wellington. They're all here for the noble cause of saving the planet.

Curtis points to the left wall of the mock TV truck. He is showing me that one wall of this operation is dedicated to following the Wellington family. Buster is on the dance floor wearing his Armani tuxedo. He's spinning his wife around the floor to the music of a 40-piece orchestra.

Another camera is focusing nearby on C.W.'s younger

twin sisters, who are dancing as well. They seem to be with some very proper young men.

One camera is locked in on C.W. at the bar, and that grabs my attention. She's wearing a beautiful low-cut shiny brown dress. Very classy, but just tart enough to attract the attention that she thrives on. She's at the bar with some preppy guy and working him like only C.W. can. I think to myself, *Enjoy these last few minutes, C.W. Trust me, it sucks having the world you thought was yours taken away.*

Everyone has been called back to their seats for the main course. The master of ceremonies has taken the stage. It's Debby Brooks, a popular comic. Behind her is a tremendous screen that projects her image throughout the room where the people who donated an insane amount are in front of the people who donated only a crazy amount. Brooks is barking her routine and the crowd is eating it up. She's tearing into some of the CEOs in the crowd and everyone is enjoying it. Right now she is crushing Brian Richmand, the CEO of Limestone Private Equity.

Brook's announces the keynote speaker, former Vice President Al Gore.

The flat screen TV shows the Wellington family sharing the table with the dates of the four daughters.

A voice reaches out to Curtis through his walkie-talkie. "Curtis, we're behind a few minutes. They're all there. Should we move in?"

"Not yet. I can't do that to Gore. Shit, the man was the vice president. Don't worry. Wellington always makes a statement at these things. As long as I have him there, it's all good."

Gore is speaking with a southern drawl and I'm sure everything he is saying is important, but shit, can the man talk any slower? When Gore is well into his speech, Curtis says into the walkie-talkie, "Any minute now. Stay loose."

When Gore finally finishes, Debby Brooks introduces the auctioneer for the silent auction. She teases Gore about the election he lost, and Gore jabs back pretty manfully. By most standards, this event is quite a success.

Curtis says into the walkie-talkie, "Okay, this is the spot I was looking for. We can make maximum impact and not ruin the event. Let's go before the auction starts."

In less than 15 seconds, 20 police officers burst into the Waldorf. They are fully armed and fully protected in riot gear for effect. It's a long march to the front of the room and the Wellington table. There is plenty of curiosity, but I bet there are plenty who think this is a gag and part of the event. However, that thought is suspended when the United States attorney approaches Buster Wellington. The DA says, "Alexander Wellington, you are being arrested on charges of violating the federal RICO act, conspiracy to commit murder, grand larceny, violating international trade regulations and treasonous acts against the United States government. You have the right to remain silent, you have the right to an attorney...."

While Buster is handcuffed, the crowd tries to converge on the table. The chatter has risen to a clamorous roar.

Sev says, "This will be a long fall from grace."

The Waldorf ballroom is huge, and the patrons from the back tables are wrestling through to get a look. The camera angle we have is well positioned and I assume that's not by accident. Wellington's wife is sobbing and trying to stay poised, you know, the WASP thing. The look on C.W.'s face is priceless. She knows it's over. She is frozen in shock. I know she is maneuvering something in her head. She's already in recovery mode and in denial about how bad things are about to get. What's the proper reaction to a family scandal, anyway? It doesn't much matter; her world is different now. It can change that quickly.

The police lead Wellington away. The oversized officers, puffed up by bulletproof flak jackets and riot gear, are plowing through the crowd, forcing a path for the man in the expensive tuxedo and shiny handcuffs. The Wellington family is close behind. It's a long way from the front of the Waldorf to the back. Sure, there are side exits, but I guess either the guards don't know about them or they have no desire to dilute the drama. Gee, I wonder which it is?

Curtis continues to give instructions to his department. Still transfixed by the TV screens, I listen to the crowd buzz and chatter with excitement.

After a few minutes, Brooks returns to the stage and gets the crowd chuckling and comfortable again. But it probably shocks the Wellingtons to discover that a huge social event can continue without them.

Sev pops his head back into the TV truck. "Coming?"

The black Escalade takes us to the federal building downtown by the Wall Street area, near the Brooklyn Bridge. When we enter, I can tell that Curtis is in a great mood, more spirited than I've ever seen him. Curtis says, "Sev, the politics suck, all the dead ends suck and all the scumbags we deal with suck. But I'll tell you, when you win it feels good."

Sev answers, "Yeah, but we could have picked up Wellington at his mansion and done this quietly. Did the attorneys' office need the scene to be this dramatic?"

Curtis answers, "Look, they always want as much exposure as possible. The more TV time they get, the better their chances are for running for governor or something like that."

"But guys like you prefer to go in stealth under the radar. Why did you go Hollywood this time?"

Curtis laughs. "I figured if we went big and bold, it would be a statement. So when this cocksucker Wellington reaches out to all his political and legal connections—and believe me, he will—I want all those connections to think twice.

I want them to think that for our group to prance into the Waldorf and disrupt an event of that magnitude, that the guys running this case have a sure thing. I want everyone to know we're beyond confident. Let them step up to this challenge."

"Do you have an airtight case?" I ask.

"I think so, but I've thought so before. Hey, guess what, kid? I got you some alone time with the Pope."

"Alone time with Wellington?"

"Listen to this, you're going to love it. My guys told him we would give him a one-time chance to a plea bargain."

"He's getting a plea bargain?"

"Of course not, I did this for you. We explained that a civilian who's been involved with both Wellington and Balducci would negotiate something under the radar, something unofficial. We told him it was you. You're going to be listed as family friend. Since you were cooperating with us and you can be considered a family friend, Wellington bit. He had to agree to waive the right to an attorney and respond to some preliminary terms you were going to present him. If we were close on these preliminary terms then we would talk officially. But right now, this is what we got."

"He agreed?" I ask.

"Even better. He suggested he bring his daughter in, the one you used to date."

They're so fucking arrogant. They figure she can wrap anyone around her finger. "I can speak to both of them?" "Yeah, they're waiting down the hall. Listen, tell me again that you won't lay a hand on him."

I tell him that I understand the situation, I appreciate what he did for me, and I'm not going to ruin anything for him. He says I've got 10 minutes with them.

Curtis completes my briefing as he leads me to the office where Buster and C.W. are waiting. The information Curtis gives me is mind-blowing. "C'mon, Buster Wellington?" I ask.

I just smile. Wellington needs to hear what I have to say and I need to say it.

Curtis leads me to some sort of sloppy police accountant's office instead of the cool room I imagined with two-way mirrors and recording devices. There are so many files most of the floor is covered. I see Buster and C.W. waiting inside. The idea of Buster Wellington needing my help is a riot. Buster Wellington is sitting on a chair, his bowtie miraculously high and tight around his neck. His head's a different story. His head is bearing all the weight, slumping and hanging heavy in hands that are still cuffed. C.W. is quietly standing next to him.

I enter the room and say, "Mr. Wellington, they told me I may be able to help."

C.W. tries to nod at me, but the effort is forced. Buster pops up and says, "Kevin. Kevin, son, you know what a mistake this is?"

"Yeah, it sounds like this is a huge mistake," I say. C.W. leans toward me and forces a smile. "I mean how can this be true?"

Wellington asks, "What do you know? What do they say they have?"

"Sir, I don't know everything, but the stuff I know is outrageous. What they're saying is crazy. If this stuff gets out there, it'll ruin you. You know how perception becomes reality. We have to stop this."

"Son, can you help us? What are they claiming?"

"Well for starters, they have info on you from all the way back in the late '80s and early '90s. How you were developing shopping centers and strip malls in New Jersey and Staten Island." C.W. looks confused and I continue. "But that can't be the case. We all know that a Wellington wouldn't be involved in that kind of real estate development. Shit, they have you owning run-down apartment buildings in the Bronx.

There's no way you would ever do such a thing."

"Son, that's not enough to arrest me. Do you know anything else?"

"Anything else? I would think that alone would be upsetting. I mean, the way you always preached how you earn money is more important than making it at all. I mean, you a *slumlord*? Ridiculous!"

Wellington is irritated and asks, "What else are they saying?"

"They say you were crushed in the real estate crunch in the early '90s. They say you owed a ton of money."

"They do, do they?"

"Obviously, there's no reason to arrest a guy for that," I say, "but this is where it gets nuts. They claim you have all sorts of financial problems. Can you imagine that? Buster Wellington with financial problems? As if! And they say they have proof of you taking the money and properties you have left and funding a bunch of Mafia guys. Ha!"

I can see Buster's Adam's apple rise in his throat. I can see he knows that I know.

"The thing that they actually can prove is that you, Buster Wellington, were working with Jimmy Balducci. Now you may not realize this, but I recently had some problems with Mr. Balducci because I found out that he killed my father." I pause, wait and turn toward C.W. "C.W., can you imagine how you would feel if you found the person who killed your father?"

She returns a blank stare and looks as awkward as she's ever been in her life. She does manage to nod once. She knew her father was a crook, but I wonder if she knew he was a killer as well.

"So it gets me thinking further. I get a plan going against Jimmy Balducci and, son of bitch, it's working and I'm getting it done. I'm closing in, and it's just a matter of time before people start making the connection, that important line that connects Buster Wellington and Jimmy Balducci." I look at Buster and ask rhetorically, "So you know what you do? You actually have your daughter call me to meet me out at the Piping Rock Country Club. I don't know what she knows at this point, but sure as shit, she knows something's up with dear ol' pops. She's going to persuade me to call off the dogs, right? She couldn't give a rat's ass about me, but for a short while she could put on a little act and perhaps persuade me, er, manipulate me." I turn toward C.W. "What was the bullshit you were spewing? 'Oh, I miss you because you're the only real person.' Holy shit, how did you manage to keep a straight face?" I turn back to Buster and say, "Mr. Wellington, do you mind if I ask you a question?"

Buster stares back at me.

"C'mon, Mr. Wellington, work with me here," I say. "How far was she going to go with me? Did you send your little princess out to have sex? Can you actually rationalize that being okay? What the fuck was going on in your warped mind? Was she going to get me thinking with my dick to drop the whole thing? I'm just a slob from Hempstead, after all, so indulge me while I ask this one important question. In lowly Hempstead, we have a name for people who send girls out to have sex. They're called pimps. But my goodness, C.W., if your dad is out there pimping you, that would mean there's a word describing you too. Do you know that word?"

That finally gets a reaction from Buster. "Just stop, Kevin." He draws a deep breath to maintain composure and says, "I understand you were sent here to negotiate some pre-terms. They had some terms to present me. What are the terms they are presenting?"

"Of course! The terms. Here they are. There are roughly five mountains of information that tie you into murder, extortion, theft and even treason. By the way, nice move getting involved with Iran. It should make really interesting conversation for you and your friends at the next equestrian event. Anyway, they have so much information, so much evidence. Yet, they're going to offer you a plea deal. Do you know what that's going to be?" There is no answer. "C'mon, take a guess."

He's fuming with irritation. "What?"

"Nothing. You get nothing. There is never going to be a plea deal. So you better get every fucking connection your blue-blood family has and get them cracking."

"I see."

"No, you don't see because now I'm going to give you my terms. You probably have thoughts of beating this rap. You probably think with some dream team of legal experts you can find a technicality and walk. Hell, even if you lose and go to jail, you might think you'll get off early with good behavior. But here's what I came in this room to tell you. I will be breathing down your neck every breath you take in this world. I can't break your back now, but man, I can taste it. That day will come. I'm the only person who hopes you find the technicality and avoid jail. Because when that happens, I will hunt you down and treat you like the low-class scum you have always been. All these years you've been hiding behind expensive wine and Italian suits, but in reality you're a tiny little person and you don't measure up to anyone in Hempstead. Man, heart isn't birthright. You were always the poorest guy in the room. I just had to understand that. But I'll tell you what, I can make this whole thing disappear. Even after everything I just said, I can make this all go away if you do one thing for me."

Buster's face is red with anger, but he's out of options. "What do you need?"

"It shouldn't be too tough for you. I need my father, I need my sister and I need Rocky. You bring them back to me and I'll make this go away."

Naturally, there is no response.

"And C.W., my guess is you are really in for a rough ride now. All the manipulating you've been doing throughout the years may come back to bite you now. You think the social crowd you've been hangin' with is inviting you to dinner? Well, maybe you'll be a novelty at first, but if I were you I would expect a degree of separation from the people you think are your friends now. Trust me, that shit stings. But keep your chin up; there's got to be some 80-year-old billionaire who's willing to take you in and give you the things you've grown so accustomed to. As for you and me, you don't have to be concerned. Believe me, I understand more than you think. I'm willing to do anything to revenge my father's killing, and you were willing to get in bed with me to help protect your father. I have to live with a lot of consequences since I went on my quest, and you have to live with being the whore you are."

A detective pops his head in the room and says, "You folks have to wrap this up. Are you done talking?"

I stare as intently as possible at Buster Wellington. "I've said everything I need to say tonight. But we're not done talking, not by a long shot. Mr. Wellington, I look forward to the next time we meet." I look at the detective and then back at Mr. Wellington and say, "Please, don't ever hesitate to call me, Mr. Wellington. Really, if you need anything, I'll always be a close personal friend to this family."

I turn my back on the Wellingtons and leave. The detective leads me down the hallway where Sev greets me. My throat is swollen and my breathing isn't stable. I feel so shitty, so frustrated and so helpless.

Sev notices that I'm not myself. He asks, "Are you okay?"

I attempt to tell him I'm fine, but when I try to move my mouth to say something, nothing comes out. Emotions are overflowing and I think I'm going to start blubbering like I did in the hospital room. Somehow I manage to keep it together.

Sev sees me shaking. "Kevin, let's grab some air." He leads me out the front door, past the armed security guard and out into the federal building courtyard. It's dark and the night is clear and warm. Sev and I walk along the streets and, thank God, he's not pushing any conversations. We walk past the closed retail stores and continue down to the construction site where the World Trade Center is being rebuilt. We've walked a good 10 minutes without talking. Finally, when I know I'm past crying, I say, "Damn it Sev, it's not enough. I got to get him."

"We've been through that; we made a deal with Curtis. Right?"

"Yeah Sev, we made a deal."

"C'mon, you took out Jimmy Balducci, you orchestrated a chain of events that got everyone on Industrial Road their lives back. Don't be too tough on yourself."

"Sev, I got Rocky killed. You can't understand how that feels."

"Oh I don't? Remember, I told you I trained a battalion that slaughtered innocent children. Believe me, I know how much you hurt right now. I know."

"How do I make it stop?"

"Son, it never stops. You hope it dulls, but it ain't ever going to stop. When it happened to me, I just put my head down and got sucked into Kosher World. I let my life get wasted. Twenty-five fucking years. Don't you waste your life."

He's silent for a minute, and I don't know what to say. Then he begins again. "Listen, I don't know what amount of time anyone has on this planet. The thing is, it's not how many years you have, it's what you do with them. You may be upset you lost your father and I don't blame you, but understand this: he had a successful life. He had a great kid like you and he spent his working hours defending something important, making our world better. That's what I was doing, too, but after my mistakes, I wasted my life in Kosher World. Not anymore."

"What do you mean?"

"Curtis wants me back."

"Special Services?"

"Yeah. With Curtis having such a big job, I know we can get things done the right way."

"You sure that's what you want to do?"

"It's really the only thing for me. And for you."

"What?"

"Yeah, Curtis wants you, too. Remember that he wanted something from us for going after Balducci? Remember he said he would ask us for something later?"

"Yeah, I remember, but I didn't think he was going to force me to be his slave."

"Yo, hold on. It's nothing like that, not at all. The choice is all yours. You don't want in, no problem. You can walk away, no strings attached. He's just asking you."

"As much as I appreciate Curtis offering me this, I'm not sure it's really my type of thing, you know?"

"No, I think just the opposite. I think this is right for you. I think you can be awesome at this. I think you can use your life to do something that makes a difference. Look back at what you just did. Guys have been taking shots at Balducci for years, but you got it done. And with a letter opener at that. Shit, you dug yourself into drugs and gambling and used them as weapons. I saw what you did and so did Curtis. You can be great at this."

"I don't know."

"Listen, right now you're hurting because of Rocky. You're wondering if you can just put this all behind you and start from scratch. What you have to understand is that there is no normal life for you any more. Normal took the bus. Think about it. If you ever found another girl, if you ever had a kid, you'd always be looking over your shoulder. A lot of Balducci's fucked-up friends aren't making any money any more, and they could be blaming you."

"Yeah, I guess there are some circles where I'm not that popular."

"You think Bino might have a kid brother? Shit, look how you reacted when you found out who killed your father. Are you the only person in the world who needs a pound of flesh? And while we're on the subject, how about Zog?"

"What about him?"

"Cut the shit. You killed the guy and dumped him in a camp in Albany."

"Fuck, how'd you know about that?"

"Please, strictly amateur stuff. They went to turn that camp into summer cottages on a lake. The bulldozers picked up the body, and Curtis found out about it in no time. Then we found all sorts of shit that tied you to it. Man, you have a lot to learn. Don't worry, me and Curtis took care of it. But the point I'm making is every time you feel normal, every time you think you can have a normal life, something will stir up your past. So either you put a fucking bullet in your skull or figure out a way to make your remaining life mean something. But it ain't going to involve a house in the suburbs with 2.3 kids and a Golden Retriever."

"So then what do I do?"

"You insulate yourself in the job. You become the best Special Service soldier in the world. You forget about life as you know it and get satisfaction from doing good. I hated the last 25 years and for the first time, I'm looking forward to tomorrow. I sure would like it if you were there with me. If it's not for you, I understand."

I ask him if I can take out Wellington if the fuck gets out of jail on a technicality or gets time off for good behavior.

"I don't think that would be a problem. Look, Curtis has something special going here. He gets results and there's not a lot of red tape that he can't cut through. Curtis has the trust of a lot of people. At the end of the day, people want to be associated with the wins Curtis can produce and are less likely to fuck with him. This time, it might be worth playing the game because we have a shot to win."

"When does he need my answer, Sev?"

"Whenever you want, but if you answer soon, we can be partners. I hope you don't mind I made that request."

I'm thinking, *I bet my father would have been real proud if I followed him into the district attorney's office.* There was no better feeling to him than when he was fighting the bad guys. In that way, I still feel him in me and I like that. I feel the pride of fighting the bad guys. Shit, if Dad knew how I did it, his head would've exploded, but I did take out some lowlifes. Maybe I should keep on doing what I'm good at. I remember what Cliff told me a lifetime ago and say aloud, "Talk about being on the point of a sword."

Sev looks at me with one eye closed. "Huh? You mean the letter opener?"

I shake my head. "Naw, it's nothing. Let's go get some waffles."

Sev frowns slightly. "You mean pancakes. Waffles are pancakes that have been run over by a truck."

"Well, I'm willing to attempt pancakes. How about blueberry pancakes?"

Sev says, "Hmmm, they might be acceptable. I'll keep an open mind to that."

"This partnership might just work," I answer.

Sev puts his arm around my shoulder and it feels good.

THE END